SALVATION

Visit us at www.boldstrokesbooks.com

By the Author

Sanctuary

The Rarest Rose

Salvation

SALVATION

by

I. Beacham

2016

SALVATION
© 2016 BY I. BEACHAM. ALL RIGHTS RESERVED.

ISBN 13: 978-1-62639-548-0

THIS TRADE PAPERBACK ORIGINAL IS PUBLISHED BY
BOLD STROKES BOOKS, INC.
P.O. BOX 249
VALLEY FALLS, NY 12185

FIRST EDITION: APRIL 2016

CREDITS
EDITOR: CINDY CRESAP
PRODUCTION DESIGN: SUSAN RAMUNDO
COVER DESIGN BY JEANINE HENNING

Acknowledgments

Huge thanks as always to Cindy Cresap, my editor, for her guidance, words of wisdom and ever present sense of humor. Also, but never least, to the entire BSB team for their continued support.

Dedication

To Cindy P, the delightful American in England.

Thank you for your generosity of time,
and for sharing those intimate and painful memories.
I hope the book has done them justice.

Prologue

It was her fifteenth birthday, but she knew there would be no celebrations of that fact, no wonderful surprises awaiting her. Not this day.

For today, sitting alone at the back of a small English church, hardly daring to breathe or move, she listened to the dull tones of the vicar. He stood in the middle of the aisle, behind a small coffin, and lamented the untimely death of a young life cut short in its prime. His funeral oration was constantly broken by the weeping of a woman—a mother—who could no longer hold her grief.

The birthday girl wrung her hands and watched as a young man and woman, seated either side of the mother, attempted to console her. She knew who they were. They were the dead girl's older siblings.

Beside them was the father who looked far older than his years. For a second, she wanted to flee and run outside, but she knew she couldn't. She needed to be here. She also knew she must remain quiet and not alert the family and small contingent of friends that she was present. That would never do. So she slid lower on the hard wooden pew and prayed for invisibility.

She thought of the glorious autumn day outside and how there was still heat in the sunshine. It was a day when she would normally have grabbed a good friend and the dog, donned her walking shoes, and headed into the hills to enjoy the last vestiges of good weather before the anticipated onslaught of winter. But today, inside this church, the contrast could not have been greater. Everything in here was dark, cold, and dull. The brilliant sunshine struggled to push its light through dirty stained glass windows, an occasional successful shaft of blue and green light splintering over the coffin.

She lowered her eyes as the weight of guilt bore down on her again. Would she remember this day for all her birthdays to come? A small price to pay, she reasoned.

A bell rang out high above the church, announcing the end of the service. She glanced up to see four men now carrying the coffin on their shoulders. They moved reverently down the aisle toward her, and to the hearse that waited to take the precious contents to a final resting place. She considered how incongruous it was that it took four men to carry her classmate, a girl who had been built like a reed, willowy and tall. Behind them, came the family procession, and despite the organ music that now played, it did nothing to blanket the sound of sobbing.

Every fiber of her body absorbed the tragedy before her. She wanted to cry too, but her empathy was redundant for it was not wanted here. She quickly looked away, but not before she caught the raw expression of loss and grief on the mother's face. She bit her lip to stem her emotion. If they saw her here, it would be awful. Dear God, let this be over soon, she prayed.

They passed, but behind her, she heard a commotion, and then a rustle of clothing and movement to her right. Glancing up, she found the dead girl's mother hovering over her, and before she had time to stand or do anything, she felt a hard slap cut across her face. Red-brimmed eyes full of loathing bore into her.

"You stay away from me and my family. You hear? You stay away!"

The daughter and son were suddenly there, wrapping their arms around their mother protectively, pulling her away. The daughter spoke gently. "This isn't helping, Mum. Come on."

As quickly as the small scene played, it was over, but not before she caught the disapproving faces and stares leveled at her from the congregation. She closed her eyes and hung her head in shame.

Then she waited.

Only when she knew everyone had left the church, and heard the hearse and accompanying vehicles drive off, did she dare stand up to leave. As she moved, her body ached and felt tight and slow like it did after a long school run. She headed toward a small car park where she could see a smart, casually dressed middle-aged man waiting.

He leaned against the side of an expensive, highly polished car smoking a cigarette. As he saw her walking toward him, he flicked the cigarette onto the tarmac and ground it in with his heel before facing her.

"Well?" he asked.

"I did it, Dad."

He looked hard into her eyes before raising a hand and gently placing it on the side of her face where she had been slapped. His eyes softened.

"I'm proud of you."

He pulled her into his arms and hugged her tight.

CHAPTER ONE

Twenty-four years later.

Claire unloaded the bags of manure from the back of her old Jeep and into the wheelbarrow. Every muscle in her body ached, and she questioned her sanity. She really should have just ordered this load, and the rest, and had the stuff delivered. No doubt she would have smiled coquettishly at the deliveryman and got him to take the heavy consignment all the way down to the potting shed and dump it there for her. But oh no, she had to keep going back to the garden center like an ant on a mission and doing ten-bag loads at a time. It was all the weight she dared put into the Jeep at one go. Any more and she'd be driving home on the back wheels with the front ones up in the air like a biker doing a wheelie. It would be fun but not really beneficial for the vehicle's chassis.

She sighed as she locked the vehicle and then began yet another wheelbarrow expedition down the sweeping and expansive lawns toward the small wooded area where the shed stood. The trouble was this garden ate manure like a prizefighter beefing up for a heavyweight boxing match. It needed huge amounts to sustain it and keep it at its best.

The large gardens belonged to no small abode. The Devonshire estate wasn't quite the stately home, but a very large property. Over the years, it had morphed its way from imposing home, to boarding school, and then a run-down hotel. It had finally been rescued, fully modernized, and converted into a dozen or more luxury apartments.

Most were owned, but a few rented. Claire's task was to keep the gardens in tip-top condition. A job she enjoyed, although her body wasn't quite agreeing with her at this time.

As she unceremoniously dumped the manure outside the shed with the other bags, she looked up as someone called her name. She saw Mr. and Mrs. Connell waving from across the lawn and slowly heading toward her. They were in their nineties, and the oldest occupants of the house. Both still sprightly and mentally alert, every morning they walked the grounds, hand in hand like young lovers. Claire started to grin. She was very fond of them, even though Mr. Connell could talk nineteen to the dozen. This time, Mrs. Connell got the first words in.

"Good morning, Claire. I just wanted to say thank you for repotting my houseplants. They're already looking more spirited. The bigger pots have done the trick."

Claire had willingly volunteered to repot half a dozen plants for the couple. Mrs. Connell's hands were now plagued with arthritis, and what had once been an easy task, no longer was. Claire's apparent success quite empowered her. She was still new to the world of gardening, and while she seemed to have mastered the basic tasks of maintenance, some of her other garden creations had withered on the vine...literally. She seemed quite good at repotting, and that sort of thing. The rest would surely come in time. Gardening was a learning process. However, there would be no more talk of her potting successes as Mr. Connell's verboseness was off the leash.

"I like what you've done with the herbaceous borders, my dear, and I love the crop of tulips and daffs. Spring flowers, always my favorite. They look marvelous. Although," he continued, "didn't you plant yellow and red tulips for this year?"

Claire just managed to get a nod in.

"They're all yellow," he said. "Not a red one anywhere. I don't understand it. I mean, I don't mind yellow tulips. They're very pretty, but if the packet says yellow *and red*, and no red come up, then isn't that wrongful sales, or something. What do they call it these days, Grace...something against the Sales Act...mis-advertisement? I suppose it could be fraud."

Well practiced patience sounded in his wife's calm response.

"George, I'm quite sure the red ones will come up. They're just a little late, that's all, and it really is still early in the season."

Claire caught the look of amiable suffering Grace shot her.

"Well, if they don't," he continued, "I think she should ask for her money back. I mean, red is red, and when they grow yellow—"

"Isn't the weather glorious, Claire?" Mrs. Connell had decided everyone had heard enough of red and yellow tulips.

Claire laughed. They never failed to lift her spirits, and she marveled at the way Grace had learned to curb her husband's verbal defecation.

She glanced at the cloudless day and the strong blue sky. It was glorious weather. "Yes, and it's only the end of March. You can already feel the heat in the sun," Claire agreed. "They say we're in for a lovely summer."

"You know what I like about good English summers?" George could never be tethered for long.

"No, dear."

"I like what it does to us Brits. We all become such nicer people, so much friendlier. It's fascinating really, that just a few sunrays can have such an effect. We're normally such a miserable nation. It almost makes you love your fellow neighbor."

"Not ours, it doesn't." Grace's dour response was pointed.

"No?" George looked at his wife, shocked.

"We live next to Michael Cooper. Deaf as a post and plays his music far too loud."

"I never hear him," George said.

"That's because you're deaf too."

"Oh." George nodded. "Quite. Well, the sunshine makes you love *almost* all of one's fellow neighbors."

"You really do talk rubbish sometimes, George."

"I can't help it. I've always been like it," he acknowledged good-heartedly. "But you still married me, dear."

Grace put her hand out and affectionately tugged his arm, "That's because you have other qualities that make you irreplaceable."

His eyes softened, and the depth of love Claire saw there made her heart twist. It was a love that everyone sought in life, and yet so few attained. His words were low and velvet.

"You think so?" He cast his wife a roguish smile.

"Don't be silly." Reserved as the admonishment was, Grace was loving every moment.

Claire thought it hard sometimes to picture that this man had made a fortune running a large scaffolding business. He'd had a fleet of trucks with the unforgettable signage of "Connell's Erections" slapped on the vehicles' side. Claire could still remember these from her childhood, and it had been her father who had pointed out that the Connells came from an era long ago when naivety reigned. They had been old-fashioned then. Wonderfully, they still were.

"We'll leave you now, dear," Grace announced. "I can see you're busy, and we only wanted to say thank you."

As they ambled away, Claire could still hear George rattling on about the weather and how he really did think the world was full of happiness when the sun came out. She saw Grace reach out and hold his hand.

She stood a while and watched them cut across the lawn. It was only when they disappeared around a corner that she glanced over to her right and up toward the house.

Like a snap of fingers, her state of bonhomie evaporated. It was replaced by irrevocable misery that nested in the pit of her stomach. The rapid change in emotion did not shock her. She had grown used to it. A familiar rawness that was never far from her thoughts paralyzed her. For a moment, her feet felt like they were putting down roots and she might never move again.

George's words of happiness played in her mind. They made her depressed.

He said the sunshine made everyone happy. But Claire wasn't happy.

Her happiness had been stolen.

CHAPTER TWO

There are moments in life one never forgets, the memories that stay forever. Memories burnt into consciousness, that hold every second of every happiness, every pain, as if it were yesterday.

And so it was for Regan Canning.

For her, the big burn started early one evening when the doorbell rang.

She was expecting prospective buyers coming to look at her house, which she had placed for sale over three months ago. Instead, she opened the door to find two police officers who informed her, with as much compassion as they could, that her only sibling was dead.

Simon, her brother a few years older, had apparently taken himself off to a field somewhere down south, sat in his car, and shot himself.

It was what brought her now, two days later, all the way down from Yorkshire to Devon. She found herself alone in her dead brother's apartment, still reeling with shock and wondering where on earth to begin.

Though the day was warm, Regan was cold as she gazed out the sitting room window of the second floor apartment. Grudgingly, she accepted that the place wasn't too bad. It was well located amidst other apartments and all within an old and well modernized, large hilltop property. Her diffident opinion allowed her to accept that the view was impressive too, if you ignored the single row of parked cars in front of the building. Beyond them, and with great theatrical aplomb, the eye was taken down over cedar treetops and to the sea bay in the distance where the afternoon sun glistened like iridescent pearls.

It was clear to Regan that the ocean view was what had drawn Simon to this place. He had always had an obsessive and magnetic pull to water.

But at this moment, the scenic vista was doing nothing for her.

She expelled air through pursed lips and felt like she was going to burst. Damn it, she was tired. She hadn't slept at all last night. The drive down had been long, the traffic heavy, and just for sheer entertainment value, one of the car tires had blown on the motorway. It hadn't helped her mood when she'd gone to replace it only to find she didn't have the key to the wheel nuts. The air had turned blue as she cursed a society that actually had to lock the nuts on car wheels to stop light-fingered criminals from thieving them. As for the key, she had absolutely no idea what she'd done with it.

The outcome of that little adventure had resulted in her driving off route to find a garage which had announced the tire was now beyond repair, and she'd had to front up for a new expensive one. Her interaction with the man from the garage had been terse. He'd spoken to her like some brainless moron, telling her she should always keep the wheel key in the car. She knew that...now.

How she'd wanted to tell him she was actually quite clever and possessed not only a double first from university in pure mathematics, but a PhD, too. But she hadn't told him because it wouldn't have changed his attitude. Instead she accepted she should be grateful for small mercies. She had made it down here to Devon in one piece.

Her thoughts returned to Simon. Ever since she'd been given the news, it was all she could think of. He had always been the golden boy who got everything he wanted, and more, with minimal effort. Maybe it was because she'd been born on a Saturday and had to "work hard for a living." Despite all her efforts and brains, she'd worked like an Aussie drover, and yet nothing seemed to have slotted into place for her. People said she was successful too, but she wasn't anywhere in life she really wanted to be.

For all her brother's success, he had topped himself, and was now gone. Was she supposed to be racked with grief, tear sodden and demented? She wasn't. She was red-hot poker angry, and the tiredness of her awful journey had done nothing to take its edge.

"You selfish bloody fool."

The heavy words fell from her lips as she continued to stare out the window. "How could you do this?"

She wondered why her brother hadn't contacted her, given her some warning that things weren't good. But there had been no desperate phone calls, no impending signs of things to come. Of course there hadn't. They hadn't spoken in ages. In childhood, they had been almost twin-close, but adulthood had ripped them apart. Their careers, life choices, and moral compasses had grown very different. Even the manner of his death spoke of the latter. She could never do something so dramatic, so violent, and leave others to pick up the pieces.

"How typical of you to die like this. Always me, me, me." She vented out loud, convincing herself she wasn't going mad but trying to release some of the bottled up tension. She'd have to say a lot more if her tactic was going to work.

"You could leave a suicide note in the car, but could you leave me anything? No. You've given no thought for how I'm going to feel. You selfish, selfish man."

She wondered if he *had* thought of her, and how she'd be the one to sort things out afterward. There was no other family, only distant relations neither of them had seen or spoken to in years. Had Simon grown to dislike her so much that this had been his final snub?

Regan turned away and glanced into the room looking for inspiration for where to start. She didn't get any because the place was a shambles. Whatever had possessed her brother to take his life, his mind must have been deranged for the neglected, slovenly scene that met her, clashed with the meticulous, annoyingly tidy man Simon had always been.

Everything was bedlam. She couldn't even see the carpets. There were huge amounts of papers scattered all over the floor along with dirty plates, half drunk cups of tea, and the remnants of takeaway fast foods that now held the beginnings of some cultural growth. In the kitchen, dishes were left unwashed, and rancid food lay untouched in the fridge. The place looked like a penicillin farm, and the smell was appalling. It had to have been like this for some time before Simon did his party trick. How the hell did he get into a state like this?

His bedroom was no better. His clothes, expensive and bespoke, lay crumpled and scattered on the floor along with dirty laundry. The bed, with its luxury satin sheets that hadn't been changed for a while, was unmade and crumpled. Everything showed the signs of a frenzied mind.

Regan was thinking how polar opposite to Simon this all was when her cell phone rang. She recognized the number and let it ring out. She was in no mood to talk to the man at the other end. He would want to talk to her about her resignation. She didn't want to discuss that now, or truthfully, ever.

Back in the sitting room, she heard a sound from the garden and crossed to a side window. She saw a woman with short ash blond hair sitting on a mower, cutting an expansive well-manicured lawn which ran the entire side length of the building. It stretched down a gentle slope to a copsed, wooded area. The thick woodland held an array of beautiful trees—cedar, cooper beech, and horse chestnut. At the one end, closest to the sweeping driveway up to the apartments, lay a small shack with a tin roof almost hidden by the foliage, surely the gardener's shed. To its left was a covered area where garden machinery was stowed.

She watched mesmerized as the mower moved left and right across the lawn. If it was supposed to have a hypnotic, calming effect on her, it was failing miserably. Obsessed with why she was here, she continued her one-way communication.

"You bastard, Simon. You were always the showman. You couldn't just take an overdose. I bet you never even thought about the poor sod who'd find you?" She exhaled noisily. "As if I haven't enough problems of my own."

And she did. Everything in her life was in turmoil right now, even before Simon's demise. She was trying to sell her home, she was changing her job, and she was getting rid of a lover. Now she was also sorting out her brother's affairs. Weren't big brothers supposed to look after their younger siblings? Hers hadn't. From their teenage years, she'd known she was the more sensible and mature. It hadn't been an issue then, and she'd rather liked the early signs of the woman she was turning into, responsible and levelheaded. The contrast with Simon, who was carefree with his "whatever" approach to life, had always brought comment from family and friends who thought the two balanced each other well. And for a while, they had. But then their diversity had stretched too far until they both rankled each other, and grew apart.

As she ran a hand through her hair, she noticed that the gardener had stopped and was looking up at her. Regan stepped back from the window. The gardener's attention felt intrusive, as if her privacy was being invaded. It only fueled her anger. She knew it was a stupid reaction, but she was irritated and tired, and didn't care.

Her phone went again. It was another number she knew. This time it was from a woman she had no intention of ever speaking to again. She ignored it, even when it rang again and again. Karen was nothing if not persistent.

Regan's poor mood escalated, and in an attempt to stop herself boiling over the top, she began grabbing all the dirty dishes and half eaten silver boxed curries from around the place, and headed for the kitchen. She tried to discard the remains of food in the bin, but it was full. Thankfully, she found an unused bin liner under the sink. It was one of two things that had gone right today. The other had been Simon's efficient and respectful letting agent who had handed her a duplicate key as quickly as possible when she'd arrived.

As she started filling the sink with hot, soapy water, the doorbell rang. It was a halfhearted ring that could almost have been missed. Regan froze and stared at her rubber-gloved hands which held a dishcloth. The last visitors to her door had brought nothing but bad news. Was this likely to be any different? She decided not to answer it. Anyone important had her number, not that she was answering. She badly needed to be left alone, just for today. If she could get this over, then tomorrow she'd be ready to face whatever needed doing. Besides, it was probably someone to tell her she'd parked in the wrong numbered space out front.

The bell went again.

For crying out loud, just go away and leave me alone.

There was a sharp knock on the door. She gripped the sides of the sink.

What part of "I'm not answering the door" are you not getting?

A small thought crept past her temper. *What if it's the police?* She didn't think so. They knew her number too, and could call. She went to the window and checked the car park. No police car.

As she turned, a floorboard creaked.

The unwanted caller knocked on the door again. The tenacious bastard wasn't going. She would have to answer it.

"What?" Regan demanded as she flung open the door, all social graces discarded.

She found herself facing the woman who had earlier been mowing the lawn. She was small and fresh faced with disheveled hair, and smelled of grass. She had hazel eyes and was smiling.

"Hello. You must be Regan, Simon's sister. I saw you up at the window. I didn't think you'd be here today. We were expecting you tomorrow."

Regan watched as the woman then shook her head as if embarrassed.

"I'm sorry. I'm Claire. I'm the—"

"—gardener," Regan interrupted. "Yes, I saw you mowing."

Claire tipped her chin forward in acknowledgement, and Regan caught her looking at the rubber gloves she was still wearing. It seemed to upset her.

"I really wanted to get here first and try to tidy the place a bit before you arrived. I'm sorry you've had to come and find this. I know the place is a mess."

It was undoubtedly the combination of shock, the lack of sleep, the bad drive down, and the fact her nerves were on edge, but Regan's barely held temper started slipping. She'd answered the door stressed because of the persistence of the caller. She'd braced herself for more official unpleasantness because her brother had blown half his head off. Instead she was facing a complete stranger cheerfully addressing her by her first name and who was daring to suggest she trespass into this apartment.

Who was this woman and what had her relationship been with Simon? It sounded like she had a key to the place. Was she another of his adoring floozies? If she was, this was another strange change in her brother. He'd always favored women with curvaceous hips and ample breasts. This one possessed neither.

"You have a key?"

The abruptness of the question took the smile off the gardener's face. It childishly pleased Regan.

"Yes. Simon gave it to me."

"Why?"

Regan figured she might as well find out now what Simon's interest in this woman had been. The gardener was visibly thrown by the blunt direction of inquiry, but she remained polite.

"His business sometimes took him away, and I'd pop in and water his plants."

Regan glanced around. There were no plants here now. She wondered what other *needs* the woman had tended to.

"I just wanted to say I'm very sorry about Simon…"

So she's come to pay her respects. This didn't endear Claire more, and neither did the reemergence of her cheery smile. Regan wasn't one for well-meaning respect. She saw a sanctimonious piety that denoted a duty to be performed, that bloody need for people to tell you how sorry they are when things go horribly wrong. She also didn't like this woman's over familiarity. It was why Regan didn't invite her in.

"…and to see if you are okay," Claire finished.

Okay?

The word snapped in her head like an elastic band, and Regan's emotional grip started slipping. She looked down at the grass cuttings being shed on the hall carpet. Claire caught her looking and bent to pick them up.

Regan wanted this person gone. Her response was abrupt.

"You're going to have to forgive me. Okay is not what I'm feeling right now. My brother has committed suicide, and I've had to drive all the way down here from Yorkshire to sort this mess out. I am not *okay*. Frankly, I think it's a stupid thing to say to anyone in my shoes. Okay?"

Claire had the decency to look stunned.

"Of course. It is a silly thing to say. If there's anything you need, any help, anything at all, please just ask. You'll find me around in the garden or in the potting shed which is down—"

"Yes, I know where it is. I can see it from the window."

Regan wanted Claire to spit out her condolences and commiserations and go. She was struggling to remain civil and heard the harshness in her voice. So did Claire.

"Yes, of course."

Claire actually looked awkward and uncomfortable, finally realizing that she wasn't welcome.

It was time to bring this all to an end.

"Well, thank you for your offer of help. I appreciate it, but if you don't mind, I've only just arrived and I'm rather busy. I've got a lot to do."

Claire smiled again sympathetically. "Well, you know where I am."

"I've got that. Thanks."

Regan couldn't close the door fast enough.

As she returned to the kitchen, her phone went again. It was the Alex Griffin, the man she'd worked for. He'd been trying to get her all day, no doubt to talk about her resignation. As before, she ignored it and attacked the washing up with force.

"That went well, not," Claire mumbled to herself as she walked down the building stairs and back outside. She flicked the grass cuttings she'd picked up outside Simon's door into the air, and thrust her hands in her cargo trouser pockets as she all but marched down to the potting shed.

Have I just been spoken down to? Yes.

She thought of the way Regan looked her up and down more than a couple of times. It wasn't a nice experience. It was disrespectful. Claire could only surmise Regan didn't rate gardeners too highly in the pecking order of life.

Damn her.

All Claire wanted to do was introduce herself and let her know she wasn't alone. She wanted to let her know she was around to help if necessary. Simple politeness. What had she got? A face full of rude, bad-mannered behavior.

Goddamn it.

Where was the easygoing, relaxed, and charming nature of Simon? Well, nowhere was it written that siblings had to be alike. But Simon had often spoken of Regan as being "naturally friendly, a bit like a Labrador."

More like a ruddy Rottweiler.

He had said she was kind, with a bubbling sense of humor and even-keeled.

Stuff that.

The Regan she'd just met was definitely listing to one side. She couldn't have been more uncongenial and inhospitable if she'd tried.

And then there was all that fuss over the damned house key. What was that all about? She'd only mentioned that she wished she'd sorted things out a bit for Regan before her arrival…a decent thing to do given the circumstances. But Regan had made her feel like a thief, someone unwanted entering a property she had no right to be in. Simon had given her that key a long time ago, and it had never been a problem. He had trusted her implicitly. Surely Regan saw that?

Obviously not.

Claire hadn't lied. In the beginning, she'd used the key to water plants when Simon was away. Later on, as his mental state deteriorated, she confessed she'd used it more than once or twice to check up on him. In the months that led up to his suicide, he would lock himself away in the apartment for days, sometimes weeks, on end.

She always gave him his space, but there were times her concern overruled his privacy. He wouldn't answer his phone or door, so she would slip into the place to make sure he wasn't ill. Sometimes Simon had known she'd done this; sometimes he hadn't. He never chastised her or asked for the key back. He'd seemed grateful that someone bothered about him.

Claire growled as she threw a bag of fertilizer artfully and well-practiced into the wheelbarrow.

"Fork!" she exclaimed to no one in particular as she tossed the garden implement onto the top of the manure and started to push it all toward the front of the building.

"Spoke down to me."

She listened to the barrow wheel squeaking on its journey and deliberately avoided looking up at the window where she'd seen

Regan earlier. Usually, the rhythmic sound had a cathartic effect on her, but not today. By the time she arrived at the flower bed destined for her attention, she was still rattled.

For a while, she tried to focus on the job at hand and push all thought of Regan from her mind, but with little success. Maybe she should have left her alone. The signs had been there. She knew Regan was in, but despite several rings and knocking on the door, she hadn't answered. Common sense should have warned her that Regan wanted to be alone, but she'd ignored it. She should have walked away and let her have the first day to settle in and get some sleep. But Claire hadn't. She'd wanted her to know there was at least one friendly face around.

Claire didn't feel very friendly right now. As she knelt by the flower bed, she cussed as she pushed a plant into a hole she'd dug a second ago.

"Don't you dare die on me. I'm not in the mood. You will live and flourish."

The last plants she'd put here had withered. They had been a bad "job-lot" from a nursery. In fairness, the woman selling them had said they weren't good and had thrown them in free with an order. Claire had been so sure she could nurture them into growth. Wrong.

The awful meeting replayed in her head. Regan was physically like Simon. She had the same intense dark brown eyes, chiseled features, and strong jawline. Her eyebrows were shaped, but heavy. She had identical jet-black hair that she wore at shoulder length. Here the similarities ended.

Regan had full lips and an olive complexion. Claire had always thought Simon too pale. She had a long, graceful neck, yet there was more than a touch of masculinity to her, for she was tall with slim hips like a boy's. Regan didn't seem to try to counter her androgynous image. She'd worn a tight fitting white cotton blouse tucked into brown leather belted blue jeans. Claire didn't think anyone would call her beautiful, and yet she was striking to look at.

The act of gardening slowly granted Claire a more therapeutic disposition. As she turned the soil with her fork, she grew more rational and compromising. Regan had to be under a huge amount of stress. She had to be emotional, and the drive down must have been exhausting. She could only imagine what Regan had thought when she'd opened the door and found Simon's place in such a mess. No wonder she was short-tempered.

Claire cursed herself. She'd wanted to go into the apartment and at least clear out the fridge, but she'd held back because of the manner of Simon's death. She'd worried about entering his place in case the police wanted it left alone. She had planned to leave some of the basics for Regan, like tea, coffee, milk, and so on, plus a note of introduction. If she'd done that, none of this unpleasantness would have happened.

Understanding where Regan's behavior came from was one thing, but in Claire's eyes, it didn't excuse it. She didn't like the way Regan had looked down her nose at her, as if she were a second-class citizen. This was not a good start.

"Well. I'm sorry, Simon. I have a feeling your sister and I aren't going to get along," she muttered under her breath.

Claire decided she'd done her bit. She'd made herself known, and it was up to Regan to make the next move. If she needed her, she knew where she was. Regan was a grown woman and could look after herself. Claire would leave her alone now. She was friendly, but not stupid. Why attract another frosty onslaught?

It was a shame that their introduction bordered on the disastrous. Claire had wanted it to go well. She and Simon had been good friends and grown close. She'd looked forward to meeting, and liking, his only sibling. That hadn't happened, and Regan's snub hurt. Claire guessed they probably wouldn't have much to do with each other, but if they did bump into one another, she'd be polite. This she would do for Simon. Who knew, maybe when the dust settled, things might improve. Claire hoped that would happen because there were things Simon had told her that she thought Regan should know. Claire hoped the opportunity would arise later that would allow her to impart that information. Right now, things didn't look inspiring.

She dug a hole for another plant.

❖

When Regan had finished the washing up and done as much cleaning as she felt capable of, she drove into town to get groceries.

She saw Claire pottering around the front of the building as she left but chose to ignore her. She was still there when she returned, and now, as Regan stood at the window with a welcome cup of tea, she surreptitiously watched her going about her work.

Regan still bristled at the easy familiarity that the gardener had projected with regards to Simon, his apartment, and her.

In no forgiving mood, she unreasonably built a dossier of additional things to dislike about the woman. There was her accent. It was too clean, too south. It clashed with her northern one. Southerners always acted like they owned the country. This was probably because most of the country's wealth was disproportionately amassed down here. It was the money that had drawn her brother. If he'd stayed north, he might still be alive today.

Claire even carried herself with that self-assured arrogance most southerners had. Gardeners were expected to loll and amble. She didn't. Though short, she stood erect, alert, with a confidence that didn't seem to fit her occupation. Now if she'd been a garden designer? Yes, that might have fit better. They came across as authoritative and assured on television programs. If Claire was ever going to fit that bill, she'd need to at least put a comb through her messy hair.

Regan watched her stand up from a flower bed, grab the fork, and start digging. She sipped her tea as she contemplated that somewhere inside the unattractive clothing was probably a fairly good-looking woman. Was gardening attire ever meant to be fashionable? Regan wasn't sure, but somehow the fatigue cargo pants and oversized light blue denim shirt with its badly frayed collar and rolled up sleeves looked too heavy for the petite build. Everything about Claire spoke small. Her size, her face, her overall appearance…they were all elfin like. Even the wheelbarrow was huge next to her. She really didn't look like any gardener she'd seen.

Regan drained her cup and walked back into the kitchen to wash it. She was ready to unpack the few things she'd brought down with her, and then try to work out where to sleep. It would probably be the second bedroom. There was no way she could sleep in Simon's bed, even with clean sheets. That was probably where he'd imbibed in his libertine ways. She wondered if Claire had spent time there. She was still thinking that when she eventually went to bed.

When she awoke the following morning, she felt refreshed. She'd had a welcome and undisturbed night's sleep. It made her more amenable, and now, as uncomfortable as it was, it also brought about a shift in her attitude toward Claire. She couldn't help feeling the slightest tinge of guilt regarding her standoffish and unsociable behavior toward her yesterday.

As the day wore on, so Regan's feelings of shame grew in increasing proportions. She realized she ought to put things right. She had been an emotional mess when she'd met Claire, and her infamous flash temper, a negative side to her otherwise perfect personality, had ascended where it really shouldn't. As she was getting older, her temper *was* slowing and getting better. Regan reckoned another fifty years and she'd be as temperate as the Dalai Lama.

From midday onward, she kept an eye out for Claire, but unlike yesterday when she'd been everywhere, today she was nowhere in sight.

Mid afternoon, she decided to take a break and go down to the shed to see if Claire was there. She wasn't, so she strolled around the manicured gardens hoping to find the suddenly elusive gardener, but with no success.

What she did find was a dark-haired woman, probably in her forties, sitting in a chair lounger on a patio outside a ground floor apartment. The woman appeared to be enjoying the sunshine. She saw Regan and waved to her. Regan wandered over.

"Do I know you?" the woman asked, raising her hand to block the sunlight from her face.

It was difficult to not miss the thin hand and wrist that disappeared into the arm of a cardigan. The woman was almost skeletal, and her skin stretched tight over her bones. Regan noticed a thick tartan throw wrapped around her legs. Though she was good-looking, her delicate frame made Regan think of the models that starved themselves to the point of death just so they could be alluring to the media and the fashion trade they moved in. Regan never understood that. Why did people think that looking like a stick insect was attractive? Maybe she didn't "get it" because she'd never had weight issues and was naturally slim.

"I've just moved in," she answered. "I've only been here a short while. I'm Regan."

"Ah." The woman didn't offer her name.

"It's a beautiful day," Regan said.

"Yes, I love the heat...warms the bones."

Bones were all the woman was made up of, and Regan knew without question that she was ill. There was pallor to her face and a frailty that didn't seem right for someone so young. She noticed a corded alarm connected to the chair and attached to the woman's clothing. It was the sort of device used to warn and protect, to alert that someone vulnerable or ill had fallen or moved. Before Regan could fathom why such an item might be present, or who would be alerted, the woman spoke as if sensing her curiosity.

"I've not been well. I caught a virus in Egypt, but I'm getting better." She smiled, and the wide eyes that locked on to Regan were the deepest blue she'd ever seen.

"I'm glad to hear it."

She was, for there was vulnerability in the woman that naturally drew Regan's compassion. "I didn't catch your name," she asked.

The strangest look crossed the woman's face and she didn't answer. Instead, she closed her eyes and placed her head back on the chair. She didn't say anything else and appeared to fall asleep.

Regan stood there for a minute, puzzled. It crossed her mind that the woman was deliberately avoiding giving her name and that she was feigning sleep. But as Regan watched her chest rise and fall with her breathing, she knew she was wrong. The woman was genuinely tired, and Regan did not doubt that she was convalescing.

Not wanting to disturb her, Regan quietly stepped back, and moved away.

CHAPTER THREE

The following evening, as dusk began to fall, Regan decided to go down to the gardener's shed and leave Claire a card saying sorry. Despite looking for her all day, she hadn't seen her. Maybe Claire only worked part-time?

Regan's guilt trip had produced a decent card with flowerpots on the front. She'd written some appropriate words of apology, including an invite for Claire to pop in sometime for a cup of tea. Whether Claire would do that, she didn't know. Regan's behavior had been bloody awful. Now she just hoped she could put things right. She had a feeling she'd at least have ample time, for until Simon's affairs were sorted, she was here to stay. Everything was overwhelming and confusing, and she could see no beginning to the unenviable process of dealing with Simon's death, let alone an ending.

There were so many issues to deal with, and, of course, her own. When she sold her house, where was she going to settle? Was this someplace she'd like to stay on given she wanted to move as far away from Yorkshire as possible? As irrational as it was, this was where she preferred to be. Though faced with the awfulness of sorting her brother's estate, the issues that faced her up North were simply intolerable. It wasn't a question of wanting to run away; she needed to start again, and somewhere fresh. An unpremeditated thought crossed her mind that Devon didn't seem such a bad place to lick wounds. The South suddenly seemed better than the North.

She ambled down to the shed, and everything looked dark under the canopy of trees. The wooden door was unlatched and half open.

She strained to hear any sound or movement within. Hearing nothing, she slowly edged her way inside and her senses were assaulted by the earthy smells of soil and plants. The lack of light contrasted with the outside brightness, and her eyes struggled to acclimatize to the strange world she now entered. Unsure of her balance, she reached out to steady herself, and in doing so, she knocked over several clay pots that rolled and rattled noisily along a workbench.

A voice cut through the darkness.

"I hope you haven't come to steal my herbaceous perennials." It was Claire's.

Shocked, Regan turned to where the voice had come. She squinted and could just make out a shadowy figure seated over in the corner of the shed. She thought she'd been alone. To discover she wasn't, made her feel uncomfortable, like a thief caught with hands in a jewelry box.

"What are you doing here?" Regan's question had all the sophistication and subtlety of a moron.

"I'm the gardener. This is the potting shed. The two are inextricably linked."

Claire's voice was calm and measured.

"But it's late."

"I like to talk to my plants. My days are busy; the evening provides the opportunity."

Regan didn't know what to say.

"You aren't, are you?" Claire asked.

"What?"

"You aren't some nocturnal thief intent on robbing me of my prized saplings. If you are, I warn you that I'm very protective of my seedlings, and you'd better leave now because I won't answer for my behavior."

Regan hoped Claire was joking, although she didn't sound it. She squinted, still trying to adjust to the dark. She could now make out the pots she'd knocked over, their soil spewed across the bench top. Next to them were other rustic pots of varying sizes, an assortment of hand tools, and an opened bag of compost.

"An answer would be nice." The quiet demand held authority.

She looked over toward Claire, targeting her voice.

"I thought you'd gone home—"

"Your intent?"

Claire didn't sound too hospitable, and Regan couldn't blame her.

She could make out Claire's shape becoming clearer. She was sitting in an old dark leather armchair with a book on the side arm. She wondered how Claire could read anything in this light.

"Have you come for the key?" Claire asked.

Regan winced. She wanted to put the other day as far from her mind as possible, but Claire wasn't letting her. She'd had a dreadful start with her and behaved like a childish prat. Claire told her Simon had given her the key, and he wouldn't have done that if he didn't trust her. What a stupid frame of mind she'd been in.

"No. I came to say sorry for being so offensive." She held the card up.

Claire said nothing, and Regan saw her raise steepled fingers to her lips.

This wasn't going very well, and she was nervous. She tried to lighten the mood.

"I see you read." *Bloody hell, what a stupid thing to say.*

Claire thought so too. "Strange as it may seem, a lot of gardeners possess that ability."

Her voice was low and soft, but Regan heard its edge.

"Look, that's not what I meant."

"What did you mean?" Claire asked.

"I meant you read books."

She was growing more accustomed to the dark, and she saw Claire's eyes widen. Regan had come to apologize, but she was upsetting the woman again as surely as she had during their introduction. It was time to do some fast backpedaling.

"I meant," Regan said deliberately, "that these days everyone seems to read stuff on Kindle or other electronic technology. It's refreshing to actually see someone who still reads *real* books. You know, something you can hold and flick the pages."

Claire remained silent.

"That's what I meant," Regan repeated. *Pedal faster.* "And I also like your subject matter."

Regan could now read the bold title on the book cover. It was one she recognized, having read it recently. It was a lesbian novel. The discovery surprised her. She hadn't considered that Claire might be gay. A few days ago, she was convinced she was one of Simon's adoring floozies. Who else would have a key to his apartment?

"She's a good writer," Regan said.

"You've read her stuff?" Claire asked.

"Everything she's written so far. I'm a bit surprised though."

"Surprised?"

"I assumed...well, Simon, he was a bit of a woman killer. He'd shag any female that moved."

"Even the gardener." Claire looked at her like she was an idiot. Why was every word coming out of her mouth attached to her foot? Regan needed to finish what she'd come down here to do and leave before she did more damage. She edged forward and gingerly placed the card on the top of the book.

"Look, it's all in there, but the other day, I think I was in shock. I was tired and upset. I'd had the worst journey down, and my anger was looking for a target. You got tagged. I'm sorry I took it out on you. You were just the poor sap who came to the door first."

In hindsight, "poor sap" wasn't the nicest term to call Claire.

"Poor sap?" Claire echoed.

Regan could almost imagine herself digging a huge hole. She sighed. "I think I'm making things worse, aren't I?"

"You just might be."

"Poor sap isn't what I meant," Regan stuttered.

"I know what you meant." Claire stood. "I think you should sit down before you implode." Claire wasn't smiling, but she seemed less hostile and defensive. Regan sighed again.

"Would you like a coffee?" Claire's question sounded like a cordial invitation before a business meeting. But at least it was a step in the right direction, for which Regan was grateful. She couldn't expect the woman to welcome her with open arms after the reception she'd given her.

Claire pointed to an upturned crate which Regan accepted as an invite to sit down.

"Rustic, but practical," Claire stated. "Simon used to sit there a lot."

Regan took the weight off her legs and watched as Claire reached across the cluttered bench to switch a kettle on. She thought about Simon and how he might have come here often to sit and talk. Claire had said *a lot*. What might they have talked about? Somehow the image of her brother in his expensive suits, sitting here in a musty, soil ridden environment didn't quite gel, but she had no reason to disbelieve Claire.

"A friend of mine passes these books on to me," Claire said as she spooned instant coffee into mugs. "I don't know how long you plan to stay, but I've a few you can have if you like. I take it…" she turned to Regan, complicity on her face, "that you are of a certain persuasion?"

Regan somberly placed a hand over her heart, as if confirming allegiance to an inner circle of some sacred order. "I am of the sisterhood, yes. Didn't Simon ever mention me; tell you that I'm a lesbian?"

"Simon mentioned you all the time, but never told me that. He was too much the gentleman."

Regan snorted with contempt. "Simon talked about me? I can only imagine those conversations. We weren't too close." She caught the way Claire looked at her as she passed her coffee, like her comments were small-minded and puerile. Claire didn't answer, only pursed her lips slightly before changing the subject.

"How are you getting on?"

Claire returned to her armchair, and Regan clung to the mug and its warmth as she thought how to answer that question. She couldn't stop the sense of suffocation from creeping over her. She might as well tell Claire.

"I got a call this morning. I've got to go and identify his body tomorrow. They wanted me to do it today, but I just can't."

She thought of the phone call earlier informing her that the autopsy was complete and now asking her to identify the body. The woman on the phone had been courteous and sympathetic saying that if she didn't feel she could do this, then there were other ways, but the latter would slow the process down.

The process. Her brother had become a procedure, something to be dealt with. Everything that Simon had been was now gone, extinct, and it felt as if he were dematerializing with each passing day.

"Ah, that's not good. Will you be all right?" There was empathy in Claire's voice.

"Sure. It's just the shock. I knew this was coming, but you're never ready, are you? I will be tomorrow."

"If you need anyone—"

"—I'll cope. Thanks."

Claire had softened, and Regan was thankful. It gave her a chance to show she could be quite pleasant on occasion.

"Beyond that," Regan continued, "I'm not sure how I am getting on. It seems like a mountain of work, and I don't really know where to start. Logic tells you to arrange a funeral, but I can't do that because the death hasn't been registered. Until the coroner's office allows that, nothing moves. I know there's going to be an inquest because it's such a violent end. That apparently won't happen yet. I guess this will all take some time, and I could be here a while."

She watched Claire slowly push back in her chair and glance up, apparently in thought. When she looked at Regan again, she sensed nothing but understanding. She was glad her temper hadn't made her demand Simon's key back the other day.

"It's early days," Claire said.

Regan knew she was right, but she still felt like she was moving in molasses. "It's all the decisions I have to make. When they allow me to bury him? Do I do that here, or up north? He loved it here, and there's no one who cares, except me. Mum and Dad died years ago, and I'm the only close family left. I suppose whatever decision I make will be it, but I still want to get it right. I've got to apply for probate, but can't do that yet either. I've got to sort his banking and business stuff out. She shuddered as she thought of the workload, and worse, all his debts. There were so many. She wondered how much Claire knew.

"Listen to me, rattling on. You don't want to hear this."

Claire ignored the comment. Instead she asked, "Have you got a solicitor?"

"No, I was going to do that today, but the call threw me." Normally, Regan was an organized person. She would make lists and then work her way methodically through them. She seemed incapable of doing anything right now. She figured it was the shock.

"I don't want to intrude, Regan, but you might like to have a word with Albert Marshall. He's a good local solicitor, very efficient, resourceful, and not too expensive. He's got a lot of experience in this area and used to work for the coroner's office so he'll know what he's doing. I can dig his telephone number out if you're interested?"

Regan's relief must have shown. "I'd really like that. Thanks." She'd actually been going through the phone directory looking for someone before the dreaded phone call. It was overwhelming how many solicitors were out there. Picking the right one was like choosing the winning number in the Lotto.

"Okay, leave that with me."

"I'll also need to find out how long I can stay in the apartment." The questions and issues were rolling off Regan's brain like a ball downhill. "I'm not even sure if the rent's been paid. Not much else has…the paperwork is such a mess. I didn't talk to the agent about that the other day, and he didn't say anything."

"I'm sure the agent will be very sympathetic. Just give him a call."

Regan finished her coffee. "Other than that, everything is peachy." She tried to sound upbeat. Claire didn't seem fooled.

She glanced at her watch. It was getting late and Claire would want to go home. She stood to leave. "I'm sorry. I'm keeping you. I only popped down to leave you that card."

"You're not keeping me. I'm often here till late."

"There's no one to go home to, then?"

Regan cringed the second the question left her lips. It was an indiscreet and prying question, especially to someone she barely knew. Claire would probably think she was a lesbian in heat looking for a quick lay. She wanted to retract her comment, but it was too late. However, Claire didn't look offended. She only shook her head, but not before Regan caught something cross her face. It was gone before she could identify it, but whatever she saw, it wasn't good. Regan didn't delve.

"Thank you for the coffee, and for listening. I hope you can forgive me."

Claire moved alongside her as they stepped outside. "Apology accepted."

Regan smiled.

Claire tapped her shoulder. "If you ever want a coffee or to just talk, I'm pretty much always here."

"You weren't earlier. I've been looking for you the last few days."

Claire shrugged. "I've been away on business, but normally I'm here, amidst my pots, talking—"

"—to your seedlings."

Though restrained, Claire almost grinned.

Regan hadn't liked this woman when they'd first met, but perhaps she did now? She'd let stupid prejudices cloud her opinion, not helped by lack of sleep, and a temper she really did have to learn to control.

Once outside, something struck her.

"How do you do that?" she asked.

"Do what?" Claire said.

"Read in the dark?"

Claire smiled. "I wasn't. I'd stopped some time before you showed. You caught me napping. But there's a small lamp to the side. I use that if it gets too dark in there."

"Oh, I didn't see that." Now Regan understood.

"Obviously."

"It's quite cozy, then?"

"I like it," Claire said, her voice betraying her amusement.

Regan walked back up the lawn.

Claire remained standing under the canopy of trees, observing Regan's boyish figure swagger up the hill. It amused her how cocksure and confident her walk was. She watched her until she rounded the corner out of sight.

Claire ruefully conceded that this meeting had gone better than the last. Could it have gone worse? Doubtful, she thought. She wasn't sure what she thought of Regan now. The question about whether she had anyone at home had thrown her. It hadn't offended her, but it had made her aware that Regan was not someone she wanted to confide in…not like she had with Simon.

She really wanted to like Simon's sister. To not like her seemed like a betrayal of his memory. In fairness, this time she'd seen some of the gentleness he'd spoken of when describing her. Regan had behaved better, and Claire's own restraint and sharpness had been taken in good spirit. This had allowed Claire to warm to Regan and served as a means to remove some of the earlier unpleasantness between them.

However, it did not mean she was lowering her guard. She wasn't sure what her opinion of Regan was after only two dealings. The first one had been bloody awful, and the second arguably better. Who was the real Regan? For now, Claire would reserve her opinion, and keep her powder dry.

She thought of Simon, and how she missed him. Their talks had been frequent and always with such warmth. Most evenings, especially of late, he had taken to coming down to the potting shed and joining her for a coffee. On rare occasions, he would turn up with a bottle of wine and they would share that.

There had never been any impropriety between them. She wasn't wired that way. It had been two lonely people sitting together and chatting. Sometimes they had laughed, sometimes they had cried. They just listened to each other's woes, but always amidst a closeness of trusted companionship.

She was able to open up to Simon, and he had willingly become her sole confidant. What he didn't know about her wasn't worth knowing. He had talked too, not just about things present that had, in hindsight, killed him, but of things past. He was full of regrets, mostly to do with Regan. He had spoken of how close they were as children, and how they had both shared a passion for all things mathematics. This had been inherited from their parents, both scholars of the subject. As they'd grown older, Simon had used his passion and moved into the financial sector. He'd worked in the city as a commodities broker. He'd proved himself a natural and made huge amounts of money. But he had grown arrogant and allowed his close relationship with Regan to drift and tarnish. She had hated his capitalist over-indulgences, his waste of money on the excesses of the good life, and worse, his sneering disrespect toward those with less.

He had confessed much to Claire, especially about his immaturity. He had explained how Regan always valued the smaller things in life. He had found it annoying, and when he'd grown successful, he had deliberately taunted her. Everything had changed as the recession kicked in. It had robbed him of every last penny. Simon had discovered at cost what finally really mattered in life, and had seen how right Regan was. He'd spoken to Claire at length of how he longed to put things right between them but didn't know how.

Toward the end, Clare had seen how desperate Simon was, how his failed finances and burgeoning debts were swallowing him up. Where she could, she'd tried to help. It hadn't been much. Claire hoped their talks had helped him to find resolution, to forge a way out of his situation, if only to declare bankruptcy. Nothing had helped. In the end, Simon had found his own answer.

There was so much Claire wanted to share with Regan, to let her know how much Simon cared for her. She hadn't told her any of this because she didn't think Regan was ready to hear it. She was still festering with anger. That much had been evident even tonight. Claire thought it would be wiser to tell her these things when, and if, she got to know Regan better. These were things that ought not to be spoken by a stranger. An element of trust needed to be present.

It was getting dark, and Claire decided she should go home. She also wanted to dig out Albert Marshall's contact details. She knew him through her father and thought she'd have a chat with him first. She could quietly apprise him of the situation, and if Regan chose her recommendation, it would make things a little easier.

But there was one last thing Claire had to do before she could leave. She glanced up the lawn toward a ground floor apartment. The curtains were closed. She was safe.

Claire loaded two large pots containing an assortment of blossoming spring flowers onto the wheelbarrow and then pushed her way up to the patio that edged the lawn. There she unloaded them and placed them where she thought they looked best. She removed a plant that needed attention. She would sort that out tomorrow.

Job done, she stood a while and listened to the wind lamenting through the treetops. A familiar veil of hopelessness swept over her as she stared at the closed French doors. She could just make out her own reflection looking back at her. Her face seemed blurred, like a ghost.

Like my life.

The other side of those doors, barely yards away, was the woman who had once loved Claire with fervor. Years ago, she had tenaciously sought Claire out and captured her heart. A willing captive, Claire had returned that love with abundance, and for a while, they had lived a dream, their lives entwined and their existence blessed. But then something had happened that had driven the love away.

Claire longed, yearned, for that love to be returned again, but she knew it never would. It was gone. A chapter in her life was over. She would still love from a distance, but that was all it could ever be now.

Friends had told her to step back. They had said that it was wrong to hang on to a love when the other person no longer loved you back, and worse, hated you. They told her she was wasting her life. But Claire knew that real love, *her love*, stayed true, and that time could not erode it. Her friends had not understood. They did not understand that where love is given so is the power to hurt.

Claire pushed the barrow back to the shed.

At least she had her work. Work was what she needed, and lots of it. Work restored her, and it preserved her mental stability. It delivered her from her darkest thoughts.

It was her salvation.

CHAPTER FOUR

How Regan managed to walk into the apartment building, she didn't know. It was only when she got inside the entrance that she was forced to stop, simply to get breath.

She had just come from the morgue where she had identified her brother's body. Nothing in all her thirty plus years had prepared her for that. Afterward, she'd been like an automaton, programmed only on driving home safely, parking the car, and then making it to the apartment where she could break down in private. That was the plan, but like all good ones, they didn't always work out. There was also the principle of mind over body. That was clearly not working, for her body was about to go into meltdown at the foot of the foyer stairs. She knew she wouldn't make it up them and that she was about to burst into uncontrollable tears. Their onslaught was only temporarily placed on hold as someone spoke to her.

"Hello, I've seen you around a few times. Just moved in?"

The voice was friendly and belonged to a portly, rather matronly built woman with brown hair that was parted in the middle and tied back in a neat bun. It was difficult to gauge her age, but Regan thought she was probably in her mid forties. She had a kind face and deep brown eyes, and she was smiling as she came up to Regan. Try as she might, Regan couldn't return the warmth. The woman frowned and laid a hand on her shoulder.

"You all right?"

"I'm Simon Canning's sister." Her words faltered, as though she had a speech impediment. She thought it was a silly way to introduce herself. Why hadn't she said she was Regan? Maybe it was because Simon was prominent in her mind right now. Maybe it was because the tears she'd held at bay for the last hour suddenly welled, and she knew she was about to make a fool of herself.

"Don't you say any more. I know." The woman's bubbly personality changed. Her joviality gave way to subdued understanding as her face creased with concern. Regan tried to reassure her that she was all right—except she wasn't.

"Forgive me," she stuttered. "I've been to see Simon..." She couldn't finish the sentence.

"To identify the body? Oh, love."

It was like trying to stop a runaway train with a feather. Tears ran down her face, and her chest started to heave as she broke down. It was embarrassing, and there was nothing she could do. She tried to say sorry, but the words wouldn't come.

"Right. You come with me," the woman said.

A warm, comfortable hand took hers and led her to an area just behind the main entrance, and out of public view. There Regan sobbed her heart out as the woman put her arms around her and hugged her tight like a mother. She couldn't remember the last time she'd been held like this, but it felt so good, so natural. Regan stayed in the shelter of those arms for several minutes until she felt her control return.

"I'm sorry. I bet you didn't expect that when you said hello." Regan pulled herself together.

"Can't say I did, but none of us get to pick our moments when life throws us a wobbly." The woman handed her a tissue, and she wiped her face.

"By the way, I'm Sally...Sally Tyne. I live in apartment two down this corridor." Sally pointed to a ground floor corridor behind her.

Regan put her hand out, an automatic act of sociability. She considered it meaningless given the woman had just mothered her.

"Hello, Sally Tyne. I'm Regan Canning, and I'm staying in Simon's place while I try to sort things out."

Sally grimaced as she cupped Regan's hands in hers. "Well, that's not going to be pleasant...losing a brother like that." There was a lull before she continued, "Are you all right now or do you need another tissue?"

"I feel better, thanks. It suddenly came over me. It's been a bloody awful morning."

"I can imagine. Well, actually, I can't. Didn't you go with anyone?"

Regan shook her head. "I wanted to do it by myself. I thought I'd be okay. I guess I should have at least taken a taxi and not driven." She paused. "I hope I never have to do that again."

"Once is enough in anybody's lifetime," Sally agreed.

They moved back into the foyer, and as they did, an official looking woman in a smart dress and tailored jacket, holding an expensive brown leather satchel under her arm, came down the stairs. Regan heard Sally mutter *no* under her breath.

The woman targeted Regan, totally ignoring Sally.

"Ah, good afternoon." She thrust a hand forward, which Regan shook without thinking. She was doing a lot of that today.

"You must be Miss Canning, Simon's sister?"

Before Regan had time to answer, the woman introduced herself.

"I'm Cynthia Tennerson, the local councilor. I called on you the other day, but you weren't in. Someone here told me you'd arrived, and I've wanted to introduce myself in case you needed any assistance."

Regan was lost for words. Why would a councilor have any interest in someone not from the area? The councilors she'd come across were busy enough without adopting passers through. It was intriguing that she was on first name terms with Simon.

The councilor continued in a matter-of-fact way, smiling cordially. "I can appreciate how awful things are for you, at this time. I just want you to know you're not alone and that if I can help, I will. I'm only sorry this is a quick call as I'm just passing. We have a bit of an emergency on our hands at the moment. What you might call a council crisis, as it were, so I can't stop, much as I'd like to. Simon was such a kind young man. I'd rather chat to you and see what can be done. I'm sure you understand." She exhaled noisily. "I tell you, sometimes this job takes over everything else and you question why you do it."

"Why do you?"

Regan heard the sarcasm in Sally's voice. The councilor ignored the comment.

"But you do what you can for the constituents. It's why I took the job on, to help sort out people's issues, make a difference." She rattled on like a machine gun. "And if I didn't do it, who else would? There aren't many people out there prepared to put the hours in that I do. Anyhow, I popped in to leave you my card. If you need any help, you can contact me. That's what I'm here for."

Cynthia reached inside her jacket pocket and produced a card which she thrust into Regan's hand. "You keep this with you, and any official problems, anything you're having trouble with, you phone me. I know all the movers and shakers in the various departments. I can help ease things through." As she walked away, she said, "It's been delightful to meet you. Ring."

Sally waited until Cynthia left the building before announcing, "What would we do without her?"

It was a disingenuous statement, and Regan could see Sally was unimpressed.

When Sally realized she was being scrutinized, she merely shrugged. "*Cynicism* is a word written for her." She laughed, more for herself than Regan's benefit.

"I'm wondering if I've won a prize. Why has she been looking for me?" Regan said.

"You should have asked."

"I would if I could've got a word in."

Sally's smile returned. "I'd better be off. I've got to pick up a prescription before the chemist closes."

Before she moved, she tapped Regan's elbow. "I really liked your brother. He was always polite and helpful. You just remember that I'm only down this corridor," she repeated. "Regan, anything you need, you just call. Don't forget...and you don't need my business card."

Seconds later, Regan was alone in the foyer. She walked up the stairs, thinking about the kindness of strangers. She'd instantly taken to Sally. It was difficult not to given her kindheartedness and compassion. She had a genuine reassurance that if she ever did need help, Sally Tyne was a person she could turn to. It lifted her spirits to know there was someone in the building if she needed anything.

As she got to her door, she studied the card still in her hand. The name Councilor Cynthia Tennerson stared back at her. She'd called her brother a kind young man. Why? She couldn't imagine Simon having anything to do with someone like Cynthia. It was also interesting that Sally didn't like her. Regan wasn't too sure either.

❖

I'll knock on the door. No, I'll ring the bell. No, I'll just push the solicitor's details under her door.

Claire stood outside Regan's apartment debating the best way to get Albert Marshall's details to her. She tutted to herself and considered how pathetic her deliberations were. How many times had she pounced up here to see Simon and never given ringing the doorbell a second thought? She'd always been made welcome.

The trouble was she couldn't stop thinking about the last time she'd stood here. There had been no welcoming reception. This accounted for her current indecisive nature, and why she was having second, third, and fourth thoughts. If only Regan was out, her task would be easier. She could post the detail under the door. But alas, she was in. Regan's car was parked out front. Claire tutted to herself again.

All you have to do is ring the bell and hand her Albert's number and then go. That's it. Just do it.

The brain decided. The body disagreed, and somewhere in the next second, Claire was in the act of bending down and pushing the piece of paper under the door when it opened revealing Regan.

"Gotcha." Regan seemed amused.

Claire stood quickly and tried not to look shocked. "I was just passing."

Regan arched her head and peered around the door. "But it's a dead end. The corridor goes nowhere."

Rumbled. Claire held her hands up and gestured surrender. "I admit it. I was about to push the solicitor's details under your door—"

"So you wouldn't have to talk to me—"

"I didn't want to disturb you—"

"You were avoiding me in case I bit your head off again like last time you were here."

Claire was not going to admit that Regan had it nailed. She didn't want to add anything negative to Regan's already horrific day. She'd seen Sally who had mentioned how upset Regan had been earlier, and why. Sally was many things, but she was not the gossipy type. She held confidences tighter than the Ministry of Defence and inter-ballistic missile systems, but she'd been concerned about Regan *having to deal with all of this by herself and not knowing anyone.* Sally had told Claire because she knew how close she'd been with Simon and thought she ought to know his sister was having a bad time.

"No," Claire lied. "I thought you might want some time to yourself after…" Claire stumbled over the choice of words.

Regan smiled as she filled them in. "Identifying Simon."

"Yes," Claire said awkwardly. "I didn't want to intrude."

"You're not. I saw him this morning, got back here, and cried a lot, but I'm fine now…I think."

Regan didn't mention Sally, and Claire wasn't going to drop her in it. She held out the piece of paper with Albert's details on it.

Regan stepped back. "Come in." She took the paper off Claire as she passed.

"This is great. I'll phone him today. I really want to get things moving."

Claire looked around. The place looked better than it had for a long time, but there were huge heaps of clothing and paperwork everywhere, all interspersed with what she assumed was some of Regan's stuff. It was now a tidier mess.

"Try to ignore the mess," Regan said, unconsciously mind melding with Claire.

"Bit difficult."

It wasn't tactful, but Claire couldn't hide the truth, and her dry comment raised a chuckle from Regan.

"I've made little channels that I can walk through. It's a bit like being a hamster and making tracks in the straw."

"You don't strike me as the hamster type."

"I'm not, but I'm having to innovate." Regan's answer matched Claire's deadpan humor.

"Well, if the system works."

Regan looked at her as if she were mad. "I have no idea. I'm just trying to put stuff into obvious piles and hope for the best. The truth is I'm overwhelmed by the amount of paperwork. There's so much of it. Where's it all come from? I know Simon had no office so all his business paperwork is here, but look at it, Claire. This is more than that. This is like walking into the home of someone with an obsessive hording disorder, someone who never throws anything out. Simon was always hyper tidy and ordered, but this?"

Regan threw her hands up in despair.

"He must have been losing his marbles. I don't think he's ever thrown away a newspaper or magazine. I've been trying to clear some of it out to make more room, but it all seems important. It's like a document archive. The police have told me that there's a load more in the trunk of his car." Regan paused and stared at the room. "At least I've discovered the carpet."

"Where?"

"That little bit, over by the window." Regan pointed.

"Oh, yes." Claire could just make out a small patch. "It's quite a nice color."

"I thought that." Regan gave a half-hearted laugh.

Claire knew the talk for what it was. Regan was putting up a front. She was struggling to hold her emotions in check, and Claire sensed they were bubbling just under the surface. Regan probably wanted to sit down and cry. The task facing her was not an easy one, nor pleasant. Right now, this was not a nice place to come home to. It wouldn't be until some of the documentation disappeared. She hoped Albert would be able to help.

"If only I could find the one bit of paperwork that matters," Regan said.

Claire heard the shift in Regan's tone. The wry humor was replaced by seriousness.

"What?"

Regan continued. "I keep looking for a letter, or something. Simon could leave a suicide note in the car, but he couldn't leave anything for me...his sister. I know we weren't close at the end, but for Christ's sake, why didn't he do that? I just wish he'd left *me* something, anything. I know it sounds stupid, but whatever he would have written, it would have been a last contact with him…something personal between us."

Claire wanted to sit down with her, instead of standing just inside the door. But a quick glance around the room revealed the hopelessness of that wish. Every chair seemed to have something on it, and there was nowhere inviting to have any therapeutic chat.

Regan looked devastated. It was as if all the emotions and revelations of Simon's death had culminated into that one moment. It pained Claire to see it. She realized for the first time, that for all Regan's anger and dismissive behavior toward Simon, she was hurting and suffering from his loss. It made Claire warm to her. She'd thought Regan didn't care about Simon. She was wrong.

There was a brief silence in the room, and Claire didn't know what to say. When she'd heard what Simon had done, she'd briefly wondered if it had been a spontaneous act. When she later learned *how* he'd killed himself, she realized he must have thought it out. He'd managed to get hold of a gun from somewhere. That would have taken planning. Regan probably thought the same. If planned, why no note or letter to a sister? It did seem cruel.

She placed a supportive hand on Regan's shoulder, half expecting it to be pushed away, but it wasn't.

"I really know how to lift a mood, don't I?" Regan said.

"I think you're handling all of this remarkably well," Claire said softly. She admired Regan's ability to hold things together. It was bad enough being the sole executor of an estate when things were straightforward, but this? Claire wondered how anyone could identify a body with half its head missing, but Albert had said amazing things could be done when the body was *cleaned up*, post autopsy.

"Can I get you something to drink?" Regan asked. "One of my hamster tracks leads to the kitchen."

Claire smiled, but declined the offer. Sometimes you could sense when someone needed company, and that a chat around a drink would be good. This was not one of those moments. Regan was tired, and it was obvious she wanted to sort a solicitor before the day was out. Claire wasn't going to delay her. She'd achieved what she'd wanted anyway, which was to pass her the details, and to check she was not curled up in a corner fighting demons. Simon would want her to keep an eye on his sister. She couldn't let him down.

Claire dropped her hand from Regan's shoulder and edged toward the door. As she did she caught sight of a business card on a side table. It was Cynthia Tennerson's. That was another thing Sally had mentioned, how the super efficient councilor had *regrettably* introduced herself to Regan. Sally was never one to hide her feelings. Claire was no fan of the councilor either.

"Regan, don't feel any obligation to use Albert. If you find someone better, I won't be upset."

Claire stuck her hands in her cargo pockets overwhelmed by a sudden crisis of conscience. What if Regan didn't take to Albert? But she knew her doubts were unfounded. He was a gentle, sensitive man—for a lawyer. Her father worshipped the very ink Marshall dipped his proverbial feather quills in, and wouldn't consider using anyone else for local matters. She'd spoken to Albert that morning. He'd implied he'd act for Regan if she wanted.

"I'm going to call Mr. Marshall now, Claire. Thanks."

As she turned to leave, Regan added, "Seriously...*thank* you. It would have taken me ages to find someone in the directory. At least this feels like a step in the right direction."

Claire could see how grateful she was. She was glad she'd made the effort to help.

As she headed down the stairs, her thoughts returned to Cynthia Tennerson. She really hoped Regan wouldn't have much to do with her. Simon had met and loathed the woman, keeping her at a distance. She remembered a conversation they'd had down in the potting shed.

Simon had thought her "an uptight shrew that needed a good bedding." When Claire had asked if Simon was up for it, he'd replied, "Shit, no! I may be broke, destitute, and up to my nuts in debt, but I still have taste. Give me some bloody credit, Claire."

Claire pivoted and headed back to Regan's. She rang the bell. Regan answered almost immediately.

"Did you forget something?"

"No, not exactly." Claire was about to surprise herself too. "Look, I don't suppose, if you ever feel like a break from your hamster runs, you'd like to walk down into the town and have a coffee? There's a shortcut through the trees and a trail that goes straight down. It's a lovely walk...comes out on the coastline."

"I'd love to."

Claire stared her straight in the face. "We had a bad start. Try again?"

"Yeah, I'd like that." Regan looked relieved.

"That's sorted then. You let me know when you've got the time, and we'll stroll down."

"Thanks. I will."

When Claire left again, she felt better. She'd never believed in first impressions. Her life had been full of wonderful people she hadn't necessary liked when she'd first met them. So giving Regan another chance seemed appropriate.

Besides, this was the right thing to do, to be there to help and support her if she needed it. She was giving Regan another chance... for Simon.

I hope you're watching, Simon. I'm doing this for you.

She returned to the potting shed.

CHAPTER FIVE

Claire did not see Regan for days, apart from an occasional wave in the distance. Her offer of a stroll downtown for coffee had not been pursued, and she started to accept that Regan's initial delight at the invitation was born out of basic politeness and nothing more.

Cynthia was about, too, and more than usual. Although she hadn't seen the two of them together, it worried Claire that she might be trying to get her claws into Regan. Even though Regan probably wouldn't be around long, the thought of the two of them becoming chummy turned her stomach. She was no fan of Cynthia and hated seeing her around at the best of times. She didn't want Cynthia "corrupting" Regan with her stuck-up snobbery and vile opinions.

Simon had seen through her straightaway when his path had crossed hers. He'd bestowed on her some chivalrous deed which he later confessed to Claire he'd regretted. It hadn't taken him long to realize she was an unpleasant, manipulative woman with a slanderous tongue. Though he never told Claire what had been said to make him form such an opinion, she guessed Cynthia had probably badmouthed her. It was no secret that Claire disliked her, but Cynthia *loathed* Claire.

She hoped Regan would assess Cynthia similarly. If Simon's assessment of her was correct, then she was no fool and as astute as him. But Claire had yet to see the sister he'd so often described. If Regan did befriend Cynthia, the last thing Claire wanted was the reemergence of Cynthia in her life. She'd had enough of the woman years ago, and the memories burned deep.

Despite their announced amnesty, Claire remained wary of Regan. As the days increased since the coffee invite, she saw it as a sign that she would be wise to keep some space between them. She was just thinking how "Distance is King" when Regan appeared at the potting shed door.

"You in here?"

Regan entered the shed smiling, and Claire felt some of her earlier reservations disappear.

"I am," she answered redundantly. Though Regan's voice was upbeat, Claire sensed something was wrong. Regan was tense.

"How are things?" Claire had wanted to ask if she was okay, but the last time she'd used that word, she'd almost been burned to the ground. She watched as Regan stepped over to the wooden bench where Claire was pricking out young seedlings. She leaned on the bench, sighed, and then wasted no time in getting straight to the point.

"Good news, bad news. The police have contacted me to say they can release Simon's car, but the officer has warned me that it's a mess. The bullet went up through the sunroof, totally wrecking it, and there's a lot of blood...and other stuff, all over the insides."

Claire could imagine what "the other stuff" might be.

Preoccupied, Regan picked up a tiny terracotta pot containing a small-leaved foliage plant and looked at it absentmindedly. "They said the car's repairable, and they want to know what I want to do with it." She bounced the pot up and down in her hand like a rubber ball.

"And what do you want to do?"

"I don't know. The car's not that old. I *do* know I don't want it. The officer said I can scrap it if I want, in which case the vehicle pound will take care of that and give me the scrap value. That's such a waste, isn't it? It's a perfectly good vehicle, albeit with a violent past." Regan grimaced. "It's not about the money, Claire, but I suppose I ought to sell it, but can it be sold? It would have to be cleaned. You know, remove all the...from the..."

Regan continued to bounce the small pot up and down.

Claire stepped forward and caught the pot in mid flight. She placed it gently back on the bench.

"Sorry," Regan said, crossing her arms and placing her hands under her armpits as if to stop herself doing any further harm. "Hope I haven't hurt it."

"It's probably brain damaged, and now thinks it's a tulip."

"Oh, it's a tulip?"

"No," Claire answered dryly. "It will be a trailing plant...if it lives that long."

Regan wasn't listening, her mind elsewhere.

"Oh, damn. I guess I'm going to have to go and get the car, but I sure as hell don't want to drive it."

I wouldn't either, Claire thought, and that was one thing she couldn't bring herself to volunteer to do. But she could help. "Would you like me to make arrangements to have it collected? There are people who clean cars and can make them look new again."

"The officer said that." Regan looked hopeful.

"And I know a man who runs a garage. I'll see if he thinks he can sell it."

"Who would want to buy a car with a history like that?" Regan asked.

Claire frowned. "I wouldn't, but there are plenty of people out there that couldn't give a toss as long as it goes, and the price is right. Let me make some phone calls."

Regan picked up another pot. "You are good, you know. First you find me Albert, who is wonderful by the way, and now this. Why?"

Claire gave a half smile. "I'm a local and know who's who. Because I like to think someone would do it for me if I needed help, and because of Simon."

Regan nodded as she distractedly tossed the pot in the air again.

"*And* because I want to protect my plants," Claire added as she removed the tiny pot from Regan's hand for a second time. "You really have to stop harassing them. They're going to grow up with complexes."

"Sorry." Regan reached out and touched a plant's leaves. "It's difficult to think of a flower with psychoses."

"Step away from the pots," Claire half joked, as she gently pushed Regan back outside.

"I haven't forgotten, you know," Regan said.

"Forgotten what?"

"About walking downtown. It's just I haven't felt like doing it, but I'd still like to if you're up for it. You are, aren't you?"

"Yes." Claire had thought she wasn't interested.

"I expect you thought I wasn't really interested."

"No, not at all," Claire lied. "I know you're busy." Regan did look shattered, and Claire felt a tinge of guilt for having thought so selfishly.

"I've been sorting stuff, getting it ready to hand to Albert," Regan added. "I don't want you to think I'm being rude and ignoring your invitation as if it doesn't matter. It means a lot. It's just that I've wanted to make a start, and I've been on a roll. If you don't mind me messing you around, I will get back to you. Will that be all right?"

"You're not messing me around, Regan. Take your time."

Claire warmed to her. Regan didn't have to explain things, and it was clear she really wanted to meet up for a coffee.

"What's that smell?" Regan sniffed the air.

"What smell?"

"That earthy sort of smell, the one that makes you check the bottom of your shoes to see if you've trodden in something nasty."

Claire sniffed too, and then made a face.

"Ah. I think that's me." She wiped her hands down the front of her cargo pants and shrugged. "I've been top-dressing the beds all morning, lifting bags of manure and forking the stuff in. It's all over me."

Regan's eyebrows lifted as she bent in toward Claire and sniffed again. She scowled.

"It's not a good smell, Claire."

Claire was being played with. She could play, too. "There are two types of shit in this world, the good shit and the bad shit. I have worked with both. This is the good shit."

Regan grinned. It pleased Claire to see her relax.

"But what's it like being surrounded by shit all the time?" Regan asked.

"It's a living."

"Do they pay well?"

"I get by."

Regan dissolved into childish laughter, and Claire thought how attractive she was when she laughed.

❖

Regan was seated on the floor in the middle of Simon's apartment.

Albert Marshal had suggested she initially place all the paperwork into general heaps of similarity. For example, share certificates, equities, UK securities, asset trusts, and so on. She wished she understood half of what she was handling. The world of finance was like a foreign language, and one she had no comprehension of. The only heap she did understand was the utility bills. There were loads of red letters from the electric, gas, and water companies, but even that was strange. They were all dated over six months ago and nothing since. The apartment was still being supplied and nothing had been cut off. She wondered what had happened. Had Simon paid the debts off? If so, with what? One look at his bank statements told her he was skint, and had been for some considerable time. She'd phoned the utility companies to check, but they all confirmed that everything was paid up to date. It was confusing.

She wished some of the other "heaps" had been paid, too. Regrettably, Simon was in debt everywhere and owed a lot of money. Several institutions had already started debt recovery schemes, and the paperwork from them wasn't pleasant. It wouldn't have helped his already fragile state of mind.

Albert advised that many of Simon's liabilities would have to be written off. He'd also confirmed that she would in no way be held accountable for any of this. In truth, Regan never doubted that. She was not responsible for her brother's fuckups. But it was reassuring to hear a man of the law say so. At least, if she could sell Simon's car, it would go toward paying off something.

She stared at the paperwork. It had taken her hours to get this far, and she'd barely made a start.

Albert was prepared to deal with it all. Just shove it into bags and get it down here, he'd said, but Regan didn't think that was fair. She could at least sift through some of it for him. It would also help her to understand more about Simon, and what had tipped him over the edge.

What was becoming apparent was the level of deception Simon had been involved in. It didn't make good reading. It seemed her brother had sweet-talked friends and close colleagues into some very dodgy investments. There were letters from bankers and investment companies advising him to be cautious, and not to take too great a risk given the current financial climate. Simon had ignored them all, and taken risk that was far too high. Even she could see that. It was greed that had driven him on. *Simon, you fool.*

Another alarming trend was the frequency in which the name de Vit kept turning up. It was everywhere. The more she saw this name, the more it made her insides curdle. It was on the paperwork for corporate investments, for stocks and shares purchasing, and money lending. Whoever the de Vits were, Simon had been in deep with them.

There was plenty of communication from them to him, invitations to join schemes or advising on *new, exciting opportunities.* Unlike so many of the other financial institutes, none of their correspondence counseled caution. Far from it. They were suggesting that speculation in a slow market had the potential to reap huge rewards when the upturn came. They actually praised Simon for his shrewd insight and ability to see prosperous ventures. It chilled Regan. It was like watching her brother slowly being pulled into a black pit by some heinous, faceless creature.

Regan did not doubt for one minute that Simon was master of his own destruction, but some of the correspondence she'd read almost made you believe that water was liquid gold.

The name de Vit was prolific. It became a name Regan dreaded reading, for it seemed to be behind every bad investment Simon made. They had also lent him disgusting amounts of money that he had no possibility of repaying if things went wrong.

And how things had gone wrong. The investment company had quickly called in the debts, and when Simon struggled to pay these back, they had turned the screws on him to such an extent, he had felt there was only one way out—to take his own life.

Regan began to hate the name de Vit.

CHAPTER SIX

L et's have that walk and coffee."

Regan's request was wrapped in a lovely smile, and Claire dropped what she was doing in the garden. After a wash and a quick brush of her hair, she and Regan walked down the rough pathway and along the coast trail that led into town.

Claire wished the walk was longer, for she enjoyed listening to Regan chat about the different types of sailing craft they could see on the ocean. It made her realize that it had been too long since she'd allowed herself to interrupt her work and simply *enjoy* the day. Regan was a very easy person to spend time with.

They sat outside a small café and relaxed, basking in the sunshine. Coffee turned into lunch, and Claire used the opportunity to tell Regan what she'd found out about the car.

"Simon's car can be cleaned by a specialist company in Exeter. Then if you want, the garage I spoke about can take the car on, make any necessary repairs, and sell it for you. They don't think there'll be a problem. All you have to do is tell the solicitor and he'll put wheels in motion, so to speak."

"Will I have to collect it?"

"No. The garage will do that and get the car to Exeter. Have a think, and if you're happy, tell Albert. He'll keep an eye on the sale and make sure you don't get ripped off."

"It's not about the money, Claire. It's the thought of having to deal with the car myself, and possibly having to drive it out of the pound. I can't do that. Sitting in the same seat where Simon..." She didn't finish the sentence. She didn't have to. Claire understood completely. "Anyway, if this all comes together, it'll be another problem solved. One less thing to deal with." She looked at Claire and said with all sincerity, "I'm very grateful to you. Again."

Claire flicked her hand nonchalantly. "All I've done is make a few calls, and the garage has done this sort of thing before so they know what they're doing."

"Well, it's really helping me. I just want you to know that."

Claire smiled. "Okay, I've got the message."

Regan smiled back. Then her phone rang and Claire watched the smile disappear as she recognized the number. She didn't answer it. Instead, she pushed the phone to one side as if she wanted it to disappear. She announced, "Not important."

It didn't seem that way to Claire. Whoever was on the other end, Regan wasn't happy, and she could see Claire picked up on that. She tried to cover her discomfort by inspecting her short nails. It wasn't working. Regan deflected attention.

"You keep the gardens beautifully. Have you been gardening there long?"

It was Claire's turn to feel uncomfortable. The question had power to open Pandora's box. If she answered it, most of her life history would come out, and with it, her problems. This was not a topic for conversation. She answered the best she could.

"I was born here, moved away, tried a few things, and came back."

Regan accepted the minimal answer with skepticism.

"Sounds interesting. Have you always been a gardener?"

"I've always been interested in gardening, yes." That wasn't what Regan was asking either, and the look on her face told Claire that her flippant, vague responses only fueled more interest.

Regan pursed her lips. "Evasion seems to be on the menu today, doesn't it?" She scrutinized Claire with intensity, but Claire didn't give in. Regan backed off and glanced across at her phone, aware they were both hiding things. She sighed. "I'm going to have to go home soon, sort a few things out, but I'll be back. I've been here longer than I expected. You see, I'm trying to sell my house, and nothing's happening. I really need to get up there and drive things along a bit.

I'm also changing jobs. I'm a maths teacher at a school, but I'm looking for something more challenging, and I don't like the area."

Claire suspected this was just the tip of the iceberg. The unanswered call sat like an elephant on the table.

"Changing job and house at the same time? That'll challenge you. Why so much in one blob?" At first, Claire wasn't sure Regan was going to answer. It rather surprised her when she did.

"I've finished with someone…Karen. It's all gone sour, and I suppose I'm running. That's who the phone call was from."

"The ex trying to lure you back?"

"Hardly. No, she's made her mind up."

"So you're getting the hell out of Dodge?"

"Maybe it's what I need." Regan was blowing caution to the wind. "Sometimes things happen and you realize they happen for a reason. Or at least you think they do. Maybe they just give you an opportunity for a fresh start."

"And that's what you want?" Claire asked.

"Yes. A new job, a new home, a new life."

Claire heard the weariness behind Regan's words. It awoke something inside her. She couldn't remember the last time she wanted, or was able, to reach out to another person. She sensed the pain and confusion in Regan. It was something she had felt too, and for a long time. It lent her empathy, and it made her feel closer to Regan. Regan was hurting, and in her hurt, she was hiding behind barriers of anger. Remove those barriers and maybe Simon was right about his sister.

"What about you?" Regan interrupted her thoughts.

"Me?"

"Anyone in your life? A love interest?"

Claire froze. It was another question she couldn't, and didn't, want to answer. But she had to say something, if only something small. It was fair, given all that Regan had just trusted her with.

"No. There was, but not now."

Maybe it was the way she'd said it, but Claire's answer solicited a strange response.

"Dead?"

Claire held her breath before answering. "Yes, dead."

It wasn't the truth, and yet it was. It was dead love, for there was nothing left alive, and the mild fabrication avoided any deeper discussion. It was a ruse she'd become used to using, and it slotted into place with routine comfort. By not having to explain further, it blocked the pain.

"I'm sorry." Regan's voice was soft.

Claire nodded.

"Hurts, eh?" Regan said.

"Yes."

Regan shifted uncomfortably. "I keep asking you personal questions, and I shouldn't. I did that the other day, too. I'm sorry. I'm not trying to pry. I'm just naturally inquisitive, and sometimes the words are out of my mouth before my brain can stop them." She shrugged. "Sorry if I've upset you, Claire."

Thankfully, Regan's phone rang again, wiping away her mixed look of guilt and compassion. She answered it this time, and Claire was grateful she didn't have to say any more. Instead, she listened to Regan's brief responses interspersed with pauses.

"I'm in town now...Yes...Not a problem...I'll come in and sign today...What time?...Yes, that's great...Thank you...See you soon then."

Regan put the phone down and looked at Claire, her face an expression of delight. "That was Albert. He needs me to sign a document releasing the vehicle to the garage. They want to get the car out of the vehicle pound today before it closes."

"That's great news."

"Yes." Regan spontaneously leaned forward and placed her hand on Claire's. "But it means I have to dash, and I'm going to leave you to pay the bill. I'll get the next lunch." Regan stood. "I'm sorry I'm leaving you like this."

"That's fine. Go get this sorted. I'll see you later."

Regan was in a hurry, but she stopped and looked at Claire.

"Thanks for getting me out of the apartment and my hamster runs. I needed this break."

Something in Regan's manner touched Claire, and she hated seeing her leave. This was unexpected. She was so used to being alone and not caring about it. It surprised her that she didn't want this to end.

"Will you be able to find your way back?" Claire was happy to go get the Jeep if necessary and pick her up later. But Regan was fine, and silently mouthed, "Easy."

After she left, Claire didn't rush. Instead, she ordered another coffee and lazily stretched her legs out in front of her.

She thought about Regan. The angry, rude woman she'd first met was fading into the background to be replaced by someone warmer who was trying her best under awful circumstances. Claire enjoyed her company, and although their conversation at times turned heavy, for both of them, neither took offense or resented the line of questions.

Claire thought it decent that Regan apologized for her supposed forward questioning. It was an indication that Regan considered other's feelings. Perhaps she was more like Simon than Claire had first thought. From the beginning, she and Simon had got on, and she'd opened up to him with ease. Although she wasn't about to do that with Regan, there were similarities.

Totally sated, she paid the bill and then began the walk back along the coastal path, and the uphill climb.

I'll get the next lunch.

Claire thought of Regan's parting words. Normally, she avoided any socializing. She hadn't always been like that, but she'd become a hermit lately. But she'd enjoyed Regan's company and was looking forward to another get-together.

Claire wondered if they were about to become friends—if, of course, Regan hung around long enough. That was unlikely. Regan stemmed from the north and would probably want to stay up that way. It didn't stop her hoping that Regan might migrate south. It was a possibility. She thought how keen Simon had been for the two of them to meet.

Maybe he was looking down on them now and smiling.

She walked home.

CHAPTER SEVEN

*W*hat an exciting life I lead.

Graveyard humor ripped through Regan as she sat in the church and waited for the service to begin.

She hadn't expected Simon's body to be released before the inquest, but it had. The coroner's office was content that no foul play was present. At last she could arrange that one undertaking everyone normally took for granted after a death—a funeral. The wait had seemed too long to be allowed to do this simple humane act, and to find partial closure.

Regan glanced around her and saw only a few strangers at the back of the church. She had no idea who they were and suspected they were regulars that occasionally came out to bolster a low attendance, an act of kindness to make the bereaved feel better. This irreverent thought made her grin, only to be followed by guilt as she reminded herself that this was her brother's funeral. But then she thought of Simon and his skewed, absurd wit. If his ghostly spirit was around, she suspected he was by her side and laughing his head off—what was left of it.

Simon had always possessed the most obscure sense of humor at the most inappropriate times. Actually, they both had. It was something they had shared from the beginning. She realized this was probably the first positive memory she'd had of her brother in ages. What an awful time and place to experience it.

It was when the organ started to gently play in the background that she looked at the coffin in the middle of the aisle. She'd avoided it till now. As she gazed at the wooden box where Simon lay, a shadow fell over her, robbing her of her safety net humor.

Oh shit. Simon was gone, and she would never see him again. She would never have that chance she'd often longed for, to put things right between them. Now it was too late. *What a bloody mess.*

Her thoughts turned to what was becoming an obsession. Why hadn't he bothered to let her know how bad things were? One phone call and she *would* have come to his rescue—really. Despite all the crap between them over the years, he was still her brother. Why hadn't he realized that and just talked to her? But no word, nothing. She tried to convince herself that it was because he'd been in a dark place and not thinking coherently. But it hadn't worked, and didn't stem her feelings of rejection. She grew gloomy and morose, and wished someone was with her at this awful time, but their parents had died years ago and there was no other family to talk of. She was alone.

She felt someone move into the pew at her side and when she looked, she saw Claire. At least she thought it was Claire. She'd never seen her in anything other than multi-pocketed cargo slacks, denim shirts, occasional sleeveless knitted sweaters, and with her short ash blond hair sticking out at odd angles. *This* Claire was immaculate, dressed in a smart black dress with white braiding around the edges, and polished high-heeled shoes. Her hair and makeup were faultless. As she looked her up and down, she was amazed—Claire had legs. And they were shapely, too. She looked like another woman. She looked classy.

My God, she's attractive. The wayward thought shocked Regan.

"No one should attend a funeral alone," Claire said.

Her voice held such warmth. She leaned in slightly toward Regan, and the look she gave her didn't speak of compassion—something Regan didn't want. All she saw was friendship and support. Her heart lifted. She didn't feel alone anymore.

"Thank you," she whispered as the service began, and she felt a hand take hers and squeeze it. Throughout the solemn proceedings, that warm, comforting hand never left hers, and Regan was grateful.

All through the service, Regan deliberately thought of everything but Simon. She knew if she thought of him she would burst into tears. Those tears would become sobs, and she didn't want to do that again, not like she had in front of Sally. If she was going to cry, *and she was,* she would do it later when she was alone.

Instead, she thought of Karen, her ex.

She couldn't help comparing her to Claire. When had Karen ever showed any real thought for her feelings instead of her own career aspirations? In fairness, nothing like this had happened when they were together to at least give Karen that opportunity. But Regan knew at a cellular level that she would never have responded like Claire.

Karen was more for the "now" and what lay in the future. Like a skilled chess player, she was always planning her next step and anticipating what people would do and how she would react, always to show her best professional attributes. Karen was always on show. She'd turned out to be hollow. It had taken Regan time to see this. The relationship, like all Regan's others, had started on a physical basis, and that always clouded issues. Maybe her next one, she would try something different and not repeat old mistakes.

She wondered if Karen even knew her brother was dead. Maybe that was why she kept phoning her, like the other day when she was having coffee with Claire. She hadn't bothered to reply to the message which simply said, "Call me."

There were no similarities between Karen and Claire. Karen was selfish. Claire wasn't. She was unpretentious and sincere and willing to extend her affection for Simon to Regan. She was here for her. Regan couldn't begin to express how she felt as Claire turned up at her side today. Karen would probably have apologized profusely stating she couldn't make the funeral because of a work commitment she couldn't alter.

It was only when the service and interment were over, followed by the requisite thanks to the vicar, that Regan had a chance to speak properly to Claire. They stood in the church car park.

"Thank you for coming. I didn't know I needed someone until you turned up."

"Couldn't let you do that by yourself. Besides, Simon was my friend, too."

"Yes, he was."

Claire's innocent comment disappointed Regan. It was ridiculous, but she wished she'd said she was here for her. Regan accepted that she probably was, but more as support.

"What are you going to do now?" Claire asked.

Regan didn't understand the question. Did Claire mean now, or in the imminent future? Her head felt like cotton wool, and she found herself interpreting words as if they were foreign. Claire seemed to sense her vagueness.

"I mean, are you going to go back to the apartment, or would you like to go and have lunch, my treat?"

A small voice whispered inside her. *Karen and Claire.*

Part of her really wanted to stay with Claire, but another part, and stronger, wanted to be by herself.

"Would you think me very rude if I said I just want to be alone?"

Claire shook her head in understanding.

"I think I'm just going to go for a drive and think about things." Regan wanted to be alone so that now she could think about Simon, and probably dissolve into tears. They were waiting patiently.

"Not at all," Claire answered. "Sometimes we need time to ourselves."

Regan caught an undertone in Claire's words. It was unintentional, but the nuance was present. It reminded her of that moment in the potting shed when she'd inappropriately asked Claire if she was alone, and later when she'd revealed that her partner was dead. Regan felt the presence of something more now. It was clear that Claire understood what she was going through because she'd experienced it too. Its footprint was still heavy, and it made Regan inquisitive to find out more. But today was no day for probing.

"I don't think I'd be great company anyway." Regan's smile felt false and empty. If it showed, it didn't bother Claire.

"No problem. There's a lovely coast drive if you follow the town road through, with plenty of nice places to stop. Not too much traffic."

Regan liked the sound of that. She would pull over somewhere and watch the ocean. She would imagine Simon doing the same. After all her anger toward him, it felt odd but welcoming to know she felt close to him today. Wasn't that what funerals were supposed to do? It was working. Little memories were seeping back in, ones where the two of them had been close. She was remembering what had made her love him all those years ago. Yes, she would stop at the ocean and remember how much Simon loved the sea.

She was glad she'd decided to bury him here. She knew it was what he'd have wanted.

She spontaneously reached out and hugged Claire. "Thank you for being here, and thanks for understanding I need space right now. Maybe we can catch up tomorrow?"

"I'd love that. I'll leave it to you to make contact. You know where to find me."

One final smile from Claire and she walked to her car and drove off.

Regan cast a final glance back to the spot where Simon was buried before leaving in search of the coast road.

Claire drove home with Regan's words buzzing in her head.

"I didn't know I needed someone until you turned up."

The simple sentence acted like a catalyst inside Claire. Something unlocked inside her.

It was an obvious enough comment to hear from Regan. She was alone and vulnerable at her brother's funeral. Who wouldn't be grateful for someone turning up? But Claire considered what the comment had meant to *her*. Regan had said *you*.

Regan had needed her. How long had it been since she'd felt needed? How long since anyone had told her? The words unexpectedly lifted her spirits. She fought not to read too much into it, but her thoughts were flooded with the memory of how good she'd felt the other day at the coffee shop too when they'd had lunch. Claire had been happy. That was not an emotion she'd walked hand in hand with for a long time. Something *was* shifting.

In church, she had reached out to Regan to hold her hand. It was a spontaneous action that, on the surface, was to be expected. It was a compassionate response in support of someone in grief and hurting. But Claire knew better. She reached out because *she* needed to. Something within her had wanted to feel a connection again to another living being. The way she'd felt as Regan hugged her also lingered.

Claire contemplated what all this meant. It was obvious. She was changing. She was coming back to life again. For too long, she'd become the antithesis of her real self—sociable, full of life, and expressive.

If she was helping Regan, then in no small measure, Regan was helping her, too. Odd, she thought, that someone she'd not liked at the beginning should turn out to be a channel for her own resurrection.

Claire drove onto the road that led to where she lived. It didn't feel like a home to her. She'd bought it quickly and because it was close to the apartments and where she worked. It was a nice enough place, but she always hated coming back to it because it made her feel so damned lonely. She still wasn't used to being alone. It was *one* of the reasons she spent so much time at work.

However, today she'd play things differently. She was going to change out of her posh frock and not go back to the gardens. She didn't feel like working. Everything could wait until tomorrow. She'd put some music on, put her feet up, and read a book.

As she parked the Jeep and locked it, she hoped Regan was coping with the sad day.

❖

The *process* of dealing with Simon's affairs was moving forward, and things were slowly getting done, but it didn't stop Regan from feeling very low as she returned to the apartment after the funeral.

She knew what she was feeling was perfectly natural. No one felt ebullient after burying someone. She'd hoped the time alone as she'd driven along the coast road would have lifted her spirits. It hadn't, and now, here in Simon's place, it felt like the walls where crushing in on her. She had to get out.

"I'm not going to mope. Simon wouldn't want me to do that," she said to herself as she decided to take a walk around the garden. Fresh air and taking advantage of the beautiful sunny evening would help. Even though she'd declined Claire's company earlier, a small part of her hoped she'd see her, but her vehicle wasn't here. Regan suspected she'd taken the rest of the day off. She'd mentioned she might.

Regan ambled directionless around the front of the house. She walked over to a waist-high rock wall and leaned on it. For a while, she studied the view down to the bay. Her thoughts turned to Claire.

She was so thankful she'd come to the funeral. Until her arrival, Regan had sat there alone like someone with a body odor problem. Claire had turned a miserable occasion into something more bearable.

Regan still couldn't get over how smart Claire was. She was a pretty woman anyway, but dressed like that today made Regan realize how bloody attractive she was. It was a shock to see the gardener metamorphose into such a stunner. Regan scolded herself. She sounded like a right snob, thinking a gardener couldn't be classy away from herbaceous borders.

She wasn't a snob. If anything, she was anti wealth. She loathed those people who had so much money they never had to worry about it at all. She wasn't a socialist either. She just hated the gap between the haves and have-nots. It always seemed to her that the rich got richer, and the poor got poorer. What always got her going was the way some of the rich took advantage of the poor. She thought of the bankers and industrialists on their huge salaries while others worked equally hard, but for far less. It was these beliefs that had brought about the clash with Simon. She'd accused him of betraying his moral foundations.

Their parents had taught them to treat people fairly, and never take advantage. Wasn't this what Simon had turned against? He'd gone after money, fleeced people, and it had done him no good.

In a way, it was why she'd chosen to teach maths at school instead of trying for a university position that would have challenged her more. She had wanted to share her knowledge. Simon had called her an idiot, accusing her of wasting her potential. He'd wanted her to follow him into the world of finance.

In a perverse way, she could now see he'd been right, but for the wrong reasons. She had no interest in investment, of speculation and assets. But she could see her original career track was wrong. While being a teacher was a wonderful vocation, it didn't challenge her. She was beginning to understand that she needed to grow her knowledge and push its boundaries. God had given her brains and a passion for maths. She wanted to see what she was capable of. It was one of the reasons why she'd given her notice at work.

She pushed herself away from the wall and strolled around the side of the house.

Crossing the lawn, she saw the woman she met the other day, the one who avoided giving her name. She was seated in a chair on the patio. Regan strolled over.

"Hello again."

This time, the woman was slow to look up, and when she did, she stared at her blankly.

"I'm Regan. We met the other day?"

Nothing appeared to register with the woman, and her face remained expressionless. Then something flickered in her eyes, and she became more animated. She looked over at the trees on the boundary of the property as if searching for something.

"Can you see them?" the woman asked.

"What?"

"They're always there in the trees, hiding. They think I can't see them, but I can. They keep watching me. I don't trust them."

Regan looked over to the trees concerned, but saw nothing. She'd read in the local newspaper that there was a spate of burglaries farther down the hill toward town. She wondered if "light fingers" were heading this way and staking the place out? Judging by some of the cars parked, there were definitely some moneyed people living here. That would not go unnoticed by the criminal element. Perhaps this was what the woman was referring to?

Sally appeared through the French doors.

"Hello again," she said warmly as if greeting an old friend. "You having a chat with Rosie?"

Rosie.

Now she knew her name. She watched as Sally replaced a blanket that had fallen off Rosie's lap and wondered what the relationship was between them.

"Don't want you catching a chill, do we?" Sally tucked the blanket in around her before turning back to Regan. "So it was you Rosie was talking to the other day. She said she'd been chatting to someone, but I didn't know if she'd dreamt it." She bent down to Rosie. "This is Regan, Rosie. This is the lady you met the other day, the one you said was nice."

Rosie wasn't listening. "What are these?" She pointed to a multitude of flowers in a terracotta pot.

"They're forget-me-nots, Rosie, and petunias." Sally pointed out each.

"They're so beautiful, all the colors," Rosie said.

"Yes, they are," Sally replied.

"Do I like them?"

"Oh yes, Rosie. They've always been your favorites."

A warning bell went off in Regan's head. *Do I like them?* It was a strange thing to say, and from one so young?

Rosie was in a world of her own. "They're beautiful."

Regan didn't have time to contemplate the surreal conversation. Sally was speaking to her.

"Everything, okay? I heard it was Simon's funeral today. Sorry I couldn't be there, but it's not always easy to get cover."

Get cover? Was Sally a nurse? It made sense. Rosie told Regan she'd been ill when they met.

"It went better than expected, I—"

Rosie interrupted.

"They're in the trees, watching me."

"What are?" Sally glanced over toward huge cedar trees.

"The monkeys. They're all over the place," Rosie said.

"Oh, them again," Sally said lightly. "I'll sort them out and make them go away. They won't bother you then." Sally took it all in her stride, as though this was everyday conversation. Regan grew aware that whatever was wrong with Rosie, it was serious.

"You live here then?" she asked Sally. "This is apartment two?"

"Yes. I'm a live-in full-time carer," Sally added, anticipating Regan's next thought.

Rosie pointed to the flowers. "What are these?"

Sally answered patiently. "They're forget-me-nots, and petunias, Rosie. They're your favorites."

"They're beautiful."

Regan felt curious, yet awkward. There were questions she wanted to ask but couldn't, not in front of Rosie. Sally seemed to sense that.

"She's been quite chatty lately. I think it's the warm weather," she explained. "This is unusual though. It's normally morning when she's more lucid. In the evenings, she closes down."

Sally was about to say more when Rosie shifted in her chair and grew agitated. This time her attention was focused on the potting shed. She fidgeted in her chair, and her face grew dark. She stared hard for the longest time, her eyes growing wide. Sally followed her gaze and frowned.

"She's still there," Rosie spat.

Sally said nothing, but Regan felt her unease.

"You'll keep her away from me, won't you? You won't let her hurt me again?"

Regan saw Rosie shiver, and wasn't sure whether it was because the sun was fading, or it was something more sinister. Was she afraid of Claire?

"It's her fault. It's her fault. I hate her. Don't let her near me."

Rosie tried to lift herself from the chair, but Sally placed a steady reassuring hand on her shoulder and bent down to face her. Compassion and understanding oozed from her as she spoke firmly.

"I'm here to look after you, Rosie. I will never let anyone hurt you, and I won't let her near you."

Sally looked up at Regan. She couldn't hide her discomfort. It was almost as if she wished Regan hadn't witnessed the scene. "I think we'd better go in now, Rosie. It's getting chilly." Whatever had just happened, Sally had no intention of explaining. As she helped Rosie to stand, the blanket fell to the ground, and Regan quickly picked it up and placed it on the empty chair.

"Thank you, Regan."

She watched as Sally guided Rosie carefully back through French doors and into the apartment. Rosie was thin and frail, and Sally needed to support her.

Just before she closed the doors, Sally glanced at her, her own awkwardness still present.

Regan couldn't stop herself. "Pretty bad, then?"

She referred to Rosie's condition. Rosie had talked about a virus she'd caught in Egypt. Whatever she'd contracted, it didn't seem to be getting better. Forgetfulness was one thing, but hallucinations were another, and neither appeared to take Sally by surprise. It appeared routine behavior.

"Couldn't be worse." Sally's answer was somber.

Sally gave a final wave. Regan reciprocated.

The door closed.

The confirmation of Rosie's condition, its seriousness, upset Regan as she walked back to the apartment. The way Sally had said it left Regan in no doubt that the prognosis wasn't good. Rosie was very ill.

Her thoughts turned to the strange scene she'd witnessed and the comments she assumed were leveled at Claire. Though her name wasn't mentioned, who else would it be down at the potting shed? It alarmed her, too, the way Sally acted in such a defensive manner, as if she needed to protect Rosie. Why would she protect Rosie from Claire? Had Claire hurt Rosie? It was mysterious.

As Regan walked through her door, she couldn't stop thinking of the look on Rosie's face.

It had been one of real fear.

Regan nearly collided with Cynthia Tennerson as she walked out of her apartment in search of Claire.

Cynthia thrust a bunch of flowers into her hands and looked genuinely chastened. "These are for you. I feel awful for not having been in touch. You must think I'm dreadful."

Regan didn't think anything. In fact, she hadn't thought of the councilor much, other than to wonder why she'd seemed so interested in her the other day. The gift of flowers only increased the mystery. Maybe now she might solve it.

"They aren't wonderful," Cynthia referred to the flowers, "but they say it's the thought that counts." She pulled a face. "Truthfully, you've been on my mind a lot these past few days. I know you've had the funeral, and I just wish I'd been more supportive. I feel I've let you down. I hope you can forgive me."

"Thank you, Councilor, but—" Regan's attempt to gain some answers was thwarted.

"Oh, call me Cyn. Everyone else does."

"Well, thank you, Cyn. These are very beautiful." Frankly, they were more than that. Cynthia would have paid top end for them. "You shouldn't have come all the way over to do this."

Cyn play-acted the guilty look. "I can't lie. I wanted to give you these, but I was also in the building visiting someone. Killing two birds with one stone."

Regan grinned. At least she was honest. "You're always here; you should move in."

Cyn laughed amiably. "Maybe I should. It'd save a lot of time. There's a parishioner who's made a complaint against the council. And he's got good reason to. We're going to have to sort a few things out. He's raised his concerns, and I think the least we can do is listen, and then act on them. That's what this business is all about, serving the community."

Not for the first time, Regan thought Cyn bordered on the pious.

"Once this is all sorted," Cyn continued, "you'll probably never see me again…with luck. But I wanted to give you these because of Simon."

Cyn was like a caricature. All her mannerisms were over-the-top like some comedy act. She was the sort of woman Regan wouldn't like to be in a room with for too long. She sapped energy and was too loud. But she'd now stopped laughing and appeared more serious and contained as she reached a hand out to rest on Regan's arm.

"I can never thank Simon enough. He was so kind. He came to my rescue late one night. My husband had a heart attack and was rushed to hospital. I was returning home from there in the early hours when my car broke down on one of these awful country lanes." She sighed. "It was raining hard, it was pitch-black, and I was stressed beyond words. I'd rushed out so quickly I didn't have my cell phone. I suppose I was panicking, and I won't deny I was shedding a few tears when your brother turned up. He was wonderful. He sorted out roadside assistance and took me home." Cynthia's hand squeezed Regan's arm. "If I can help you just a little bit, it will feel I'm returning the favor."

"I didn't know."

"Didn't he tell you? I thought he might have. It's not every day you get to do such a deed. Still, no matter."

"Is your husband okay now?"

"Oh, Oliver's in fine form again. But seriously, is everything okay with you? Are you managing? Bloody awful way to lose a brother." Her words were clipped and sharp.

"I'm coping fine, but thank you for asking." Regan knew she had to be polite. "Would you like to come in for a coffee?"

"No, I won't do that. I've got a disgusting amount of work to do, and I'd like to get some of it sorted before the weekend. And I expect you've got better things to do. Maybe next time, eh?"

Guilty relief flowed through Regan. Cyn really wasn't the type of person she naturally gravitated to, but her heart seemed to be in the right place...if you could just get her to shut up and stand still for a minute.

Cyn turned to leave just as Claire appeared. Regan felt the temperature plummet in the corridor. The smile that rested on Claire's face as she rounded the corner disappeared faster than a rat up a drainpipe as Cyn, disapproval exuding every orifice, deliberately scrutinized Claire up and down. When Cyn's detailed inspection finally made it to Claire's face, the two of them locked stares like two gunfighters waiting for the first finger twitch. Regan had to be a blithering idiot to miss that the two disliked each other intensely.

Claire, rock still, watched Cyn with defiant eyes as she passed her. When she knew she was out of earshot, she dourly said, "Nice flowers."

If ever there was an insincere comment, this was it.

Regan attempted to lift the oppressive, electrically charged atmosphere.

"I was about to come and find you."

"I found you first." Claire's face relaxed, and her customary grin returned. It seemed the memory of Cyn was evaporating.

"Have you got a minute?" Claire asked. "There's something I want to do in the garden, and it needs your input."

It sounded intriguing, and Claire wasn't telling. Regan put the flowers inside the apartment, locked the door, and followed her down the stairs. What was she up to?

Claire took her to the back of her Jeep and showed her a large potted plant.

"It looks like a rhododendron," Regan said.

Claire was impressed. "Right first time. I've just fetched this and thought we could plant it somewhere nice...to remember Simon."

Regan was shocked. It was a lovely idea, to plant something in the garden that would forever remember him, a sort of memorial. For a moment, she couldn't speak.

"I haven't done the wrong thing, have I?"

Claire looked worried.

"No, no," she spurted. "I'm just taken aback. This is such a bloody lovely thing to do, such a kind thought, and so unexpected. Simon would love it." Regan's thought seemed stupid. Simon would have to be alive to love it.

Until then, Claire had been pulling the pot forward, getting ready to lift it from the back, but now she stopped. She wiped her hands down dirty slacks and turned, placing her hands on Regan's shoulders. She looked deep into her eyes, her face serious.

"This isn't just for Simon. It's also for you."

"Me?" Regan said.

"I wanted to do this for you, too."

Claire's gaze was intense. "You've had to do so much. It's been horrible. You haven't stopped since you got here. You've been very brave."

It was instantaneous, like a raging fire. The minute Claire's hands touched her shoulders, Regan felt the intimacy of the moment, the closeness of Claire's face to hers. She could feel her breath on her face. It was a shock, and she felt awkward, like an inexperienced teenager. Her heartbeat rose and she felt it hammering in her chest.

Regan couldn't hide her embarrassment and felt her face redden. What would Claire think? She watched as some form of recognition dawned on Claire's face, who withdrew her hands and stepped back, behaving as if nothing had happened. But something had. And both of them realized it.

"Right," Claire coughed. "Do you want to pick a spot and then we'll dig it in?"

Regan's breathing calmed as she surveyed the area to the side of the house. She managed to regain her composure and pointed to an area near some trees. "What about there? The soil will be acidic, and rhododendrons like light shade; the trees will provide shelter."

Claire seemed back in her comfort zone. "Okay, now I'm really impressed, a mathematician who also knows her plants."

Regan shrugged. "What can I say? I'm multitalented."

"Fork." Deadpan, Claire handed her the garden tool, then lifted the plant. "Let's go dig."

Claire did most of the dirty work as Regan took enjoyment out of directing the project.

As she stopped for breath, Claire joked. "I can tell you're a teacher."

"How so?"

"You're bossy."

"Is that a fact?"

Claire's eyes danced with devilment. Regan loved it. She also liked the way the sunlight played in Claire's fair hair. She looked very pretty.

Bloody hell, what's happening to me?

Regan felt as if her gravitational center was shifting, and she was being magnetically pulled toward Claire.

This isn't supposed to happen, and not so soon after Karen. Get a hold of yourself, Canning.

She realized she'd been staring too long at Claire who now leaned on the fork watching her.

Regan covered her tracks. "What type of rhododendron is it?"

Claire appeared oblivious to Regan's distraction.

"You have to ruin the moment," Claire said.

For a minute, Regan thought she knew she'd been having wayward thoughts.

"How the hell do I know what type it is?" Claire clarified.

Regan breathed a sigh of relief and joined in the apparent joke.

"You're a gardener. You're supposed to know this stuff."

"Well, I don't. Latin was never my strong subject. I like it because of its color, not because of some stupid name no one can pronounce." Claire reached out to hold a bud in her hands, studying it closely. "These are apricot-pink now, but they turn the most magnificent yellow. You wait till next year when it's seated in."

"I may not be here next year," Regan said.

Claire looked at her, the intense gaze of earlier returned.

"Then you'll just have to come back, won't you."

It wasn't said like a question; it was more of an order. Warmth permeated Regan, the probably innocent comment feeding her undercurrent of awakening desire. Again, she forced herself to focus.

There was something she wanted to tell Claire. It's why she'd been about to find her before Cyn arrived.

"Look, now the funeral's over, I'm going to have to go home. Tomorrow. My house isn't selling, and I need to go back and rattle a few boxes. There are other things I need to sort out, too."

"You are coming back, aren't you?"

Did she hear disappointment in Claire's voice? She hoped so.

"Funny you should ask me that. I rang the letting agent this morning to ask if I could take over the rental of Simon's place. There's still a lot to be done here, and the inquest could be weeks, maybe months away. If I ever manage to sell my place, I'm going to need somewhere to live. I might as well stay down here for a while and take my time working out where I want to live and work. To be honest, I rather like this area."

It occurred to Regan that there were many more reasons for staying than she'd had when she arose this morning. "And I know this sounds silly, but I feel close to Simon." *And you.*

"What did the agent say?"

"He said he'd talk to the owner and get back to me. Do you think there'll be a problem?" That now mattered to Regan.

"No, I don't think so."

"You sound pretty sure."

"I'm sure the owner will be happy to have someone renting so soon after..." Claire didn't finish what she'd been about to say.

"Simon's suicide," Regan whispered dolefully.

"Sorry. That was a bit tactless."

"It's okay. You're right," Regan said more brightly. "He'll just see it like a business."

Claire nodded.

They finished the task and both stepped back to admire their work.

"This is a nice place for Simon's plant," Regan said.

"It is," Claire said.

Regan looked at the bush with the trees in the background. If Simon was looking down, he'd love this.

She glanced up at the house, and her attention fell on the patio where Rosie normally rested. She wasn't there. It was probably because the sun hadn't appeared today, and the air was cooler. The French doors were open, but she saw no movement. She spoke without thinking.

"What do you know about the woman that lives up there? Rosie?" Regan's focus remained on the doors.

"What do you mean?"

"I just wonder who she is and what's wrong with her. I've met her a few times, and she's obviously not well. She's got a full-time carer, Sally. I just wondered how long she's been ill and if you knew anything about her."

When Regan didn't get an answer, she glanced back at Claire. She was staring at the place, her face blank. All except her eyes. They were full of pain.

When Claire realized Regan watched her, she shrugged and turned her attention to gathering up the empty pot and tools.

"I try not to get involved in other people's business," she said.

The comment was blunt, and it came out defensive. Regan thought how out of character it was. For a split second, she worried that Claire might think her a busybody, but then she remembered the way Rosie and Sally had acted the other evening, and how everything had been directed toward the shed. Claire's strange behavior only added to the mystery. Regan was convinced that something linked the three of them together. Whatever it was, Claire wasn't being drawn into any conversation.

Regan wished she hadn't said anything, for the bonhomie which had rested so easily between them only seconds ago was now gone, and Claire was already walking back toward the potting shed.

"I think we're finished here now, Regan. Do you want a coffee?"

Regan didn't think the invite was meant. It was more politeness. Something told her Claire didn't really want her to say yes. She followed behind Claire with the fork, and the brief walk seemed long.

She inanely wondered if whoever had discovered the coffee bean ever realized how important it had become as one of the main cogs that drove social interaction. It was the panacea of all things. Except she didn't think it was right now. She would have accepted the offer moments ago, but there was an unwelcome atmosphere, and she couldn't decipher it. All she knew was that it was to do with Rosie, or Sally, or both.

"Thanks, Claire. I better not. I plan to leave early for home tomorrow, and I've got to sort some things out first."

Only now did Claire stop and turn. She was smiling, but her smile didn't reach her eyes, and Regan knew it was forced.

"You're going to be missed."

This time, Regan knew Claire meant it. It tempered her unease.

"I'll be back, Claire. Keep the coffee pot on."

"I will."

"And thanks again for Simon's plant, and for doing it for me, too. It means a lot."

It did. She wanted Claire to know that.

When it seemed they'd run out of conversation, Regan left and Claire waved as she turned for the shed again.

Confusion filled Regan as she entered the foyer and headed for the stairs.

She didn't understand what had just happened. Claire had acted strangely and for no apparent reason.

Neither did she understand her own *interesting* emotions. One minute, Claire was just the kindhearted gardener showing all the signs of developing into a friend. Then—ta-dah!—she was showing on Regan's radar as the next possible mate? And so soon after Karen?

But was it really that soon? She and Karen had broken up some time ago.

It fascinated Regan that this time around she wasn't eyeing someone as "sex on legs." Not that Claire wasn't attractive, but she was looking at her differently. More long term if she was truthful. It was an interesting development for Regan. She knew she wanted to mature, but this was quick. *Am I getting old?*

She wondered if Claire might be interested in her. She wasn't sure, but when she returned, she'd put out a few feelers and see what might happen. It gave her something to look forward to.

When she finally made it to the front door, she was thinking about packing, and the long drive home.

CHAPTER EIGHT

Regan rose early. She wasn't looking forward to traveling up north and would have given anything for an excuse to get out of it. But it was no good. She knew she had to go home, if only to sort out her own affairs which recently had been put on the back burner. Now they were screaming out for attention. Nothing more was happening here, no coroner's findings, and until that happened, she might as well go home and sort out the mess up there.

For a starter, Alex Griffin, headmaster of the school, was blatantly ignoring her handwritten letter of resignation. Despite the warnings she'd given him that leaving was on her mind, he'd acted as if it was never going to happen. She hadn't left him in the lurch; there were other teachers who could cover her absence and plenty who would answer the job vacancy.

Her one fault with Alex was that she'd avoided facing him at the time. She had sneaked into his office when he was out and placed her letter on his desk. She'd then run. He'd left her numerous phone messages, and no small amount of e-mails, telling her to get in touch with him. All professional and in headmaster tone, he stated he wasn't going to act on her letter until they had spoken face-to-face. Then with more warmth and friendship, for they had always got on, he'd said whatever was wrong, maybe it could be fixed. In his gloriously deep Scottish accent, he said the school needed teachers like her and he was damn well going to fight for her.

She knew she would have to see him when she got home. Alex was a good, decent man, and she owed him that. He would want to know why she had left in such a manner. What on earth was she going to tell him? That she had been having an affair with the deputy headmistress, a married woman—that the affair had been going on for several years? Would she tell him that it was now over and she couldn't stand being at the school anymore, seeing her every day? That would simply drop Karen in it, and Regan, pissed off though she was, couldn't do something as underhanded as that.

She'd always known her affair with Karen wouldn't work, but she'd hoped. Karen was such a voluptuous, damned attractive woman with a huge capacity for…sex. Well, Regan couldn't deny it. The latter fit right in with her own carnal urges, and she'd found herself more than accommodating on that front. Karen wasn't just a gorgeous physical specimen displaying all the swarthy dark looks of her Italian heredity; she was also very smart, very imposing, very impressive— frankly *very* everything. And here was the problem.

Karen was headmistress material in abundance, and she wanted Alex Griffin's job when he retired in the next few years. She was always ready—at the drop of a school boater—to put her career first and place education to the fore. Noble though that was, it left Regan living in the margins. How many canceled dinners, holidays, weekends, were the victim of some scholarly crisis arising?

It had also been difficult for Regan to handle how secretive Karen was about their relationship. The "don't touch me or look at me that way at school" routine had driven Regan nuts. Karen hadn't wanted to be out and proud. That would damage her chances of accession to head. What would the parents, staff, governors think? It had been a huge event for her to announce her marriage was on the rocks, and that she was moving out and "sharing a place" with Regan. There had been the constant explanations of "needing a separation from Mac," the errant husband, and being lucky to have such a *good friend* like Regan Canning who could let her rent a room for a while. The fact they had then bonked every available non-school minute of the day rather pushed the concept of friendship to extremes.

Regan did understand Karen's predicament. Being homosexual in the UK was no longer the huge compromising issue it had once been. But there were still pockets of resistance to the newer lifestyle, and regrettably, some of those pockets did reside on the board of governors. This had driven a wedge between them, and in the end Karen had gone back to Mac. That had hit Regan hard, especially after all the times she'd listened to Karen saying what a prat he was, and real lowlife.

There was also the house. It wasn't selling, and until that happened, Regan was financially stuck and unable to move on. She'd always known she needed to declutter a bit, maybe sell some furniture and shove other stuff into storage. Less is more, and it would make the property look bigger. Then there was her hallway. It was dark. Karen had said it was like entering a catacomb. Regan had planned to brighten it up, but then Simon died. Now the estate agent was confirming that the mausoleum effect might be putting people off... first impressions and all that. There were so few people out there house hunting anyway, given the recession.

She gave a final glance around Simon's apartment before leaving. It was tidier, but there was still so much paper to go through. She'd already handed some over to the solicitor, but she knew there would be more he would need. She just couldn't believe the volume of paperwork, and nothing in any order. So she put what she thought might be the most important into two unused potato sacks and decided to take them home with her. When she wasn't facing Alex, painting hallways, shifting furniture, or avoiding Karen, she could sort through it.

As she drove away from the front of the apartments, she passed Claire coming the other way. They waved at each other. Claire's huge smile made her smile too. It stayed there long after she'd driven onto the main road and begun her pilgrimage home. She allowed her thoughts to stay with Claire, something she was beginning to enjoy.

Regan was drawn to her. She was paying more attention to things Claire said and did. She was already missing her.

She grinned to herself. She was driving home, contemplating the chance of a relationship with Claire. She started to laugh as she recognized that her modus operandi in life's quest for the perfect mate was changing. Where once her head was turned by the attractive femme fatale, all of which usually ended in disaster, she was actually looking for something different now. She wanted a relationship with more depth. Not that Claire was lacking in beauty. Her flawless appearance at Simon's funeral showed otherwise. That was the first time that Regan had really looked at Claire, and she liked what she saw. But equally she knew that Claire could be dressed in a Mickey Mouse outfit, and she would still be attracted to her.

It excited her that little things suggested Claire might feel the same way about her. Yesterday, when they'd been unloading the rhododendron from the back of the Jeep, Claire touching her had sparked something interesting. She was sure Claire felt it, too. Then, when she'd told her that she was leaving today for home, Claire couldn't hide her disappointment. It was only when Regan said she was coming back that she saw the relief flood Claire's face. Regan so hoped the attraction was mutual.

She cross-examined herself. Was *she* ready to move on, and into another relationship? She thought she was. In truth, she and Karen had been over for a long time even though they'd stayed together and gone through the motions hoping something would kick in and resolve their problems.

Regan didn't want to ruin anything. She didn't want to embarrass Claire if she wasn't interested in her. How many times had she misread signs and wrecked things? She knew she didn't want to lose Claire's friendship if that was all it was going to be. Regan wanted Claire around.

She reminded herself that Claire had a past. It was a past that held a dead lover. Was Claire ready to move on?

But the lovely Claire was also an enigma.

She seemed to live in the garden. In the short time Regan had been there, she'd see her out there when she got up in the morning, and she was still there when she turned in at night. Regan was an early riser and had the habits of a night owl. She didn't need much sleep. This morning, she'd left very early. It had only just started getting light, and yet she'd seen Claire arriving. Regan already wondered if Claire didn't sometimes spend the night in the shed, but she shook her head in disbelief. Though the weather was unseasonably warm, it wasn't that warm, and who would want to stay over in a potting shed? She suspected Claire was throwing her life into her work to forget her deceased partner. It made Regan want to reach out and help her.

She was also intrigued about Rosie's strange comments the other day and more, Claire's odd behavior last evening in the garden. Regan couldn't make sense of it.

Eventually, the long drive ended. When she entered her house, it smelled musty, and she realized how badly the hallway needed work. It was like entering a burial chamber—not exactly what was needed to invite potential buyers to want to see more. She would fix this. She'd get paint tomorrow and make a start.

First, she needed a cup of tea, and then she'd go through the mail. A neighbor had gathered it up and put it on the kitchen table. Most of it was junk mail, the odd postcard from a friend on holiday, and an annoying mass of free local newspapers that came weekly. The neighbor had forwarded any mail she thought important, but left the rest. Neither of them had thought she'd be away for so long.

As she flicked through the post, she froze.

One envelope grabbed her attention. It wasn't large, and her name and address were written in blue ink. She recognized the writing. It was Simon's. For a moment, she just held it in her hands, almost afraid to open it. She studied the post date. It was the same date that he had killed himself.

Controlling her breathing, she opened the envelope slowly. She used a kitchen knife with surgical precision. Inside she found one piece of folded paper, and an old black-and-white photo. She glanced at the photo first. It was a holiday snap taken by their mother when they'd been on a beach at Blackpool. She was sitting on a donkey that Simon was leading. They were laughing and happy. She remembered it being taken. Regan stared at it for a few seconds more before the draw of the letter overwhelmed her.

As she opened it, she saw the heading *My dearest Regan.* Her eyes watered, and it took a while before she could read it.

My dearest Regan,

My lovely kid sister—by the time you get this, you'll know what I've done.

I've never been a great letter writer, and this is likely to be the worst one you'll ever have to read. I'm sorry. I've got myself in such a mess.

I found the photo some months ago and I've kept it close. It reminds me of all the good times we had together when we were growing up. I ruined all that, didn't I?

I want you to know you are the best sister anyone could ever have. Every time I look at this photo, I find myself thinking so much about the times when we were growing up. We were such similar souls then, and close. I've missed that very much, but I see now that the choices I made in life drove us apart. You tried to stop me, but I stupidly went after the golden chalice with all its immoral glory and false wealth. I should have been like you and stayed on the right path, true to the values we grew up with. You always were the strong one.

Sis, I've been a complete arse, and I've let so many people down—many of my friends. They've lost everything because of me. I can't believe what I've done, and I don't know how to put things right. Mum and Dad would be ashamed of me. The worst thing I've done is to hurt you. I pushed you away. I hope you can forgive me, and please don't be angry with me, although I know you will. Just remember I love you, Sis. I know I haven't shown that for years...but I do. I've never stopped. I'm so proud of you, and I only wish I'd taken more time to tell you that.

Hang on to this pic, and please, when you think of me, remember the good times. Think of Batman and Robin.

Love you always,

Simon.

Batman and Robin. They'd played this as kids. Regan was always Robin to Simon's Batman, as he rescued the weak and fought for justice as the Caped Crusader. Then, she would have followed him to the ends of the earth. That's probably why he wanted her to remember.

She held the letter to her heart and started to sob. He *had* remembered her. He'd written her this letter. He loved her.

As she cried, all the vestiges of anger left. Now she could grieve—for the brother she had lost—the brother she had loved.

CHAPTER NINE

One minute, Claire was alone outside her potting shed and topping up the engine oil of her sit-on lawnmower, the next, Regan was there. She crept up to her like a stealth missile, swift and silent—and welcomed. It surprised Claire that her mood changed so quickly from vague disinterest in dull inanimate machinery, to uncontained delight at seeing her back.

While she'd been away, Claire had tried not to think of Regan, but invariably, her thoughts always turned that way. Despite their awful introduction, she longed for her return. She had grown used to her and missed her company.

She stepped back from the engine casing and wiped her mucky hands on a dirty rag. The potential for her to get oil over Regan's light green blouse did not stop her from being grabbed by the shoulders. Regan grinned liked an inmate of a local funny farm.

For an infinitesimal second, Claire thought she was going to kiss her on her lips, but Regan only delivered an awkward peck on the cheek before pulling her into a tight bear hug.

"I'm back," Regan announced.

"I can see that." Claire felt her breath on her neck.

Regan hung on to her for ages before releasing her.

"What's that for?" Claire asked.

"I've missed you." Regan seemed amused. "Have you missed me?"

The question was direct. It wasn't one of those throwaway ones that you weren't really required to answer. Regan was waiting for her response.

It was a daft question because Claire was hardly going to answer "no." It wasn't a polite, socially acceptable thing to do. But she wouldn't have to lie, for she had missed her. While she'd tended the hedges, the lawns, the borders, and the compost heap, her thoughts had been on Regan and what she might be doing. She imagined her redecorating her hallway and progressing with the house sale. Her return to the school had featured in there somewhere, too.

Claire also contemplated how quickly Regan had become a welcomed presence in her life. She'd crept under her skin. How did that happen? Hadn't she deliberately allowed herself to become cut off and distant from anything remotely emotional and animate? She'd let friends fade into the distance. They hadn't wanted to, but she'd backed off. They wanted her to *talk*. She didn't.

Claire figured there were many reasons why Regan succeeded where others failed. She recognized that raw pain and shock that Simon's death delivered. Something in her had wanted to reach out to Regan to try to help. Time was also a factor. It had passed, and in doing so, she had healed. Claire's frozen emotions were thawing, and Regan was merely proving a catalyst for her own reemergence into the life-stream. She was also her friend's sister, and that gave her a free pass.

"Well?" Regan pushed.

"Okay, I admit it. I've missed you."

"Are you sure? You've had to think about it. You don't have to have missed me. I've been nothing but a pain in the arse since I got here."

The response was upbeat and cheerful, but Claire heard doubt in the words. She couldn't have that.

"Yes. I have really missed you."

"You're not just saying that?"

"No. I have missed you."

Claire started to laugh. That was another thing. She laughed a lot in Regan's company. It felt good. She'd always had a sense of humor, but she hadn't had much to laugh about lately.

"Things have been altogether too peaceful around here," Claire said. "And there's been no one around to torment my plants."

Her enthusiastic reply appeased Regan who seemed to run out of words. They stood looking at each other, until Claire could stand it no longer.

"Okay, are you going to tell me how things have gone, or do I have to use telepathy?"

Claire wanted to know so much. Had Regan sorted out the decoration of her home and was anyone showing any interest in buying it? She wondered if her ex had made contact with her. If so, had it turned into an awful experience? Regan didn't need more turmoil. And what if her old school convinced her to return? Regan might go back north for good. This was something Claire was trying not to think about. She wanted Regan around so she could get to know her better. Besides, Regan owed her lunch.

"There's something I want to tell you," Regan said.

Claire cringed. Maybe she was going back north.

Regan sounded serious, and it didn't help when she suggested they go into the shed for a coffee. This was something they needed to sit down for? Claire imagined every unseasonal autumnal leaf dropping on her. She was sure the ominous request was the forerunner of something good coming to an end. Whatever Regan was about to tell her, it was big. Claire reluctantly tossed the oil rag to the side and covered her gloom with false humor.

"Of course. Where are my manners?" She bolstered herself for the worst news as they moved into the shed. She wasn't looking forward to this.

"Have a seat."

She pointed to the usual seating arrangement as she forced herself to concentrate on switching the kettle on and throwing instant coffee into two mugs.

Her attempt at diversion didn't help her when Regan came and stood next to her by the bench. She was so close, their bodies touched.

Claire blushed. Her breathing turned labored. Never had water taken so long to boil.

"I've only just arrived back, and I had to come and see you. I want to tell you what happened."

Regan's voice was low, serious.

Here it comes.

"Simon sent me a letter."

"What?" This wasn't what Claire expected.

"Simon. He wrote me a letter before he killed himself."

"He did?"

Claire stopped messing with a spoon. Shock and relief combined as she faced Regan.

"It's good, Claire. He sent the letter home. It's been sitting there all the time I've been down here. The postmark was the day he died. I must have just missed it."

Claire thought her heart was going to burst. "Oh, Regan, that's wonderful." She studied Regan's face. Whatever Simon had written, it had healed wounds.

"It's only a page long, but in it, he tries to explain things. Most important, he writes how much he loves me and that he's never stopped caring." Regan hesitated. "I suppose this should be in the past tense."

Her eyes watered. Claire instinctively wrapped an arm around her shoulder, suddenly aware of how her body responded to the closeness. It made her nervous, and she wondered if Regan sensed it.

"I'm happy for you."

"It's made all the difference, Claire. He bothered to write. He thought about me, even at the end when things were going crazy. I still wish the stupid fool had phoned me. I know I could have done something, but...I can't tell you how much this means. I thought he'd forgotten me, and that he didn't care."

"Simon never forgot you, and I was never in any doubt that he loved you very much. He was always telling me that. He used to say you were the Dynamic Duo."

"What?" Regan frowned.

Claire removed her arm and returned to making the drinks. "That's what he called the two of you, something to do with being kids and playing games."

Regan wiped her eyes on her sleeve. "Oh, the silly sod. When we were kids, we used to play Batman and Robin. I was Robin because I was shorter. We spent hours in the holidays annoying the neighbors who were really evil enemies of Gotham City. I remember several of them waved us off when we moved. We weren't popular."

Bless you, Simon. Claire wished she could thank him for putting something right at the end.

Regan moved over to the upturned beer crate and sat down.

"You said he used to talk about me a lot?"

Claire smiled as she stirred their drinks. At last, the moment had arrived when she could share what Simon had told her. She'd wanted to tell her from the beginning, but until now, Regan hadn't been ready to hear. She handed her a coffee and sat down opposite. Claire sipped her drink before starting.

"He used to sit exactly where you are now. We spoke about a lot of things, but you were never far from his thoughts. He talked of you all the time. It was clear he adored you. You were perfect in his eyes."

"Perfect?" Regan said, "I didn't think he liked me anymore. The last few times we saw each other we did nothing but argue, and both of us said some bloody awful things to each other. It's why we stayed apart. It was easier."

"Simon became very reflective in the last few months. He was full of regrets and said he felt guilty for the things he did and said to you. He blamed himself for everything. He knew your anger was you being defensive because he'd hurt you, something you'd never expected from him. You'd loved each other so much. He told me he threw that love back in your face and betrayed your trust."

"I never understood why he did that."

Claire gave an empty laugh. "I don't think he did either. He once said he felt like a snowball rolling downhill and gathering speed. He couldn't stop the momentum, and it kept taking him places he didn't want to go. He knew he was doing the wrong things but couldn't stop. He pushed you away because you saw this. It made him feel bad, and he felt he didn't deserve you."

"That doesn't make sense."

"He wasn't making much toward the end," Claire said.

"He told you all this, but not me. Why?"

Claire shrugged. "Sometimes it's easier to talk to strangers rather than face the people we love and who we've hurt most. I think he was confused and desperate. He couldn't think rationally anymore. When all his financial ventures failed and the vastness of his debts hit him, he went into shock and couldn't cope. Sometimes he would sit here, talk, and make no sense at all. Other times he was more meditative and spoke with such clarity. All I can tell you is that he loved you with all his heart."

"What a waste, Claire."

Claire didn't answer. It was a waste.

"He talked a lot about the two of you growing up and how close you were. He spoke of your parents and how it had almost destroyed him when they were killed in the car accident. He thought it was where he started to go wrong. You became the strong one, and even though you both grew closer, he always felt he should have been more robust because he was older. He felt weak. When an opportunity came along for him to do something he excelled in, finance, he grabbed at it without thought."

Regan listened. She hung on every word Claire said.

"He spoke a lot about the passion you both shared for mathematics and how competitive you were." Claire hesitated.

"What?"

"I'm not sure, Regan, but I think Simon was always a bit sad for you."

"Sad? How do you mean?"

"He said you were brilliant at the subject—gifted—and he thought you'd sold yourself short by ending up teaching the subject at school level. I think he felt you should have stayed at university after your doctorate and done something more mentally stimulating. He never felt you were entirely happy with your choice of career."

Regan was uneasy. "He was right. I didn't realize it then, but as time's gone by, I see the mistakes *I've* made. It's one of the reasons I've left the job. This is my chance to make some changes. I can't believe Simon saw that. I thought he was so self-focused."

"Maybe once, but not toward the end." Claire studied the liquid in her mug. "I'm sure there are other things I'll remember, but you remember this. He adored you, Regan. If this shed could replay the conversations Simon and I had, you'd never doubt that again."

"Thank you." Regan's voice was so quiet, Claire almost didn't hear.

"Now tell me, what else happened back home? What are these changes you want to make?" Claire asked.

Regan put her mug down and spread her arms open wide as she exclaimed, "I've been busy. Where do I start?"

"Start at the beginning."

"I went to see the headmaster, Alex Griffin. No stress. I told him I needed to leave because I want a new career direction. Not quite the whole truth, but I couldn't say it was because of my affair with Karen, his deputy. I didn't mention her at all. I just said I wanted to reconnect with my studies and go back to university if I could. I told him I want to combine teaching at that level, and research. He tried to sweet talk me into staying, but finally accepted I want out.

"I've also thrown a disgusting amount of paint on the walls of my house and put a load of furniture into storage. I've obviously done something right because I've had a few interested people since, although no one has made an offer yet, but the estate agent is happier. It's got her off my case."

Regan's smile grew. "Another good thing is that the rental agreement for Simon's place has come through. I can't tell you how happy that makes me. It feels good coming back. I feel close to Simon here, and I like being in his place, even more now I've had his letter and heard what you've told me. So, Claire, I'm afraid you're stuck with me for the unforeseeable future."

The unforeseeable future.

Claire's spirits lifted. Regan was planning to stay around for a substantial amount of time. She wasn't planning to return north.

"Can you handle me being around longer?" Regan was staring at her.

Claire was so ecstatic, she almost laughed. "I can, although I'm probably going to have to arrange a security system for my seedlings."

Regan held her gaze long enough for Claire to feel her face flush again. She diverted her eyes and pretended to concentrate on downing the remnants of her coffee. When she looked up again, she could see something was worrying Regan. She was frowning. She hadn't been a moment ago. Claire was about to ask her what was wrong, but Regan was already talking.

"I've spent a lot of time sorting through more of Simon's paperwork while I've been away. It's strange."

"What is?"

"Well, there's nothing on any of Simon's bank statements that show payment of utility bills or rent. Yet there are no demands for payment, no apparent debts in those areas, but everywhere else he owed *huge* amounts of money. He was broke. I don't understand how those bills got paid. I asked the letting agent how much money he owed."

"What did he say?"

"That was strange, too. He was really vague, and it was only when I demanded he check, he just said the account was fully paid and closed. I asked how Simon paid because nothing was reflected in his statements, and he said he always paid in cash. Cash, Claire. I don't get it."

"Maybe he had a hidden stash of money. I don't know, but I shouldn't worry about it. If the bills have been paid and nothing's outstanding, I'd save your concerns for other things."

"You're right, I suppose. It's just odd."

Claire changed the subject.

"Given any thought on where you want to eventually settle?"

"I guess it'll depend on which university I pick, and if they like me. I've been looking at research posts at Exeter. I could stay here if I got in there."

The answer pleased Claire.

"I like this area," Regan continued. "Maybe when I've sold my house, I might even see if I can buy Simon's place. It's a good size, and it suits me. Do you think that might be possible?"

"Lots of the apartments here are owned. It'll all depend on whether the owner wants to sell. I'm sure the agent can make discreet inquiries when you're ready."

Regan tried to hide a yawn but failed. She stood.

"I better go and unpack, Claire. I haven't done that yet. I've brought a load of stuff back with me."

As Regan deposited her mug on the bench and headed for the shed door, Claire asked, "Have you ever been to Torquay?"

"No."

"I've got to go down that way the day after tomorrow, to deliver some stuff. Do you fancy coming with me? We could make a day of it, leave early, drop the stuff off, and then drive into Torquay and have a wander around. It's a lovely drive. We could have lunch. What do you say?"

Please say yes.

Claire could barely contain her joy as Regan accepted.

"I'd love to."

"Dress casually, Regan. I'm delivering plants so it'll be jeans and T-shirt attire for me. I'll be out front about seven thirty a.m.?"

"I'll be ready."

Claire didn't miss the obvious delight on Regan's face.

As they stepped outside into the sunlight, they both announced at the same time, "I've missed you."

Regan shrugged. Claire raised her hands to the air.

"Well, there you are. We're in tune," Claire joked.

As Regan walked off, she looked back over her shoulder. "I'm glad you've missed me. Catch you later."

Claire struggled to concentrate after Regan left.

It didn't matter what she turned her hand to, her heart wasn't in it, and she couldn't focus. In the end, she stopped, gathered her belongings up, and drove down to the town's edge. She hopped out of the car and walked along the coast.

She came to a favorite spot where a path led onto the beach. She took her shoes off and ambled across the sand toward the sea.

Thoughts buzzed in her head.

As Regan had walked away, Claire felt something tug inside her. She'd experienced a crazy impulse to run after her. She had wanted to stay with her.

Claire knew why. She recognized the feelings. They were the ones that had always been reserved for her true love.

For Rosie.

To experience this again, but for someone else, it didn't feel right.

Rosie was still alive and near. Was Claire's love so shallow to now feel like this for Regan? Lately, it felt like she was betraying Rosie. But for too long, she'd closed down and grown lonely. So very lonely. Each day had become a day to survive. Her work was an anesthetic. She would push any emotion from her thoughts. But when she wasn't working, when she was home alone, her fear would return. It was always the same. She was scared to think what her future held and that she might never love another, or be loved in return. She'd grown tired of such negative emotions. Regan was changing that. It was shocking yet exhilarating to know she still had the capability to feel anything positive.

But it was happening fast. Maybe her obsessive thoughts about Regan during her absence should have been the wakeup call, but it was the hug. Claire's body relaxed into it, and she felt a long absent warmth cocoon her. Their contact chased away a bitter chill. She could have stayed in that embrace forever. And how she kept blushing. That was a surprise, for she'd been quite one for the girls in her youth, and had taken to the mating business like a tick to a dog. She'd never blushed in her life. Claire had always been self-assured and cocky. It's what won her the love of Rosie.

All this revelation was both frightening and liberating. It scared her because she wasn't supposed to feel this. She had responsibilities; she wasn't free.

Claire flinched as she recalled the evening before Regan drove home. She had overreacted when asked innocent questions about Rosie and Sally. She hadn't been trying to hide anything, but up to that point, their time together had been fun and light. Talking of Rosie would change that and reveal more than she wanted. Claire had reacted with her usual ploy of burying her head in the hope that ignoring things would make them disappear. They were never going to.

She waded into the sea, letting the cool water flow over her feet.

She thought again of Rosie as she stared out at the ocean, watching a yacht sail by in the distance.

How Rosie had loved the ocean. It was one of the first signs that something was wrong. They'd always enjoyed water sports and sailing, but suddenly, Rosie became afraid of the water and didn't know why. The memory of a conversation returned and with it, such pain.

It was after the diagnosis, but long before Rosie stopped remembering who Claire was, and before things became really bad.

Rosie had been self-aware in the early stages, knowing what was coming at her, the cruel robber of life and the dismisser of hope.

They were in the kitchen. Rosie was agitated, and all over a can of Diet Coke.

Claire had passed her one from the fridge. It was Rosie's favorite drink, but in the destruction and mutation of her mind, she now loathed it.

Claire hadn't understood in the early days, and had gently reminded her of her fondness for the ice cold drink. The shock and realization upset Rosie. It was another thing that no longer made sense to her. She became angry and started shouting at Claire.

"I want you to leave me."

"Over a can of Coke?" Claire knew it was more but tried to deflect what was coming with humor.

"I said I want you to leave me."

"No."

"Yes. I want you to leave me now and let me get on with this alone."

"I can't do that," Claire said.

"You have to. I don't want you to see me deteriorate like this."

Claire couldn't believe what Rosie was asking her to do.

"I will not leave you."

"You have to. I want you to. I can't stand you around me seeing me like this. It's only going to get worse."

"Please stop this, Rosie." Claire had started to cry. She loved her so much. Rosie ignored her tears.

"You have to do this, and I need you to promise me something."

"What?"

"I want you to find someone else."

"Oh, for Christ's sake, Rosie."

"Promise me, Claire."

Claire shouted back at her. "Shut up. Stop talking like this. You'll live for a long time yet."

"I'm dying, Claire. Stop kidding yourself."

"You're young. You'll live a long time."

"I'll be dead and gone long before this body cuts out. I've got this shitty disease too young in life. My body will keep going like fucking Robo Cop, but *I'll be gone*. Don't you understand that?"

"Just stop pushing this in my face all the time."

"Well, stop burying your head in the sand."

"I'm not."

"Yes, you are! I am dying—dying—and I want to know you're not going to give up on life and waste away because of some stupid idea that I'm your one and only."

"But you are my one and only."

"Wrong answer. If you really love me, you'll promise me you'll find someone else…" Rosie's frustration turned to tears. "…because the thought of you being alone after I've gone frightens me more than this bloody Alzheimer's."

Claire sobbed. Rosie was tenacious.

"Promise me!"

"I can't promise you…not that. I love you."

Claire had broken down, and Rosie's anger evaporated as she wrapped her arms around her. "I love you, too, darling. I love you so much, so very much."

Pain gripped Claire's heart as the screech of a seagull overhead pulled her back into the now. The tide splashed up her legs. She stepped back.

A man with a dog walked past her but then stopped.

"You all right, love?"

His concern broke her thoughts.

"Yes, I'm fine."

He didn't look convinced, but carried on. She realized she was crying and brushed a sleeve across her face.

Rosie continued to love her until the disease would no longer allow it. It then warped her love and turned it to hatred. In her mind, Claire became someone she both loathed and feared, and could no longer stand to be around. Claire had nearly gone crazy. The only way she had coped was by shutting herself down.

Claire thought of love. Love and Rosie were inextricably linked.

Love—real love—never dies. All the romantics, poets, and philosophers spouted that. Because of Rosie, she knew it was true, but she also knew that sometimes you had to walk away from love. Sometimes you had to place it behind you in order to move forward.

Mental deliberation and time had taken her on an intellectual journey full of introspection. It had shown her reality, something she'd been asked to face long ago, but hadn't. Now she could no longer ignore it. Regan's presence was awakening her, and her mind and body were being bombarded with emotions that swirled through her like whirlpools. Her eyes were open, and life was knocking on her door, and with it an incredible array of possibilities. But her heart was duplicitous. It craved love and yet held her back. It kept reminding her that Rosie lived, and here she was having feelings for someone else. It didn't matter how many times Rosie had made her promise to move on and find another, Claire was torn.

It was a shock to have feelings for someone who wasn't Rosie. Rosie had always been her life, and she hers. Neither of them had bargained on Rosie becoming a rare statistic, getting Alzheimer's so young.

But Rosie *was* gone. She'd spoken words of truth that day in the kitchen. Her shell would hang around a long time, but the wonderful human being who she had been was dead. The woman living in the ground floor apartment bore no resemblance to the vivacious, effervescent woman Claire had fallen in love with. It had taken a long time to come to grips with this, and Claire had fought it every step.

Would she ever love again like she had with Rosie? She didn't know. She thought of Regan, and of possibilities. Might something happen between them? She didn't know that either. But she knew Rosie was right. Somehow she had to overcome this hurdle of guilt. She also knew she needed to tell Regan who Rosie was. She should have done that the other day in the garden. It might change how Regan felt about her, but relationships needed to be built on truth.

Whatever happened, Claire knew she was facing an important milestone in her relationships with Rosie *and* Regan. This was her chance of a new beginning. For Rosie's memory, she must be brave and not give in to guilt.

CHAPTER TEN

"Yoo-hoo."

Regan turned from the fresh fish counter and saw Cynthia Tennerson in the aisle behind her, waving madly. For a second, she had the impulsive desire to throw herself headfirst in with the salmon and cover herself with crushed ice, but it was too late. Cyn had spotted her and was heading her way.

"Hello, fancy seeing you here," she bellowed out.

A part of Regan cursed Simon and his good deed toward Cyn. What on earth had possessed him? But for his actions, she would happily be ordering fish now.

Cyn's shrill voice echoed like a foghorn through the store, and people turned to look. She seemed blatantly unaware.

"You're back then?"

Obviously.

"I got back a few days ago," Regan answered softly, hoping Cyn would get the message and drop the volume. It seemed to work.

"Yes, actually, I know," Cyn replied in lower tones. "The Connells mentioned they'd seen you going up and down the stairs like a demented lemming loaded up with stuff. Sounds as if you're moving in?"

"I'm renting the place now."

"Oh? So you're not returning home?"

Regan watched as Cyn put her shopping basket on the floor. She was in for the kill, and Regan realized this wasn't going to be a passing, "Hello." She stepped away from the counter so another customer could be served as she wished Simon was still alive so she could kill him.

"No, Cyn. I'm selling my home, and I plan to get a teaching job down here. I've rather taken to the area, and I like Simon's place."

"Well, you must let me advise you on suitable schools. I know all the good ones, and those to be avoided. There are some dreadful ones out there."

In all the time she'd been here, driving around the area, Regan hadn't once seen a school that struck her as particularly poor. She suspected Cyn was a snob. But it didn't really matter because she wasn't looking at school positions. She'd had time to think while back up north, and her decision to return to university life and research had been cemented when Claire told her what Simon thought. She would seek a new career and return to old roots, doing research. Maybe she'd do some grad tuition. This new path seemed exciting. She was looking forward to it, although she'd wait till Simon's estate was sorted. She didn't have to rush.

Regan hoped her *passion* for mathematics would return. Rote teaching at school had crushed it. She only hoped she hadn't left it too long and that her brain cells were still up to the challenge.

"I'm not going back to school teaching. I'm going to apply for some university posts. I feel like being stretched."

Cyn seemed impressed. "Well, I can help there, too. I've contacts all over the place. There are plenty of higher education opportunities around here, and if you don't mind commuting, you'll have a wealth of choice." She rubbed her hands together as something crossed her mind. "I've been meaning to ask if you'd like to come to dinner. As it happens, I'm throwing a little soiree tomorrow night, and I'm one down. I hate uneven guest numbers. Would you like to come? They're all locals, all professionals, and heavily involved with the community. You'll be making some great contacts."

Regan would have rather had bamboo shoved down her nails, and she was thankful she genuinely had something else—much more fun—arranged. She was a hopeless liar.

"That would be lovely, but I'm going to Torquay tomorrow with Claire."

"Claire?"

"The gardener...up at the apartments. She's got business there and asked if I'd like to go along. We're going to make a day of it."

Cyn's disapproval showed as she pursed her lips and raised a brow. "I'd be careful if I were you, the new friends you make. Some are not really the type you may wish to be seen with."

The harsh comment took Regan aback. She'd sensed only too clearly that there was no love lost between the two women. She wondered if Cyn's snobbishness stretched to those employed in less intellectual type jobs like gardening, or worse, she was a good old-fashioned homophobe. Did she know Claire was a lesbian? Was that what all this was about? Whatever it was, Regan felt a need to defend her.

"Claire has been very kind and supportive, Cyn."

"I'm sure she has." The sarcasm flowed, and the sour look on her face didn't shift. "Well, you know your own mind, and I'm not one to tittle-tattle, but just be careful."

Regan felt sure this was homophobia leaking out, and she didn't like it. The more she got to know Cyn, the less she thought she liked her. She wasn't sure.

Cyn looked at her watch. "Terribly sorry, but I must dash. There's a committee meeting this afternoon, and I need to get back to the office."

Regan's relief clashed with a sudden rise of awareness and curiosity. Cyn was at the center of all things in the area. Maybe she could answer some of Regan's questions.

"Cyn, what do you know about the de Vits?"

A change came over Cyn as she bent to pick up her shopping basket. She scrutinized Regan sharply. "What don't I know about them?" It wasn't a question, more a revealing statement. Her eyes turned cold, as did her tone. "Why are you asking?"

Had Regan hit a nerve?

"The name keeps cropping up in Simon's affairs. He was in pretty deep with them." Regan hesitated, unsure of how much to say. But given Cynthia's role, if anyone would know anything, surely she would? "I've just got questions...lots of them."

Cyn was nodding like a toy dog in the back of people's cars.

"Listen, you come and have dinner, just the two of us at my place. Oliver is away this weekend at a golfing tournament in Wiltshire, followed by some boring annual dinner. You come over and we'll talk about the de Vits. I'll tell you everything I know about that unpleasant family. What if I ring you later with details?"

Regan accepted the invitation. She could put up with Cyn if it helped answer some of her questions. Whatever Cyn knew, it was apparent she didn't like the de Vits either. At least they now had something in common.

"Good. I'll be in touch," Cyn said as she turned and left.

Regan refocused her attention on the fish counter. The positive mood she'd been in earlier, before Cyn, had gone. All she could think of was the dislike she had for all things de Vit. Perhaps now she might learn more about them.

"Bloody hell, this is a noisy vehicle," Regan said.

Claire laughed as she drove around the tight country lanes. "Don't pick on my wheels."

"And it smells of grass."

She looked at Regan with playful contempt.

"What do you expect? It is the gardener's vehicle."

"But why grass?"

"Why not?"

"Don't you pile the stuff up in a corner of the garden somewhere? That's what normal people do."

"That's the problem. I cut so much of it, sometimes I have to take the excess down to the council tip."

"It's like traveling in a mobile compost heap. If I end up with hay fever—"

"—then you'll just have to use these." Claire thrust a box of tissues toward her.

"I guess this means you don't have a nurturing side," Regan said.

"I guess this means you're a whiner."

"Why don't you have a normal car like everyone else?"

It was clear that Regan was thoroughly enjoying herself.

"Normal?" Claire said.

"One that doesn't smell of grass."

Claire shrugged. "I did once. I had a Merc."

She thought lovingly of the shiny red SLK Roadster she'd exchanged in favor of the more practical Jeep. A friend had needed to sell it fast, and it had been offered at a bargain price. She'd jumped at the opportunity. She'd cried when she'd sold the Merc.

"What happened to it?"

"Trunk wasn't big enough. I couldn't get the grass cuttings in."

"Pity."

Claire was enjoying their dry banter, too.

She was pleased she'd chosen the back roads to Torquay. The journey was longer, but it meant spending more time with Regan. The route would also take them through some of the most stunning countryside the area had to offer. Besides, neither of them was in any rush. She was dumping some plants and returning borrowed electrical equipment to a friend, but he was out for the day and had told her to drop the stuff in an outbuilding. So with no particular deadlines to meet, the two of them had the day to enjoy.

She hoped she might learn more about Regan beyond her current problems. She wanted to know what her leisure pursuits were. What did she like doing when she had time to relax? Did they share common interests? For now she was content to find out how her priorities were moving along.

"Any potential house buyers?" Claire asked.

Regan shifted to face her.

"No, but one couple seems keen. They're going back for a second viewing so that's hopeful. At least people are going around it now. My paint job must have done the trick."

"And the recession's lifting. This is always a good time of the year to sell."

"I hope so, Claire. I just want to start anew, and the sooner I get away from there the better. At least I managed to get all my stuff from school without bumping into my ex. Someone's been listening to my prayers."

Claire had wondered if Regan and Karen had crossed paths. Her own experience, albeit many years ago, reminded her that meeting up with an ex so soon after finishing was never top of anyone's want list. Emotions were always high, and things often got said that didn't need to. Regan was getting her full quota of emotions at the moment. She didn't need further stress.

"It would have been too embarrassing, too awkward," Regan said.

"Want to talk?"

"The question is do you want to listen? This is where people start jumping off cliffs like rockhopper penguins."

"Try me. If it gets too bad, there are plenty of cliffs en route."

They both smiled.

"No, you're off the hook, Claire. There isn't much to say. I went out with Karen for several years, but it didn't work out. She left her husband for me...always a bad sign. I was her first woman. Dangerous. In addition, she decided her career was more important. She's gunning for the position of headmistress. Regrettably, she doesn't want a lesbian affair to blot her copy book, so she's settled for the safe road."

"How does that make you feel?" Claire sounded like a psychotherapist.

Regan behaved like a patient. She took time before answering.

"Disappointed. I thought we were good together, but when she chose to go back to her husband, that's when I knew it was all over. He's a total prick, and I know the reunion won't last. He's had affairs all over the place, but has promised her he's a new man."

They looked at one another and scoffed in unison.

"It won't last," Regan stated without animosity.

Claire could only agree. Some scripts were chiseled in stone.

"That's my nonexistent love life in a nutshell."

"I'm sorry." Claire genuinely meant it. She knew what it was like to lose love.

"Don't be. In a way, it's been the stimulus I've needed to take charge of my life again and do something I should have done years ago. My objective now is to get back into university. I always wanted to do more research, and I might be able to teach the undergrads. Don't get me wrong, I've loved teaching high school, and I've loved the kids, but—"

"—it doesn't challenge you."

Regan looked at her with wide eyes. She appeared shocked that Claire saw this.

"Yeah," Regan said. "Teaching school, I've always felt I was heading in the wrong direction, moving away from what I really want. But I seemed to be caught on a conveyor belt I couldn't get off. I ended up at the last school, which is a really good one, and at the top of its league. It's where I met Karen. We became an item. If Karen hadn't killed me, the job eventually would. Simon was right. I wasn't happy. Now I want to try to resolve all that."

"I have a feeling you're going to do fine."

"Do you?"

The way Regan looked at her made Claire's heart miss a beat.

"Yes, if you follow your heart."

Regan nodded and relaxed back into the seat. Their conversation went quiet, but there was comfort in its silence. Several times, Claire looked across at Regan whose attention was drawn to the passing countryside. Her dark hair was tucked behind an ear, and she looked like a young teenage boy, alert and full of inquisitiveness. With her strong face and lean lines, she was handsome.

Claire wanted to reach out and touch her, but she didn't. She didn't want to ruin their growing friendship, and until she knew how Regan felt about her, she needed to be cautious. She also needed to tell her about Rosie. That might affect any changes in their relationship. Who would want a partner who already had one?

Claire chose the safety of words.

"I'm enjoying this, Regan. Thanks for coming today."

"I'm enjoying this, too. Thanks for asking."

A look passed between them that gave Claire hope. She sensed it wasn't a look of just gratitude. She took a deep breath and tried to concentrate on her driving.

Regan relaxed into the seat and closed her eyes. She didn't know if she was getting used to the rhythmic rattle of the vehicle, or whether it was the sun that fell across her face, but she became very tired. It was easy to relax around Claire. When she was with her, all her worries and problems faded. Even before Simon's death, Regan had been uptight and unhappy. *Nothing* had been right in her life. Yet here she was, sitting in a car, smelling like a blade of grass, and in a completely tranquil state of nirvana. Claire's influence was calming, Karen's never had been. She'd always flustered her.

When Regan opened her eyes again, they fell on Claire, who seemed blissfully unaware that she was being watched. Regan smiled. Claire's face was a picture of concentration as she drove. Regan found it endearing. She studied her small hands on the large heavy black steering wheel, observing the short, clipped nails. On the face of it, they seemed fit for purpose as a gardener.

Yet Regan couldn't dislodge the feeling that Claire might not have been a gardener for too long. She wasn't sure what fed that. Maybe it was because she hadn't known the type of rhododendron they'd planted. You expected gardeners to know things like that. Perhaps it was because her hands were too soft, or maybe because the gardeners she'd come across always seemed more robust and strong. Claire was gentle and waif-like. She'd mentioned that her last car had been a Mercedes. That seemed a whole lot of wheels for a gardener. She wouldn't be on much money. Had Claire had another life? Had she taken this job to heal after she'd lost her partner? When the time felt right, she'd ask her.

"You've woken up then."

Claire's voice startled her.

"I haven't been asleep," Regan said.

"I think you might. You've had your eyes closed for the last twenty minutes."

"Really?" Maybe she had drifted off. "I'm sorry."

"Don't be. You must have needed that."

Regan sat up, suddenly more alert.

"You better talk to me...keep me awake."

"I can do that." Claire looked at her, her eyes warm, her words soft. "How's Simon's estate coming on?"

Regan grimaced. "I love that word, *estate*. It sounds like someone has a large amount of property and wealth, neither of which poor Simon has. All he has are debts. I'm discovering a lot, Claire, and much of it I don't like."

"How so?"

"He seems to have sold financial packages to friends that didn't turn out too well. They lost money and then turned nasty, not too unrealistically." She had found some terrible letters from old friends who did not hold back in their anger. "There's also a lot of official paperwork that shows Simon has been hand in glove with some very dodgy people."

"Dodgy?"

"There's always one rotten name that keeps cropping up...the de Vits." She couldn't hide the bile in her tone. "I took a load of paperwork home with me to go through, and that name is everywhere. It's on the contracts he signed, the loans he took out, the investments he signed up to. I know they're big in London and Bath, but they're pretty prolific around here too. So far I've found the de Vit Walker Corporation, de Vit Investments, even one of the shopping malls is named after them."

"I'm sure they're not all—"

"Yes, they are," Regan interrupted. "They are an intrinsically rotten family with tentacles everywhere. I have no doubt that once they'd gotten a hold of Simon, they reeled him in and controlled him like a puppet. When the economy turned sour, they left him to flounder. Simon made huge mistakes, his own, but from what I've seen, the de Vits have got a lot to answer for."

When her vitriolic download ended, Claire had gone quiet, and her customary smile was absent. Regan kicked herself. She'd done it again. She'd let her notorious anger off the leash. Now she'd made Claire feel uncomfortable, and probably reminded her of her bad behavior when they'd first met. Poor Claire. She was ruining her day. She reached over and touched her arm.

"I'm sorry. It's that flash temper of mine. I don't know when to shut up, do I?" She threw her hands up in front of her. "I promise I won't talk about this again...at least for today." She covered up her embarrassment with a small half-hearted laugh. "Maybe I should get anger therapy."

"I don't think you need that." Claire smiled, but Regan noticed it didn't reach her eyes. She was being polite.

For a while, Claire didn't say much else and just drove.

Only later did they enter back into a richness of conversation on other safer topics. Regan was disappointed. She wanted to impress Claire and let her see her in a more relaxed, fun-loving state. She'd blown it.

Not long after, Claire dropped off the plants and equipment, and they drove on and into Torquay.

Once there, all memory of Regan's outburst disappeared. They strolled along the seafront, ambled around cheap souvenir shops, and both discovered they shared a love for the theater. It was revealed as they walked back to where the car was parked. There was a billboard advertising a local amateur theatrical group doing an upcoming season of Noël Coward plays.

"I love his stuff," Regan said. "I used watch all his old movies on TV with Dad."

"Me, too," Claire said. "Which of his plays is your favorite?"

Regan didn't have to think. "*Blithe Spirit*. I can watch that over and over again."

"Margaret Rutherford," Claire added.

"She was wonderful as Madame Arcati. The part was written for her."

"Was it?" Claire asked.

"No. I mean, I don't know. I was just saying, the part was written for her."

"Ah."

"And you? Your favorite?"

"*Private Lives...*and *Blithe Spirit*."

They didn't lunch in Torquay, partly because everywhere was jam-packed with tourists, and when Claire suggested they make their way home, Regan didn't object. She had a feeling Claire was keen to finish the day. She hadn't been right since Regan's over-the-top outburst in the car. Claire probably figured she was trapped with a nutter.

As they drove back, Regan decided to be brave.

"Are you okay, Claire?"

"Yes. Why?"

"Because you've gone dead quiet." Regan was ready to apologize for her behavior again.

At first, Claire didn't say anything, but then asked, "Do you fancy having something to eat on the way home? I know this friendly little restaurant that's only half an hour from the apartments. It does nice, simple food, and it's a good place to chat."

A good place to chat.

That sounded ominous. Regan was nervous.

"Am I in trouble?" Regan half joked.

"Trouble?" Claire frowned.

"You want to chat. It sounds serious."

Claire's frown disappeared. "There are a couple of things I want to talk to you about," she said.

"Oh, it definitely sounds serious." Regan's nervousness grew.

"It depends on how you view them."

Claire sounded upbeat, but she didn't look it.

"Should I be worried? Have I upset you?"

Shock crossed Claire's face, and she reached out and grabbed Regan's hand. "God, no. Is that what you think? Nothing could be further from the truth. It's because...because you haven't done anything wrong...because you're you...I need to tell you a few things about me, about..." Claire was struggling.

"About your partner."

"Yes, in part."

"You don't have to." Regan could wait.

"Yes, I do. I want to. I should have told you the other day."

"When?" Regan wasn't making any connection.

"Look, let's wait until we stop, then we can talk over a meal and a glass of wine, eh?"

Claire was nervous, too, and Regan wondered why. She cupped Claire's hand in both of hers. "No more questions. We'll wait."

Claire's smile returned, but it was a ghost smile. What was going on?

They turned a tight corner too fast, and the vehicle swayed. Claire drove out of it safely.

"You better use both hands before we end up in a ditch or something." Regan's sense of survival cut in. Besides, she was hungry, and if she was going to die, she wanted to do it on a full stomach.

Her phone rang.

It was Karen's number. She ignored it.

"Karen, again?" Claire asked.

"Yeah."

"You really ought to take her calls, or at least one of them."

Regan couldn't think why. She and Karen were finished. Anything that belonged to Karen at the house had now been returned. There was no good reason why they needed to talk. Why couldn't Karen leave her alone? Her constant phone calls were irritating. Maybe Claire was right, but she didn't feel like answering. Besides, it would only ruin a day that she was enjoying and turning out to be much more than she had hoped for. She knew she was about to learn something important about Claire. That excited her. You didn't share important things with people you didn't care for. Did you? Maybe this was where she would discover what Claire felt about her. Regan kept looking for signs, but nothing obvious was evident. It was her earlier words that were beginning to give Regan hope.

Because you haven't done anything wrong...because you're you.

It was the way Claire said them. There was affection behind the words, and Regan sensed subtext. She cautioned herself to not read things that might not be there.

"I really enjoy your company," Claire said.

Regan felt her caution blow to the wind.

"I did miss you while you were away," Claire continued, her voice low and intimate. "I kept hoping I'd see your car back, but..."

Regan couldn't believe it. Was Claire telling her she *did* have feelings for her, that her attraction was mutual?

Her phone went again. Regan cursed.

Claire looked at her with wide inquisitive eyes.

"Not Karen's number," Regan said. She didn't recognize it.

"Sorry, Claire. I'd better answer this in case it's to do with the house sale."

"Hey, Regan. It's me."

It was Karen! She recognized her deep, velvety, and sexy voice. It had once driven her crazy. It didn't anymore.

"At last," Karen said. "Whatever you do please don't put the phone down on me. You have no idea how hard I've been trying to get in touch with you. You never answer my calls or ring back. I'm using a friend's phone so you won't recognize the number."

"You're using what?" Regan couldn't believe Karen would do such a thing. She looked over at Claire, and silently mouthed "Karen."

"It's worked. It's the only way I can get to you. You wouldn't answer otherwise."

"Of course I don't answer. Why would I? We're finished. You walked out on me and went back to your husband, or don't you remember that?"

"I need to talk to you, Regan."

"But I don't want to talk to you. Aren't you getting the message?" All the time she was talking to Karen, she couldn't keep her eyes off Claire. What a bloody awful moment to call.

"There's something I need to say," Karen said.

"There's nothing you need to say, and certainly nothing I need to hear from you." Regan was livid. She heard Karen give a heavy sigh into the phone.

"Well, you're not going to like this, but I've driven down to you and I'm in town now booked into a bed and breakfast place."

"You've done what?"

"Keep your hair on. I've no intention of trying to win you back or anything. I know when something is over, but I'm determined to see you. Can we meet up?"

"I can't believe you've done this. Just go home, Karen. You're wasting your time."

"No. You either phone me and arrange a meeting or I come and find you. And you know I'll do that. You know what I'm like. I have a feeling you're going to prefer the former."

"Can't you say what you want over the phone?"

"No, Regan, I can't. I just want five minutes of your time... maybe ten."

"This is really unfair."

"I know it's awkward."

"Awkward? That's a bloody understatement."

"Want to arrange a time and place now? I repeat: I'm not leaving."

"No. I'll call you back. In the meantime why don't you go and play with the cars on the motorway."

"That's not nice, Regan."

"I know."

"Just phone me back. The sooner we meet, the sooner this is over for you. Okay?"

"Fine." Regan ended the call.

"Not a buyer for the house, then?" Claire said.

"It was Karen."

"I got that."

"She borrowed someone's phone so I wouldn't know it was her."

"Tenacious."

"Can you believe it?" Regan was exasperated. "She's down here, and she's booked into a place. She's determined to see me."

"Why?" Claire shook her head, "No, look, this is none of my business. I'm sorry, I don't mean to pry."

"No, that's okay. It seems she's tracked me down."

"What are you going to do?" Claire asked.

"I'm going to have to see her if only to get rid of her. I don't know what she wants, but she isn't leaving until she sees me. Damn it."

"Maybe she wants you back." Claire wasn't smiling anymore, and something dishonorable in Regan was pleased.

"She said she didn't...said she knew when something was over."

"Then why's she here?"

"Damned if I know." Regan's despair filled the Jeep like the convicted awaiting a hangman's noose. "I need this like a bottom full of hemorrhoids," she sighed.

Claire actually laughed. "That's a unique way of explaining things."

Regan drew her hands through her hair in exasperation. She was sure Claire had been about to tell her how she felt about her. Karen's timing was bloody inconsiderate. The moment was ruined.

"Maybe we should cancel our dinner," Claire said, disappointment on her face.

The moment really was ruined.

Regan could only agree. It was the last thing she wanted to do, but this was spoiling everything. Her mind would be on why Karen was here and what she wanted. She needed to see her and get it over with. Claire knew that.

"Would you mind?" Regan asked.

"Truthfully, yes, but I can see neither of us is going to be able to relax and enjoy dinner."

Regan hated disappointing Claire. She knew where she would rather be.

"Let's not cancel our dinner; let's just postpone it. We can have our chat later?" Regan asked.

"Okay. You let me know when you're ready."

Though Claire's response was understanding, Regan heard the disappointment in its tone. This was all such an anticlimax. Nearly everything about the day had been wonderful, but now it was all messed up. Regan fizzed like a bottle of pop.

They arrived back at the apartments and Claire parked in her usual spot by a clump of trees. Regan was glad because it offered a modicum of privacy.

Claire turned the engine off. Neither of them made any attempt to leave the car. They seemed awkward in each other's company.

"I hope you've enjoyed today," Claire said.

Regan swiveled in her seat to face her. She felt bad and wanted to put things right.

"Of course, I have, Claire. Really. I'm sorry I've ruined it with this call from Karen."

"That's okay."

"No, it isn't, and I want you to know that I *do* want to have dinner with you, sooner rather than later. I want to hear what it is you want to tell me. It's important."

"Important?"

"Yes."

"Why?"

Something snapped inside Regan. The day should have been a success, but because of her, on two occasions, it had turned into a huge disappointment. Suddenly, an impulse came over her. She felt daring. "Because all day, I've wanted to do this." She leaned over, cupped Claire's face, and kissed her. She half expected Claire to push her away, but she didn't. Regan found her mouth warm and welcoming.

"Oh," Claire said as Regan pulled back.

Regan saw her flushed cheeks and glazed eyes.

"I hope that was okay?" Regan smiled.

"I've wanted to do that all day, too," Claire said.

"I wish you had."

"I wasn't sure."

"I wasn't either," Regan said.

They laughed.

Regan kissed her again, and this time their tongues danced. She wanted to stay like this forever, touching Claire, holding her, but she knew she couldn't. She had to sort Karen out first.

"I'm going to have to go and see—"

"—Karen."

Regan nodded. "Please, can we rearrange dinner?"

"What about tomorrow night?" Claire suggested.

Regan grimaced. "Karen might still be here. What about the night after?"

"Okay."

"Hang on, no. I've got something arranged." Regan thought of the dinner arrangement with Cynthia. "It'll have to be the night after. Christ, this is irritating."

"It doesn't matter. Just ring to confirm it, okay? The wait will make it all the more enjoyable. It'll be something to look forward to."

"For me, too," Regan said. "It's a date, then, as soon as we fix it."

"A date," Claire whispered. "It's been a long time."

Regan was glad that she hadn't ruined everything. Claire looked happy and full of expectation. It made Regan want to take her in her arms and hold her tight. But she needed to go and sort things out. She reached out, took Claire's hand, and kissed it.

"Don't forget me while I'm gone," she said as she hopped out of the vehicle.

"Unlikely." Claire started the engine and drove off, leaving Regan on the driveway, cursing.

Damn you, Karen. You pick your moments. This had better be good.

And why the hell had Regan arranged to have dinner with Cynthia?

But she'd deal with Karen, find out what Cynthia knew about the de Vits, and then third time lucky, she'd go out with someone she really wanted to.

She had a date with Claire.

❖

The next day, Claire rose early and went and checked on Rosie. She did this at least twice every day—once in the morning and again at night. But she didn't bother going to work. Everything could wait. The lawns had been mowed, the borders dug, plants planted, and borrowed equipment returned. She had other things to be getting on with. Besides she didn't want to be hovering around the apartments like some lovesick voyeur with a pair of secateurs, watching out for any visitation by Karen…and that's exactly what she would have done.

Instead, she spent time surfing the Internet and booking tickets for a Noël Coward play in the Torquay area. She wanted to surprise Regan with them when they had dinner.

She couldn't believe how happy she was.

There was no more dreary loneliness or feeling of isolation. Gone was the oppressive sense that her life was slipping away and that there was nothing she could do to stop it. Her life was moving again, and she had a future.

She was realistic. She and Regan might fall at the first hurdle, but then again, they might not. Things had not started well when she'd first met her, but how they were improving.

She thought of Rosie, her beautiful Rosie. This was what Rosie had wanted her to do, to find someone else and live life. Now she understood. But it would still be a big step. Their love had been perfect. It would take time to get used to moving forward. Recognizing change was one thing, dealing with it another. The guilt would be there for a long time. Its presence proved what a wonderful person Rosie had been.

Claire was blessed the day she met her. She laughed to herself. They hadn't had a great start either.

They had met at the military Joint Services Command and Staff College at Shrivenham, where Claire had been a young cocky naval officer on a junior staff course. Rosie was one of the international affairs instructors, on loan from King's College, London. Sparks flew straightaway. Rosie hadn't liked her much at the beginning. She'd thought her a know-it-all who fancied herself too much. It was a pretty accurate assessment.

Claire was bright and didn't hold back letting people know that. She was hungry for promotion and the best jobs. Rosie never seemed impressed with her. It didn't seem to matter that Claire kept getting top grades and ended up best student; she was a constant irritation to Rosie.

Maybe Claire had been immature, but she'd enjoyed goading Rosie all the time. Everything escalated, and things had got so bad that one day Claire and Rosie decided to go out for a drink to *chat* about how they could improve their relationship. Several glasses of merlot later, they both realized that the flashing sparks were actually sexual attraction, and there was a strong possibility that they were actually in love with each other.

To *improve their relationship*, they moved in together.

That had been the beginning of a most incredible love story, and one that had continued nonstop until Rosie became ill. As the disease progressed, the person who was Rosie slowly disappeared before Claire's eyes. Her personality changed, and Claire's world fell apart.

It was strange the things that went through Claire's head. She wanted to tell Rosie about Regan. There had never been any secrets between them, and it seemed odd that this important move in her life shouldn't be shared. But Rosie wasn't here anymore.

After a light lunch, Claire decided to drive into town. There were a few errands she needed to run, and the fresh air would do her good. It would take her mind off Regan.

Several hours later, Claire walked out of a dark, musty bookshop and into the light.

She stood for a moment on a walkway deliberating what to do next. She'd achieved her main aim which was to buy a book for a niece's birthday. She'd not seen her brother's youngest girl, Alison, for some time, but she always sent her something, normally money in a card. This year, however, Claire had been hit by the inspiration fairy. Her brother had mentioned that a book on Edith Cavell might go down well as Alison was contemplating training as a nurse.

Alison was currently into the heroism of the World War I British nurse who had saved the lives of soldiers on all sides in Brussels. She'd been shot in 1915 because she'd helped Allied troops to escape German occupied Belgium.

Claire thought what noble reading matter it was as she decided to walk the longer, more scenic way down the high street back to her car.

As Claire waited to cross the busy road and walk along the river path that led to her car, she spotted Regan. She was over by the water's edge, leaning on a barrier, and looking the other way.

Claire's heart quickened. This chance meeting was unexpected, and so welcome. A smile automatically rose on her lips. Regan looked so damned attractive in her tight blue jeans and white cotton blouse that hugged her trim body.

She saw the humor in the moment. Here she was trying hard to avoid Regan, to give her the space she needed to deal with Karen, and yet they seemed destined to bump into each other. It was a sign.

Who would ever have thought, just a few months ago, that her life would be so changed by the arrival of Simon's sister? She wondered if Simon would approve if he were still alive. She had a feeling he might. They would have made a fine trio if only he'd lived. But then, she reasoned, she might never have met Regan.

A huge articulated truck drove past on the road, and Claire stepped back from the sidewalk's edge. The road was busy today. She needed to pay more attention to what was going on around her instead of daydreaming.

But she didn't care. Yesterday had been wonderful. She couldn't stop thinking about that kiss. Why shouldn't she dream? Rosie had gone on and on about her doing this. It had driven Claire to distraction. She had never wanted to listen. Now Claire was thankful Rosie had pushed her about moving on. It eased the guilt.

She quickly checked the traffic and chanced an opportunity to dash across the road. It was a slim one, and an irate driver beeped his horn at her. She ignored him and walked toward Regan. She started to cross the small patch of green grass that separated them and was about to call out to Regan when someone else did.

Claire saw a tall, attractive blond woman in a tight black sweater and hip-hugging red skirt, all of which showed off a voluptuous Sophia Loren-type physique, approach Regan from her right. She was waving.

She saw the two of them face each other and freeze. Claire stopped too. She instinctively knew she was watching something intimate reveal itself and that she should turn away. It would be beyond embarrassment if she was caught.

So this was Karen.

Claire watched her talking, but she was too far away to hear. Moments later, she saw them embrace and hold each other tight.

She couldn't see Regan's face, but she saw Karen's. She was upset and crying. Regan was wiping the tears from her face.

Claire held her breath. She stepped back and hid from sight behind a red telephone box, and continued to watch. She knew it was wrong, but she couldn't stop.

She watched as Karen drew back from another embrace and intimately placed her hand on the brown leather belt around Regan's jeans, tugging at it playfully.

Claire still couldn't see Regan's face, only Karen's. She looked vulnerable and emotional. Claire saw love, lust, passion, sadness all in one. Whatever had once existed between them, Karen wasn't over it. She was suffering. Claire found it painful to watch. This was private. She of all people wasn't supposed to see this.

She forced herself to turn away and walk back to her vehicle.

What had she just witnessed?

Regan had told her that she and Karen were over. She did not doubt that. Regan was honest about her feelings toward Karen and she trusted her. But it still annoyed Claire seeing Regan in Karen's arms. She felt no jealousy. What they had shared was in the past. But she was worried for Regan. This would upset her. She was coping with so much and did not need any emotional extra. And seeing the panoply of emotions on Karen's face, she suspected she wasn't over Regan. Is that why Karen had come? Was she trying to win Regan back, to rekindle their relationship? What other reason would she have for driving all the way south? Claire would have to wait until she saw Regan to find out.

She drove to the potting shed before going home. Though she had no intention of working, she needed to collect her pocket book. There were some numbers in it she wanted to call.

As she picked it up from the workbench, it opened to a page she'd written on earlier. It was a reference number for play tickets at a Torquay theater house. She wanted to surprise Regan when they had dinner. Maybe that would take the sting out of her meeting with Karen. Claire just wanted to make her happy, like she was feeling right now.

There was a spring in her step as she closed the shed door, but it disappeared as she glanced up the lawn to Rosie's. There was no sign of her, but Claire's jubilant feelings gave way to remorse. How could she feel happy when Rosie was so ill? Here she was planning what she hoped would be an intimate evening with Regan while Rosie, the woman she loved and would love until the day she died, remained alive and within touching distance? It wasn't easy leaving her behind.

She knew she had to tell Regan everything about Rosie. There would be no moving on until all was out in the open. Regan needed to know that whatever happened, Claire would always look after Rosie. She would want for nothing. That was Claire's promise to her love even though Rosie had accused her of being a fool.

Claire knew that in time Rosie's body would give up, but until that day came, she would never let her down. And she had Sally. Sally had been like a beacon of light entering Claire's dark world. She thanked God for her.

She looked up at Rosie's window. "Good night, my darling. Sweet dreams."

Claire blew her a kiss and went home.

CHAPTER ELEVEN

The dinner at Cynthia's was excellent. Regan knew she enjoyed playing host, but the standard of fine cuisine was unexpected. Cyn declared it was something she'd just thrown together. It wasn't. It was the sort of meal you paid a fortune for at a top class London restaurant. Regan wondered how much more impressive the meal would have been if it was to entertain local dignitaries, the movers and shakers of the area. She suspected Cynthia had missed her true vocation. She could give many of the television famed chefs a run for their money.

The level of conversation also initially matched the social chitchat of an evening out in some expensive eatery. They talked of safe, general, and mildly informative topics, all of which bored Regan rigid. She was here with an agenda, to learn more about the de Vits.

Cynthia was well aware of that, and in time she turned the discussions toward the local family.

"They've been here for generations, wealthy beyond belief, and involved in just about everything," Cynthia said. "When my father left school, he went to work for them, but got out as soon as he could to set up his own business. He never liked them…said they were like vultures with fingers in everybody else's affairs."

"Where does their money come from?" Regan asked.

"Difficult to say, but I think they used to buy property and land, sometimes businesses from those who had fallen into debt. They'd buy people out, offering slightly more money than the banks. I call them asset-strippers, the type who prey on those in trouble and take advantage. They pretty much own all the land around here and a fair chunk of real estate. They're involved in everything."

"They aren't on the council." It was more a statement of fact than a question. Regan had looked up the council and its members on the Internet.

"My dear," Cyn said knowingly, "they don't need to be *on* the council. They are like the Mafia and can control those they need to. How do you think planning permission for all their housing estates and business ventures gets passed? They don't control me." The last statement came out harsh.

"Hasn't anyone every tried to stop them?"

Cynthia gave a flippant flick of a hand. "Some have tried. They always regret it. This is a family you don't mess with. If their connections don't work, they simply throw money at a problem to make it disappear.

"Of course, they're big in London, the City. The backbone of their business these days is financial—commodities trading, corporate investments, share dealing, and so on. That's where your brother got caught. He should never have dealt with them. The odds were stacked against him from the start."

Regan thought of Simon and how desperate he would have been toward the end. Her heartache must have shown because Cynthia reached out and tapped her hand.

"You make sure you steer clear of the de Vits, my dear. Forewarned is forearmed."

Regan was glad of the temporary respite when Cyn changed the subject.

"So, you plan to stay," Cyn said.

"Yes. I like the area, and the people." She thought of Claire.

"Everything sorted with Simon's estate?"

There was that word *estate* again. Simon had no estate. The de Vits had seen to that. She curbed her acidic thoughts to answer Cyn.

"All's fine. Things are moving," she said. "I had a letter from the coroner's office this morning telling me the date of the inquest. I don't have to be present."

Cynthia nodded sympathetically. "No, it will be just formality."

It was a kind statement, and Regan almost liked her, but something in her resisted.

"I've been very lucky to have such support…yourself of course, and then a good solicitor."

"Who are you using?"

"Albert Marshall. He's a local—"

"I know Albert," Cyn interrupted, an unpleasant tone in her voice.

"You don't like him?"

Cynthia shifted uncomfortably in her chair. "Oh, he's okay I suppose. He is a very good solicitor. It's just he's done dealings with the de Vits. They tend to use him a lot."

Regan balked. "I didn't know that."

"Don't take that the wrong way. Marshall is a good man, and there are plenty around who rate him very highly. Just because he's worked for the de Vits does not mean he's in their pockets. Far from it, I'd say. The man's a Quaker, and I've never met a dishonest one. If you're in any business around here, it's hard to avoid coming across that family. I hope I haven't upset you."

Regan smiled. "Not at all. Just a bit of a shock, I suppose."

She reasoned that Marshall was a good man. Cyn had reluctantly paddled backward and announced he was, and of course, Claire recommended him.

"And Claire's been very helpful."

"The gardener." Cynthia's words were drawn out and sounded bitchy.

"You don't like Claire much, do you?" Regan asked.

She wanted to know why Cynthia thought so little of Claire who didn't seem to have an ounce of harm in her.

Cynthia did not hold back. "I don't," she said. "She's a bad lot, from a bad lot. She started off rotten, and in my opinion, very little has changed."

"What do you mean?"

Cynthia pursed her lips as she neatly folded her napkin and placed it on the table. "I really shouldn't...I'm not one to spread gossip."

Regan knew she was about to.

"But it isn't gossip, it is fact, and you're bound to hear it sooner or later, so it might as well come from me. At least this way, you get the truth."

"What?"

Was this where Cyn announced that Claire was a lesbian, and Regan would be hit by a torrent of homophobic rhetoric? If it was, Cynthia was in for it. Polite host or not, Regan wouldn't let her get away with this. Cynthia was in for a shock. She had just entertained a woman from "the dark side" in her home. She waited for the inevitable to come, but it didn't.

"I always felt she should have been charged with murder, or something."

"Murder?" Regan spluttered. This was not what she was expecting.

Cyn arched a brow, ill-hidden enjoyment slapped across her face. "Well, not murder, because she was too young and didn't actually lift a hand to anything, but she might as well have done. I think they call it antisocial behavior or harassment these days…some mamby-pamby way of softening, of excusing people's terrible behavior."

Regan couldn't speak. This development was serious.

"Claire was at the same school as me so I know. She was a school bully who pushed a young classmate over the edge. The child committed suicide because of her cruelty. It was only her family's connections that saved her. Money can buy you out of a lot of trouble. I expect that payoff bought a new school wing or something. She disappeared from school soon after that…conveniently went off to some expensive sixth form college up in London, and then joined the Royal Navy. I heard all the rumors, probably lies fueled by her family, of a very successful career, quite the high flyer, early promotions. But look at her now…reduced to a gardener of all things. How the mighty have fallen."

Regan couldn't believe what she was hearing. None of this made any sense. The Claire she knew was not the one Cyn was painting.

"One has to wonder," Cynthia continued, "why she was thrown out of the service. I mean she had to have done something damn serious for that. A court-martial, I expect. Even the family couldn't help her this time."

Regan was shaking her head. "No, this can't be right. Wealthy? Claire? She doesn't look as though she's got too much money." But then a small memory reminded her that Claire had said she'd once owned a Merc before the Jeep.

Cyn rattled on, enjoying the moment.

"Is that what you believe? My dear, don't you know? Wealth is her middle name. She's a de Vit."

CHAPTER TWELVE

S he's a de Vit."
     Cynthia's apocalyptic words reverberated through Regan's mind on a playback loop. As she drove home, she felt physically sick. It was a feeling she recognized. It was the one she'd experienced twice in her life—once when they had broken the news to her and her brother that their parents had been killed in a car accident, and the other when the police had informed her that Simon was dead. Both times the news had been unexpected and catastrophic. Both times she had been thrown into shock, as she was now. She could barely believe what Cyn had told her.
     Claire is a de Vit!
     She was a member of the family that had played such an intricate part in Simon's downfall. Though master of his own fate, all the paperwork she'd read showed how Simon had been lured in by the urbane and perfidious de Vits. Their money-making schemes had been presented with such skill and cunning, and to think Claire was part of that family disgusted her.
     Once home, she couldn't sleep and lay awake wondering if Cyn had made it up. There was no love lost between Cyn and Claire, but she rationalized that there was no reason to fabricate such lies, for they could soon be discovered. Regan knew she'd been told the truth.
     What hurt her most was the deceit. How many times had she vented to Claire about the de Vits? Claire was under no illusions what she felt about them. There had been ample opportunity for her to tell her who she was, but she hadn't. Why was that? Claire had deliberately kept that particular piece of important information to

herself. Why would she do that if not to *hide* the truth? At some point it was bound to come out, especially if they were going to become more than passing acquaintances. It would hinder any relationship, unless of course the latter didn't matter to Claire. Was that it? Claire was not interested in her, and Regan was being used, for whatever reason that was.

She thought how Claire had subtly recommended Marshall, a man she now knew was regularly employed by the de Vits. Was she being manipulated, much like Simon had? If so, how could this have happened? How could Claire take advantage of her under such dreadful circumstances, and when she was at rock bottom? What sort of person would do that?

Everything Cynthia told her that evening swirled in her mind like a vortex. Other things had been exposed, and none of them painting Claire in any redeeming light. The more she discovered, the more the Claire she thought she knew, faded. What replaced her was a woman duplicitous and dark.

She was a de Vit, and one with a dishonorable past that stemmed from a childhood built on bullying and harassment, and one that had goaded a young girl to take her own life. Claire's formative, atrocious years had apparently not diminished as she grew to womanhood. She had been kicked out of the military. That was serious. Regan saw the pattern of sour behavior revealing itself. Her eyes stung as she realized that Claire was a deceiver with a mean past, and a charlatan.

Questions filled her mind, and when she eventually arose the next day, the first thing she wanted to do was to go into town and visit the letting agent. It seemed important to find out why Simon's bank statements had mysteriously stopped showing rental payments many months before he died. She wondered too about his utility bills; nothing was owed, and yet again, there was no evidence on statements to show payments. How could Simon have paid any of these? He was too far in debt. None of it made any sense.

She wanted to talk to the letting agency office manager, but he was in a meeting. Instead she met a young girl who declared this was her first week in the job, but who seemed very helpful. She found Simon's account on the computer system and confirmed the account was closed, that there was no debt…*because the owner had wiped it.*

When Regan asked who the owner was, the girl looked uncomfortable.

"It says here," she said in a small voice, "that the owner's name is not to be divulged to anyone."

I bet it isn't, Regan thought. She was beginning to smell a rat. The building was probably part of a de Vit investment. Cynthia had said they owned a lot of real estate in the vicinity. A chill went through her. Was she now renting from them?

Regan was so close to an answer, she wasn't going to give in. She played on the young girl's inexperience.

"Oh, that's okay. I wouldn't want you to tell me anything you shouldn't. I can easily get that info from public records. It's just that I want to thank the owner." Regan leaned in toward the girl, as if telling her something personal, something she only wanted to share with her. "You see, Mr. Canning was my brother and he got himself into a lot of debt," she whispered. "He took his own life. I only want to thank the owner for his kindness. It's such a wonderful thing to do in the given circumstances."

"Oh...I'm sorry. I didn't know." The girl was embarrassed.

"No, why should you? I expect they've kept this quiet. It's not the sort of thing that gets banded around, is it?" Regan made as if to move. "Don't worry. I'll go get this information from records." She moved toward the door but then stopped, turned to face the girl, and in a low, conspiratorial voice said, "Look, no one is here. They'd never know. I can get the info anyway...can't you just tell me who it is?"

"I really shouldn't."

"I won't tell anyone, I promise. I'll just say I got it from records on file. It would just save me some time. I'm sure you can imagine my brother's death has left me with a lot to do."

Regan saw the girl weakening. She felt guilty for playing on her naïve desire to provide good customer service.

"They'll kill me if they find out. I'll lose my job," the girl said.

"I won't tell a soul where I got this from. I promise."

The girl hesitated for a second before hitting a few keys and then declaring, "It says here that the owner is Claire de Vit."

Claire de Vit. If Regan had possessed a grain of doubt regarding Cyn's information, it now evaporated. She felt sick. This was even worse. It was yet another thing Claire had kept from her. All those times Regan had talked to her about whether or not the owner might consider renting to her, Claire had never revealed she was that person. *My God, I'm renting the apartment from her.*

When she returned to her car, she stayed sitting in it. She did a lot of thinking.

She wondered why Claire was a gardener. It wasn't because, as Cyn had suggested, it was the only job she could get, and that her family had probably helped her out. Far from it. This was a woman of independent means who owned an apartment—possibly more—that pulled in a sizeable monthly income. Why would someone in her position be a gardener if not for some sinister reason?

Regan's imagination went wandering. Was this a way the family could have someone close to keep an eye on *persons of interest?* Claire would have known Simon's every movement, even his thoughts. It sickened her to think that Claire might have tricked Simon into thinking she was a friend and confidant, someone he could trust.

There was also the strange behavior of Rosie and Sally. Rosie was scared of Claire. *Don't let her hurt me again.* Sally said nothing to suggest that Rosie's fears weren't founded. What had Claire done to a sick invalid? Might Rosie have crossed the de Vits at some point? Was she too being watched? This was like opening Pandora's box. Regan's mind was flooded with crazy conspiracy theories. The frightening thing was they might all be true.

She drove home to the apartment, but when she got there, she didn't stop. She only circled the driveway to spot Claire's Jeep. There were things she wanted to say to her, but right now, they could wait. There was something else she wanted to do.

She drove back out of the apartment complex and onto the main road that led back into town. A few hundred yards ahead, there was a main junction through which all apartment traffic had to pass. Just a short distance away, she pulled over into the car park of a small timber merchant's, and waited. There she had an excellent view of the road. She was prepared to wait there all day if necessary. She wanted to follow Claire.

She didn't have to wait long. Less than an hour later, she saw Claire drive past.

Regan carefully tailed her. She kept her distance and followed her left at the junction and then through two small villages before Claire turned left again, entering into a gated community development.

She wasn't able to follow her in, but several yards past the gates, Regan pulled into a lay-by that gave her a clear view of the front of the residential building. Regan watched as Claire got out of her Jeep and walked into the front of the complex.

So this is where Claire lives, she thought.

It was an impressive place. She could make out the cars parked to the side of the building. They were expensive, posh cars. This was not the domain of a typical gardener, on a typical gardener's pay. Claire's independent means had to be substantial.

Her shock began to ferment in anger as Regan realized that Claire wore a mask and was leading a double life.

CHAPTER THIRTEEN

It was mid morning as Claire parked the sit-on mower under cover back at the potting shed. There was a summer storm brewing. The air was humid and draped around her like a heavy winter coat. When she looked up she saw how dark the sky had become.

Something wicked this way comes, Claire thought as she saw a flash of lightning and heard a distant rumble of thunder.

This was no time to be out in the open with machinery; it was an invitation to an electrical storm, and not one she wanted to proffer. She wanted to die old, and not as a burnt offering in the middle of a freshly mown lawn.

As she walked from the machine to the shed door, she saw Regan stomping down the lawn toward her. Everything about her body language told her she was fuming. She looked like an Icelandic volcano about to blow its top.

Claire figured it might have something to do with Karen's unwelcomed appearance. She drew breath, expecting Regan to start venting. But as she drew closer, some inner intuition warned her that Regan's ire was focused on her. By the time Regan came to an abrupt halt before her, a thousand warning signals were blasting *beware*. She didn't need to be a student of human behavior to recognize that Regan's anger *was* directed at her. Why? She'd done nothing, *unless* Regan had spotted her in town watching her with Karen. Claire was certain she hadn't been seen, but maybe? She didn't have to wait long for an answer.

Regan didn't shout, and her quiet, composed voice belied her barely contained rage.

"You're a de Vit," she announced.

The few words hit Claire like a southpaw to the stomach. Air sucked from her lungs as she struggled to breathe. This was not what she was expecting to hear. She swallowed uncomfortably, and a distant memory reminded her that the last time she'd felt this bad was when the consultant announced that Rosie had Alzheimer's.

Regan's accusation sounded heavy *and unacceptable.*

When Claire failed to answer, Regan said, "Don't want to answer that?"

"Yes," Claire replied. "Yes, I'm a de Vit."

She'd known in the car on the way back from Torquay that Regan might take her hereditary ancestral line badly. Now she wished it had been her who'd told her. She was going to tell Regan, along with who Rosie was, when they had dinner that day, but the opportunity was stolen by Karen's untimely arrival. Now struck with the gifts of Mystic Meg, fairground mind reader extraordinaire, she could see that Regan thought she'd deliberately tried to hide that fact.

"You couldn't tell me that, could you?" Regan said, confirming Claire's psychic abilities. Regan didn't wait for an answer.

"Neither could you tell me that you're the owner of Simon's apartment, the one who wiped his rental debts."

Claire frowned. Nobody knew this except the letting agent, and she'd left implicit instructions with him that this information was not to be released. Had someone there ignored that instruction?

"I found out from public files, Claire. Didn't you think I was going to try to find out?"

As Claire contemplated what accessible records would show she was the owner, a loud clap of thunder rumbled in the distance; the storm was getting closer. Claire felt specks of rain, but if Regan did, she wasn't moving.

"And what I found out. You own the entire bloody building."

This racehorse was bolting, and Claire needed to halt it.

"Hang on, Regan—"

"All the time I was talking to you about whether the owner of the apartment would let me rent it, *you* owned the bloody place. You never told me. I have to wonder why the secrecy."

Claire had her reasons, but Regan wasn't in any mood to hear them. She held her hands up in defence.

"Listen, Regan, this can all be expl—"

"Explain what? That you've deceived me over who you really are, that you've not told me you own all this real estate, and that *you* are now my landlady? You know how much I loathe your family, and yet, at every opportunity—and there have been many—you've never told me any of this. I'm sorry, but this strikes me as deceitful. What I'm seeing is a member of the wealthy de Vit family who is strangely playing the part of the gardener. That doesn't make any sense either. I can't begin to tell you what I'm thinking."

Claire raised a hand to interrupt, but Regan ignored her.

"Were you watching over Simon and reporting back to the family Death Star? Were his investments so damned important? I can see that if they'd been successful, he'd have made a lot of money. Were you all so frightened you'd lose a good deal, someone you could continue to suck blood out of? Are you part of that investment crap, too? Was that your role, to keep an eye on him and, as his landlady, offer him chats and sage council in a fucking potting shed? The de Vit family control mechanism?"

Claire's eyes widened in response. "It's nothing like that—"

"It looks like that to me. Keeping Simon financially handcuffed to you lot. Then when his rent fell into arrears, you felt obliged to kindly clear his debts and make him even more indebted. No wonder he committed suicide. He couldn't see a way out."

Claire's spinal fluid turned to arctic ice. She didn't like what she was being accused of. Regan was implying that she was in some way to blame for Simon's death. Her breathing quickened as a nasty taste rose in her mouth.

"You're way out of line, Regan. Listen to yourself. None of this makes any sense. Simon was my friend and—"

"Like I was."

Like I was.

The three words defused Claire's anger as quickly as it had arisen. She felt desperate and powerless. This was Regan standing here in front of her, accusing her of things that weren't right. Things that weren't true. And she was looking at her with such contempt.

This was the woman who had kissed her only days ago. How could this turn so quickly? Everything was slipping away from her.

Regan wasn't listening, and the words coming out of her mouth were wrong and twisted. Yes, she was a de Vit and she was wealthy, but it wasn't a crime. Everything could be explained if only Regan would shut up and listen.

"And now you've got me on a rental contract." Regan spread her arms out wide, a look of astonishment on her face. "You must love this. I have no idea what satisfaction this gives you because I'm no financial speculator. You'll get nothing out of me." For a brief second, Regan stopped. She frowned. "Or is this some sordid way you deal with your diseased conscience. Everything went wrong with Simon, and by being nice to me, it appeases your guilt? Shit, if it hadn't been for Cyn, I wouldn't know any of this. You were certainly never going to tell me."

Claire froze. *Oh, please, not Cynthia.*

"Regan, would you calm down and let me explain?" The minute the words were out of Claire's mouth, she knew they were wrong. One of the essential things she'd learned in life was to never ask someone to calm down when they were angry. That was like throwing gasoline on a fire. And so it was now. Regan rocketed.

"Calm down? Let you explain? I don't think so. I've learnt more about you than I care to, and none of it is attractive. This is the way you function."

"What are you talking about?" Claire crossed her arms defensively.

"I'm talking about money spoiling the child, and you certainly started young. I know what you did to that schoolgirl."

What you did to that schoolgirl. These were the words Claire did not want to hear. Her past was rising up like the Phoenix from the ashes to haunt her again. It was a blot on her past that could never be erased. She couldn't believe that this was being thrown into discussion now, but then Regan had been speaking to Cynthia.

"Cynthia told you that?" This wasn't good. The horse hadn't just bolted; it was galloping down the turf toward finish, breaking all track records.

"Every sordid little detail. You don't deny it?"

"No." Claire was numb. How could she deny that she'd bullied her classmate who had later committed suicide?

"How can you be like this? You really are a piece of work."

The storm raged above them as thunder followed lightning almost instantaneously. The rain fell fast and heavy, hitting them like air pellets. They were soaked, but it didn't stop Regan.

"I trusted you, Claire. I thought you were a friend. Damn it, I wanted to get to know you better, to see if we could have something together. But you've turned into this. Everything about you is a lie. You're not even a real gardener. You're a liar, a trickster—"

"I'm no liar," Claire shouted over the thunder.

"—a de Vit. You stay away from me. I want nothing to do with you anymore. Let me get on with my business, and you get on with yours...whatever that really is. Just stay away from me. The less I have to do with you the better."

Regan didn't wait for a response. She turned and stormed back up the lawn.

"Regan!" Claire shouted, but Regan either didn't hear over the storm, or chose to ignore her. As she watched her walk away, Claire felt a stab of pain run through her. Her heart ached.

Please turn around and come back to me. But she didn't.

Claire didn't move. She couldn't. She was in shock. Minutes ago, she'd been mowing the lawn, but now this.

The rain ran down her face and dripped off her nose.

How could this have gone wrong, so quickly? Regan had hit her with a list of supposed offenses. It was a list that, on the face of it, was true, but it contained distorted truths. It didn't help that Cynthia Tennerson had stuck her oar in everything. Claire could only imagine how she would twist everything, and with such delicious relish.

Claire kicked herself. She should have told Regan who she was, but she'd stupidly thought that if Regan knew her better, she'd be able to reason that being a de Vit did not naturally equate to being a distant relative of the Borgias. Claire had made a bad decision, and the delay had made things worse.

She shuddered as she recalled Regan's words. *"I trusted you, Claire. I thought you were a friend. Damn it, I wanted to get to know you better, to see if we could have something together."* Regan had looked at her as if she was vile.

Things seemed terminally broken between them now.

Claire walked into the shed and wiped the rain off her face.

She was shaking, and she was frightened. Had she lost Regan, even before anything had happened between them? Her heart beat frantically.

Claire needed to correct things. She *would* correct things. She didn't know how, but she'd find a way.

When Claire had thought earlier that something wicked this way comes, she had meant a thunderstorm.

How wrong she had been.

❖

Claire's bed creaked as she moved.

It was past four in the morning, and here she was, seated on the side of the bed unable to sleep. Despite the earlier storm, it had done nothing to remove the humidity, and the sheets stuck to her like gum on a sidewalk.

She peeled them off as she crossed over to the curtains and drew them back. It was just getting light, and everything looked calm and peaceful outside. Nothing moved, even the birds still slept.

This was her favorite time of the day. As a kid she used to imagine the world had faced some catastrophic disaster, and she was the only survivor. Sometimes she was the leader of a last pocket of resistance, and any minute now the metal aliens would appear out of the bushes, and she would have to fight. Years of being a sci-fi addict and watching apocalypse movies had wired her brain that way. It was probably why she'd joined the Royal Navy. They were all grown up space cadets looking for excitement and a way to avoid the mundane morning to evening work pattern. How she missed her career.

She leaned in and rested her forehead against the cool windowpane.

"What a mess," she said, thinking of the circus of events that had exploded between her and Regan.

She didn't know what she was going to do, only that she was going to have to do something. She loathed this misunderstanding. If she could just explain, she knew she could make Regan understand.

She shook her head in disbelief. She hadn't done anything wrong. All she had done was keep certain information tight, not for any Machiavellian reasons, but because she hadn't thought it was important. Not at the beginning. She heard Rosie's voice in her head, "You can be so ruddy dense at times." In their occasional moments of disagreement, Rosie would question how "someone so intelligent and professionally competent, an officer in the Royal Navy, can be so bloody thick when dealing with people's emotions."

Damn it.

She was a de Vit. So what?

Claire rather liked her family. While she was willing to accept a few of them on the peripheries had the scruples of an alley cat, most were hardworking, honest, and fair-minded. She had no idea what financial dealings Simon had entered into, and with whom. There were a lot of distant relations out there that she'd never met, or even heard of. Even her father couldn't keep up with all the de Vit tributaries. Besides, nowadays, you dealt with strangers behind the corporate name. There had been so many takeover bids, mergers, sell-offs, there probably wasn't a real de Vit left anywhere on any board. It was wrong that Regan was laying all her grievances on her shoulders. *She* certainly wasn't to blame.

Claire bristled defensively.

She owned the apartment block. So what? She rented one to Simon. So?

When Simon had rented, it had been through the letting agent. She hadn't known him from Adam before he moved in, and had only got to know him later. They'd become friends. How dare Regan accuse her of underhand surveillance techniques. Yes, she had wiped off his rental debts. She owned the frigging apartment and could do what she wanted. Simon was her friend who was in a whole lot of trouble. She wasn't going to stand by and do nothing. Isn't that what friends do? Help each other? She'd paid his utility bills, too. The poor bloke couldn't sit in the dark without heating or cooking facilities.

"You're not even a real gardener."

What had Regan meant? Claire didn't know, but something had been said.

Regan accused her of using it as a ploy to spy on people. How ridiculous. She was a gardener so she could be near Rosie.

She brushed a hand through her hair as she headed for the kitchen.

Add to this total mess the final toxic ingredient. Cynthia Tennerson. *Bloody woman.*

It didn't help that Cynthia was involved. She had a way of telling the truth a certain way, and of leaving key bits of information out. Cynthia's way was warped and spiteful. An evil thought crossed Claire's mind as she placed a mug of water into the microwave to heat up for a coffee. If only she could microwave Cynthia. She could then scatter her crisp remains all over the apartment gardens, and be rid of her. *Fertilize the bitch!*

Now I sound like a serial killer. Great. Claire looked up at the ceiling in disgust. That would certainly add to Regan's burgeoning dossier on her.

How was Claire going to put this right? She assessed the problem from her military training and figured she needed a plan of campaign. She used to be good at those.

She had to put things right. Check.

I've been nothing but a friend to her since she arrived.

She had to let Regan's infamous anger calm. Check.

I deserve more than this.

I'll approach her when she's calmer. Check.

She didn't even give me a chance to talk.

Claire realized her own anger was awake, like some rising spectral power about to go on a night walk. She certainly wanted to rattle some chains. That wasn't good either.

I'll wait until *my* temper calms. Check.

She could count on one hand when her temper had really gone off. All times she reacted badly and illogically. She did not want to do that with Regan.

The microwave pinged.

Claire threw a spoonful of coffee into the hot water, and then grabbed a chair at the kitchen table. Slowly, the caffeine infiltrated her system, and she grew calmer.

Anything said between the two of them now would only inflame the situation, and she didn't want to upset Regan any more than she had to. She reminded herself that Regan was vulnerable and emotional. She'd just buried her only sibling, and was hurting like hell. Things weren't over either. There was still the inquest. Although it was probably just procedure, Claire was in no doubt it would be weighing heavily on Regan's mind. She was also trying to forge a new life, move home and area, and look for a new career. Maybe Regan needed understanding and sympathy…as well as a bit of space.

Claire thought about the magazine articles that wrote about the most stressful moments in life. Regan's were all up there in one huge clump. Claire acknowledged that she needed to be mature about this. One of them had to. What did her father always tell her as she was growing up? *Go away and count to one hundred. It helps put things into perspective. If that doesn't work, sleep on it.* It was simple advice that had served her well in later life, especially in the Navy when dealing with sailors, and all the problems they had a habit of collecting.

But Claire would have her say too. She was damned if she was going to let Regan fire those broadsides and get away with it.

Claire thought of the rental agreement Regan had just signed. It was for six months. Those months were going to be very uncomfortable if something didn't change. A lump came into Claire's throat, and she panicked. What if Regan wanted out of the contract? She prayed she wouldn't. She would lose Regan and she didn't want to. Despite everything said, Claire wanted Regan around and in her life. But what if Regan wanted to leave? Then Claire would have to let her go. But it would be Regan's decision, not hers.

Claire's attention fell on two theater tickets in the middle of the table. They'd arrived yesterday morning. She'd been like a kid when she'd booked them, but looking at them now, she felt no joy. They reminded her of what she'd lost.

Oh, Regan. How can you distrust me? What have I done to feed this?

They'd been growing close. Now they were miles apart.

Her heart ached. She wondered if Regan was having a sleepless night, too. Nights were always the worse. Claire couldn't switch her brain off. She kept replaying things, over and over.

She closed her eyes, and for a minute telepathically willed Regan to phone her. But no call came, and Claire remained there until dawn broke.

Despite everything that had happened, all that was said, she had fallen in love with Regan. She was in big trouble.

❖

Days later, as Claire drove up to the front of the apartments, she saw the Connells standing outside talking to Regan. Black, heavy dread filled her. She didn't feel ready to see Regan, and not here, like this, out in the public arena.

For a brief second, she contemplated turning the Jeep around and driving back out the way she'd just come, but she didn't. That would be cowardice. Where was her backbone? So she braved it, parked the vehicle, and casually waved to the group as she began to walk down to the shed.

She didn't get very far. She heard her name called and saw George Connell beckoning at her to join them.

This will be awkward, she thought. She'd had no contact with Regan since that dreadful falling out. Her feet moved like buckets of mud as she turned toward them. She couldn't be rude. As she closed in on the group, she heard a lighthearted remark from Regan who then walked away, turning her back on Claire.

The snub was clear. Logic told Claire that this was what Regan might do, but the clash of expectation and actuality produced a sharp cut of pain that ran right through her. It hurt to know that Regan didn't want anything to do with her. She dredged a smile for the Connells.

"We're having a party," George said, unable to contain a huge grin.

"It's our seventieth wedding anniversary, Claire, and we'd love you to come," Grace added.

Claire heard Grace's words, yet they didn't register. She was too busy watching Regan enter the front of the building. Only when she'd completely disappeared did Claire's attention center on Grace who was waiting patiently for a response.

"Sorry?" Claire said, aware she'd not taken in a word Grace had spoken.

"I said, darling, George and I have been married for seventy years, and we're having a party."

If Grace was offended, she didn't show it. She only looked bemused.

Claire mentally shook herself and focused on the moment. These two lovely people were celebrating seventy years together. It was an incredible milestone.

"You will come, won't you?" Grace repeated. This time Claire was quick to respond.

"Love to. When?"

"Bit short notice, I'm afraid. The party's this Saturday," George said. "Can't take too long with these things, you know. We might die any day at our age."

"Do shut up, George. You can be so morbid at times."

"Sorry, dear, but you know I'm right."

Grace ignored him with saintly patience. "You will come, won't you, Claire? You're one of our dearest friends, and it won't be right unless you're there."

Claire's forced smile grew genuine.

"I wouldn't miss it for the world." She meant it.

The Connells seemed over the moon, and their reaction lifted Claire's spirits. Someone still liked her.

"Excellent," Grace said. "Party starts at seven o'clock. Drinks on the veranda. No gifts, darling."

Claire watched as they bounced away like two youngsters arranging a first party without parental presence. Again, and as always, they held hands. The show of affection reminded Claire that she was alone...still alone. She looked up at Regan's apartment window, half expecting to see her glowering down at her with the malevolence of Morgana, Merlin's dark adversary. But the window was empty.

This has to stop, Claire thought. I must do something.

Every hormonal instinct in her body told her to go to Regan now and talk. Every sane coherent thought in her head demanded she mustn't. They were both still too emotional. Sanity won, and Claire kept her distance. Instead, that evening when she drove home, she stopped off at a store and bought a card. It was for Regan. In it, she asked for an opportunity to explain. The next day, when Regan was out, Claire posted the card under her door. Such a card had worked for Regan with her. Maybe this card would have the same effect.

❖

Regan did her best to block Claire from her thoughts. It wasn't easy. Instead she channeled her energy into something more positive and concrete. She wrote letters, attaching her résumé, to several educational institutes inquiring about employment opportunities. She'd never applied for a job in her life, as in never answered an advertisement. Regan had always approached the places she wanted to work in first, introducing herself, and then seeing what response she'd get. The method never let her down, and she'd always found a job. She was hoping she hadn't lost her touch. Armed with the letters, she headed to the post office to mail them.

As she climbed into her car and started the engine, she saw Claire. Flustered, she could see she was heading her way with a deliberate look on her face. It was one that said, "I want to talk."

Well, I don't, Regan thought as she reversed out of the bay.

She slowly moved forward, but to her dismay, Claire stepped into the driveway and raised a hand, trying to flag Regan down and force a conversation.

This is not going to happen.

Regan refused to stop. She maneuvered around her and drove off toward the road.

The nerve of the woman.

Regan was livid. What part of "leave me alone" wasn't Claire understanding? She'd already had a card pushed through her door asking to talk. Regan had given that a stiff ignoring. She had ripped it in two and then binned it.

Regan let out a sigh worthy of a banshee. Despite all her intentions of a new start, her life changes weren't shaping up at the moment. Her relationships appeared to be continuing in their usual downward spiral.

It wasn't that she was asking too much out of life. Years ago when she was young and naive, she dreamed. Her dreams were greedy. Not for money. She wanted the perfect career, the perfect house, the perfect "other half." But reality had hit her like a wet face flannel, and as time went by, she realized everything perfect wouldn't come her way.

She didn't want *everything*. Not now.

She just wanted someone in her life that she could love and have that love returned. There had been many applicants, but none successful. Her relationship with Karen had failed, too. It had been all heat and sexual excitement. When their ardor cooled, there wasn't much left, and nothing of any meaning. And Regan did want *meaning*. She wanted something deeper, more spiritual. She wanted a soul mate.

She thought of Karen's recent impromptu appearance.

Regan had been on the defensive when she'd gone to meet her in town, but their reunion was not as she expected.

Karen, usually commanding and full of self-confidence, had been anxious and insecure.

"Thank you for seeing me, Regan. I know you don't want to and you'll be wondering what this is all about. I expect you think I'm going to stir things up…make things worse again. I don't want to hurt you anymore, and I know that's what I've done."

Regan hadn't answered. She stood and listened. She'd felt no desire to make things easier for whatever Karen wanted to say.

Karen seemed to understand.

"I suppose I'm being selfish, but there are things I want to say… things I must say. I want to say them in person, not via email or text, or the dreaded cell phone which you never answer anyway." Karen laughed, but her eyes welled with tears. "I want to say I'm sorry, Regan, for everything I've put you through. I want to say I'm so sorry about your brother…Alex told me what happened." Karen's emotions spilled over and for a while, she couldn't continue. Regan knew she'd never been a player of mind games and her genuine vulnerability made her reach out and take her in her arms. She couldn't quite bring herself to hate Karen.

But Karen pushed back, tugging at Regan's belt in playful fun. Regan could see it was her way of covering nervousness.

"There's something important that I have to say," Karen said. "I'm looking for other jobs, other school posts. I want you to know that so you can go back and resume your career without fear of bumping into me at school like a pinball."

"You're up for the headship; you'd give all that up?" Regan couldn't believe this. Karen was career obsessed.

"You're up for head of department if you stay. I don't want you to lose that." Karen was sincere.

"You'll be losing your chance of promotion and you've worked so hard for it. You'd have to start all over again. It'll take years. You'll have to rebuild your reputation."

Karen smiled. "I can do it. Bit of a setback, but you know what I'm like." She paused. "I wanted to tell you this in person so you'd know I mean it, and that it's genuine."

Regan knew she was a woman of her word. If she said she would do something, she believed her. Was this what was behind all the unanswered calls? But despite the gift Karen was offering her, Regan knew she no longer wanted it. She was moved by Karen's act of generosity, and she reached out in one last emotional embrace.

"Thank you, Karen, but no. I've made a decision not to go back to secondary education. I want to do something different and more challenging. I'm thinking of going back to university…see if my old brain cells can handle the test."

"Oh."

"Have you said anything to Alex yet?" Regan asked.

"No. I wanted to see you first."

"Then please don't jeopardize your career for me, Karen. Thank you for the wonderful gesture…really, but I'm not going back. I'm going to make a fresh start, and that includes my career. You stay and make a bid for Alex's job. I really hope you get it. You're made for that role. Please don't leave the school. The governors want you as his successor; you know they do."

Karen hesitated. "It just seems so wrong after what I've done."

Regan smiled for the first time. "It isn't. Simon's death has given me focus. I'm chasing new opportunities. Karen, you have my complete blessing. Go for the job."

"I guess that's it then. I said five minutes. I've kept to that," Karen said.

"Tell me, are you still with your husband?"

"I am."

"You know it won't work."

"I do." Karen nodded. "But at least I've given it the last try."

There was nothing Regan could say.

They parted on good terms. She couldn't deny she was glad when Karen left and happy she was no longer part of her life. It was over, for both of them. It had left the way clear to move things forward with Claire...or so Regan had thought. An evening with Cyn, and everything bright and shiny, turned to fool's gold. When was this bad run of luck going to stop? Karen, Simon, Claire?

She knew she was falling for Claire when, on impulse, she leaned across and kissed her in the car. It was such a frightening, yet sweet moment. She'd felt scared as her lips touched Claire's, so afraid that she might be pushed away. But Claire had responded, and the look on her face told Regan that she had feelings for her, too. Now that special moment was sour. Her bad luck run continued.

Lack of sleep strangely made Regan productive. She came up with a list of things to do. She needed to get the inquest over; that was a few weeks away. She must also get a job; that was her number one priority.

Until yesterday, she had convinced herself that she was going to move out of the apartment. She'd been ready to see the letting agent and take whatever financial penalty came her way for breaking the rental agreement. But then she got bloody minded. *No, damn it.* She wouldn't move, not unless Claire chucked her out. She rather doubted Claire would have the nerve to do that.

Regan didn't want to move out of the apartment. She was beginning to love it. Besides, it was Simon's, and it's where she felt close to him. It was all she had left. Why should Claire chase her away and deny her this small comfort?

Regan reckoned she could cope with having a de Vit as a landlady. She might even prove to be a sore in Claire's side, a reminder of the dirty deeds she'd done. All business would be conducted through the letting agent anyway, and once she was working, she wouldn't see that much of her. Maybe now Claire's true nature was revealed, she might give up her day job as gardener. Who knew? If Regan ignored her, she'd soon get the message, and leave her alone.

Regan was staying, and damn Claire bloody de Vit.

CHAPTER FOURTEEN

Parties at the Connells were notorious. They were fun, bordering on a little crazy. Claire had never been to one before, but knew enough to go hungry, and be prepared to either walk home or get a taxi. The Connells knew only glorious excess, and alcohol flowed like liquid gold, and the buffet was a feast for an entire army regiment just returned off military exercise. It was not a social you went to if you were a dried out alcoholic, or a catwalk model living on lemon grass.

The minute Grace Connell opened the door, Claire was pulled with enthusiasm into an environment that was a concoction of opposites. Everywhere there was tasteful, elegant furniture hinting of regal periods, pushed to the sides of walls. The vacated space now throbbed with excited, vivacious people, many geriatric by age, but not by behavior. The room was packed, and animated socializing was already in full swing with arms and hands waving all over the place.

Seventies disco music played in the background. Already some partygoers, who looked more comfortable holding a walking frame, were rocking around the floor with a partner to an old Tavares hit blazing out "Heaven Must Be Missing an Angel." If it was, it was actually missing a load of them, and they were all down here, for surely they were closer to more heavenly places than earthly ones. The average age of the swingers had to be eighty plus. This party was "live" in the full sense, and Claire had worried she would arrive too early.

She couldn't stop grinning as she handed Grace a gift and card that earned her a gentle reprimand.

"You shouldn't have, darling. We just want you, not a gift, but thank you anyway."

It was clear others had made the same error, for the room was crammed full with cards and unopened gifts in bright paper.

George appeared at her side, dressed in a garish flowered shirt that looked too bright for a Hawaiian beach party. He thrust a glass into her hand.

"Bubbly," he said with animation.

"She might not drink bubbly, George. You're supposed to ask first," Grace said.

"Nonsense. Everyone drinks champagne. You do, don't you?"

Claire chased his doubts away. "I do."

"There, see," he said to his wife. "You worry about nothing."

"Seventy years," Grace drawled to Claire, her face mock weary.

Claire laughed. They were eccentric, warm natured, and the most wonderful couple she'd ever come across. They were the sort of people that made lemmings think twice before they jumped. Their company was addictive.

"Go and introduce Claire to some of our friends, my love."

"Will do." George knew how to take orders. "First though"—he pulled Claire like a fellow conspirator across the room—"come and have a look at this."

They ended up in front of the mantelpiece.

"We've had a card from the Queen!"

There in the middle, positioned below a gilded mirror, was a resplendent looking card.

"I didn't know we got these. Thought one of us would have to wait until we were one hundred. Isn't it nice that she did this?"

Claire thought of the myriad of staff that the Queen employed who took care of the finer detail of such things. But she wasn't going to spoil George's image of Queen Elizabeth going through her personal diary and announcing she simply must send a card to the Connells.

"It's excellent, George. You're going to have to frame it."

"Already got one." His grin was infectious. He placed a hand on her elbow and started pushing her along again. "Now I really must introduce you to some people before Grace kills me."

"I don't think Grace would ever do that."

"No, she wouldn't, but that's our secret. She's a huge sweetie inside." He slipped his hand into hers and led her through a bustling group to what appeared to be a more civilized and quieter couple. "Come and meet Leonard and Elvira."

He gave a nominal introduction and then left them to it.

Claire learned they were *civilized and quieter* only because both had had hip operations in the last six months and were afraid to "knock something out of its socket."

Time passed swiftly, and Claire moved her way around different folk, introducing herself and getting to know them. It was called "mingling" in the Navy. When she'd first joined and gone to do her officer training at Britannia Royal Naval College in Devon, there had actually been lessons teaching you how to socialize. You were taught to move around a room and be the perfect host, or guest. There were lots of little tricks to be employed if socializing with anyone who was difficult to get to know, or God forbid, *the non-talker*. The latter was every young officer's nightmare. How many formal dinners had Claire been to, seated next to someone who could only talk about fly fishing or their geological rock collection? It was fortunate that none of the Connells' guests fit into the latter. They were the polar opposite; you couldn't stop them talking. Claire would just lob a question into the conversation, and they were off with their often wild anecdotes. How she wished she'd had some of these folk as guests during her military years. These people were a fun-loving, irrepressible, spirited lot, and she was thoroughly enjoying herself.

That was until she locked eyes with Regan.

When had she arrived? Claire didn't know, and her mingling track hadn't intersected with Regan's.

The background drone of noise seemed to disappear, and time stopped as she stared across the room at her. Her happy state evaporated, and she responded like an animal caught in car headlights. She watched as Regan's smile disappeared too, leaving her face like a fortress, impenetrable and giving away nothing.

Claire's first instinct was to run. The way Regan was looking at her, she didn't sense an easy path to appeasement or mollification. This was also not the venue for any reconciliation, assuming there could be one. But then it occurred to her that maybe this *was* the perfect backdrop for a gentle re-introduction. Neither would be able to say too much, nor want to cause a scene. They would have to talk to each other and keep things civilized. The party provided safe containment.

All good mediation had to start somewhere, and maybe now was the time to wave the olive branch, which in fairness, Claire had already done a couple of times, and been ignored. But peace talks were never easy and required many attempts before some form of treaty was achieved. Claire swallowed hard. She reminded herself she'd been a naval officer, braced herself, and moved forward. It was worth a shot.

The people she'd been chatting to thankfully melted away. It left the two of them standing alone, and facing each other.

"I didn't see you arrive," Claire said lamely, wondering how to start the conversation with Regan who glowered at her, saying nothing. This was not going to be easy. More lame talk. "The Connells certainly know how to hold a party. Are you enjoying it?"

"I was, until now."

The tone was hard, the words abrupt. Regan stared at her, and there was no warmth or friendship present. Claire's stomach churned, and she knew she had to speak from the heart.

"Look, Regan, it's been a while since we talked, and I hate all this—"

"What part of leave me alone do you not understand?"

"Can't we just talk?" Claire asked.

"I don't want to talk."

"I'm just asking for a chance to explain things."

"There is nothing you can say that I want to hear," Regan said.

"Please, Regan—"

"I'm trying to enjoy this party, and you're spoiling it. I want you to leave me alone."

This wasn't going well, and Claire felt everything getting worse. She was making all the effort and nothing—nothing—was being returned. *Damn the woman.*

"How can we fix things if you won't talk?" Claire asked.

"Nothing has changed," Regan said in a low, grated whisper.

Claire looked away, fighting the unexpected surge of anger that rose in her. She sucked at her top lip and her tone dropped low, the usual subtle warning to anyone who chose to recognize it.

"Nor will it until you give me an opportunity to speak." She was rattled and could feel her jaw tightening. *So much for safe containment.*

Regan leaned her head down toward Claire's.

"There is nothing you can say that I want to hear. Now will you leave me alone, or do I have to leave this party?"

Years of officer training and acquired leadership skills helped Claire hold her temper, but it wasn't easy. She watched as Regan stood straight and stepped back several paces.

"I'm waiting for your answer," Regan said.

Claire threw her hands up, said nothing, and walked away. Her flash of temper stayed.

Damn that woman.

Claire was the one who was shouted at down in the potting shed. She was the one insulted by accusations that were wrong. Yet she was the one trying to put things right. Had she not sent Regan a card asking to talk? Had she not tried to approach her the other morning in the car park only to be driven around? She'd tried again now, but was being treated like primeval slime. How dare Regan behave like this and totally ignore her.

Claire was of a mind to go back up to Regan and tell her exactly what she thought of her. She'd tenaciously stalk her into a corner and let rip. Oh, wouldn't she like to do that. But of course, Regan would rip back and then there would be a scene. It would ruin Grace and George's magic party. Claire was torn.

"Fight or flight" ran through her mind as she glanced at her watch. *Damn it.* It was too early to reasonably leave without being rude. Yet she no longer felt the slightest bit like a party animal.

Somehow, she managed to *mingle* for another forty minutes, noticing that Regan eyed her all the time while keeping the farthest distance from her. It came as a relief as Claire eventually looked at her watch and realized she could leave the party without hurting the Connells.

As she left, she didn't miss the look of pleasure on Regan's face.

CHAPTER FIFTEEN

They were beautiful flowers.

Regan held them to her nose and breathed in their fragrant scent. She only hoped they'd last. Fresh flowers on graves in the summer tended to wilt too quickly, but she wanted something bright and aromatic for Simon, not artificial ones, no matter how real they looked.

She reached back inside the car and grabbed a large bottle of water. She had no idea if the church had a communal watering can, and her flowers would need plenty of water to survive the heat.

As she walked from her car toward Simon's grave, she thought how she would first remove the wreaths that had been laid the day of his funeral. She could only imagine the state they would be in. She remembered visiting her parents' grave and seeing how other new recent arrivals were covered in decaying flowers. There were so many of them laid across the freshly churned soil, and yet no one had returned to clear them away. She always hated seeing that. It was as if the person laid to rest was no longer of interest and was now forgotten. It made her sad. She was not going to let that happen to Simon.

As she turned around the side of the church, she saw a woman at his grave. When she looked closer, she realized it was Claire. She froze before stepping back so she couldn't be seen.

Hell. Here she was trying to avoid her, and all the time they seemed destined to bump into each other.

Why can't the bloody woman keep her distance?

She fumed and went back to her car to wait.

As she saw Claire return to her vehicle, something inside her snapped and she sprang out of her car. Claire looked shocked.

"What are you doing here?" Regan asked.

"I came to pay my respects."

"Pay respects, or appease your guilt?"

Claire's eyes narrowed and her lips tightened to a thin line. Her voice was low. "That's way beneath you. He was my friend."

Regan knew she should walk away and ignore Claire, but she didn't feel finished. Things had been going through her mind.

"Does anybody at the apartments know who you are?"

"No."

"Don't you think that's deceitful?"

Claire stared at her defiantly, placing her hands on her hips. "No. Not really. If they knew, for a lot of them, it would change the nature of the relationship we have. Do you think the Connells would ask me to repot their plants? Or Mr. Cooper would ask me to pick up his prescription? Do you think Marie Page would ask me to take her grocery delivery in because she was going to be home late from work? I doubt it. This way, I get to hear when things go wrong, or need attention, and I can sort stuff out. It also gives me anonymity and freedom, and not for any negative reason you want to believe. Being a de Vit *does* have its drawbacks."

Regan's thoughts bounced like a pinball. "Do you have everyone's keys? I expect owning the building—"

"Stop right there." Claire raised her voice. "The letting agent holds spares, like any agent legally would. But they would never do anything inappropriate, and neither would I. I don't have anyone's keys unless they chose to give me them."

"You have Simon's." The minute Regan said it she knew it was the wrong thing. Her comment was churlish and immature. Not unexpectedly, it irritated Claire, who came back at the comment fast.

"Did you listen to me? I told you Simon gave me that."

Regan sensibly changed tack. "Did *he* know you owned the building?"

Defiant eyes softened. "Yes, but only toward the end. When all his debts started to bite and I could see he was struggling to pay bills, that's when I came clean."

"And I'm supposed to believe that?"

Claire stood a minute, disappointment in her eyes. Her reply was so quiet, Regan almost didn't hear it. "Yes, Regan, you are."

Claire said nothing more, but got back into her car and drove off, leaving Regan alone.

For someone who was determined to isolate herself from Claire, she wasn't doing very well. It was with a heavy heart as she trudged to her brother's grave to lay the flowers.

Regan did some shopping before she drove back to the apartment. She should have felt good challenging Claire, but she didn't. Her questions came from anger, and a sense of betrayal. Something tapping away at the back of her brain told her this was wrong, though she couldn't explain why.

En route home, she tried to analyze her feelings. It felt like she had lost something, and whatever that indefinable thing was, it was important. The more she thought about it, the more she realized it was all to do with Claire. Regan had lost the Claire she thought existed, the one that wasn't a fake. *That* Claire had attracted her like no other, and had filled her with a sense of something better, something that offered her a future.

Her desire for once had not been born solely of carnal pleasure or hormonal drive. It had been a solid attraction; she'd been drawn to the woman she thought Claire was. How she'd wanted the chance to try to build a meaningful relationship with her. A voice inside her had whispered that this was the one. But that desire and hope evaporated as Cyn told her the truth. To lose *that* Claire was devastating, and despite all her ice maiden behavior, Regan was struggling to get over it.

It also didn't help that she was unable to dislodge the uncomfortable fact that Claire had been to see Simon. That wasn't the act of a conspirator. She had left a tiny but pretty posy on his grave. It didn't make sense. You didn't expect a fraudster, who duped someone during their life, to then act this way after his death. Regan thought as a mathematician, and the numbers weren't adding up. Claire's behavior wasn't something that could be passed off as a guilt complex.

When Regan finally returned to her apartment, she found Simon's spare key pushed under the door. It was the one he'd given Claire.

She burst into tears.

CHAPTER SIXTEEN

It was growing dark early as ominous black clouds gathered overhead. Another storm was approaching. This was the price of a decent English summer and something every native of the land came to expect with grudging acceptance. Already Regan could hear the distant rumble of thunder.

She was sitting on the lounge sofa with the lights off, watching the lightning and counting the seconds between its flash and the thunder. They said each second equated to a mile's distance. She didn't know if that was true, but the shorter the count, the closer and louder the storm became.

Regan loved storms like this, as long as she was safe inside. A friend of her father's had actually been hit by lightning, and survived, while playing golf. He had stupidly thought to ignore the storm. Nature had reminded him that she was to be respected. She had done this by wrecking his five iron and melting most of the clothing he was standing in. He got the message. From then on, he was always the first off the course before the first raindrop touched the green.

The storm grew closer and more exciting. Regan welcomed it. Perhaps now it would steal the humidity from the air, and she would sleep better. The heat was unbearable at night. How she yearned for aircon.

A flash of light filled her room and then, barely seconds apart, a heavy rumbling. It was almost overhead. Regan watched fork lightning fill the sky, its electric fingers running in all directions. She heard the arrival of the rain which splattered on the windows and ran down them like small river tributaries.

Barely five seconds later, her room lit orangey red as lightning and thunder collided together.

Flash. Bang.

The building shook as a thunderbolt hit land somewhere close. Regan jumped up and crossed to a window in time to see one of the garden trees split and part of it fall across the lawn. The rain became a cloudburst and fell so heavily it bounced off the ground and looked like mist. It rattled noisily on the windowpanes like thrown gravel.

Dark. Light. Dark. Light.

The darkness was constantly pursued and chased away as more flashes of light and violent cracks of thunder arrived.

A prolonged series of lightning lit up the lawn again. This time Regan could hardly believe her eyes. She saw Rosie. She was standing in the middle of the lawn dressed in nothing but her night wear. Rosie wasn't moving as the rain hammered down, soaking her. She looked like a marble statue.

Damn. Regan panicked and was about to run out when a movement on the periphery compelled her to stay and watch longer. All was dark until another flash of light. This time, Regan saw Claire. She appeared from nowhere and was now holding Rosie by her thin, fragile arms. Regan watched as Rosie thrashed about in an attempt to break lose. It looked as if Claire was attacking her.

Regan hesitated no longer. She ran out. As she cut across the lawn, she heard Rosie shouting.

"Stop. Stop. Get away from me." She was struggling against Claire's grip. Regan rushed up to them barely able to see because of the torrential rain.

"What do you think you're doing?" she shouted at Claire over the thunder. Claire ignored her as she continued to hold Rosie tight.

"Stop. You're killing me," Rosie wailed as she swayed unsteadily.

"You're hurting her," Regan yelled as she pushed her way between them, forcing Claire to let go.

"I'm not hurting her...I'm trying to help her," Claire shouted back.

"Well, you're not."

Another flash of light and a bang arrived simultaneously.

"Get her inside, Regan. For God's sake, get her in. She'll catch pneumonia."

"Keep her away. Keep her away," Rosie said, her voice growing weaker. She was faltering. Claire recognized this and edged forward again, but Regan put a hand out to stop her. She turned to Rosie.

"It's okay, Rosie. It's me, Regan. I'm here now. Let's get back inside."

As she wrapped a protective arm around her, Regan watched a subdued Claire step back as if surrendering. The storm lit everything up again, and this time, she saw the naked look of pain on Claire's face. Her body language spoke volumes. She was taut like a coiled spring, and she paced back and forth not knowing whether to follow or walk away. Regan didn't know why, but a bolt of compassion ran through her. She had no time to stand and decipher it. She had to get Rosie inside and out of the rain.

As she moved toward the open French doors, she was aware of Claire following a safe distance behind. Sally appeared through the doors looking ashen and shocked. Claire shouted at her.

"Where the hell have you been?"

Regan turned on her. "Don't talk to her like that."

She had no idea what was going on, but she was incensed that anyone would speak to Sally in such a manner. But it was as if Sally hadn't heard, for she ignored everything and had already taken over Rosie's care and was leading her back inside. She beckoned the two of them in and then closed the door behind them. Regan watched as Claire fought to hold herself in check. What was this all about?

Regan surveyed the room she'd never been in before. She'd assumed this to be a sitting room, but it wasn't. It was a bedroom set up for an infirm person, and it possessed a similar set of smells one associated with hospitals. She caught the slight whiff of antiseptic and disinfectant. There was a large lifting mechanism, a hoist used by nursing staff to help move patients in and out of bed. But there the similarities of a hospital disappeared.

This was no clinical, sterile environment. The room looked friendly and warm, as if someone made a deliberate effort to create that. But it didn't rob Regan of the feeling that whatever ailed Rosie, it was serious. Before she could analyze further, Sally threw towels at her and Claire.

"Dry yourselves off. I don't want the two of you getting sick," Sally said.

A clap of thunder shook the building again. Rosie moaned.

Sally was already searching for dry clothing for her. As she did, she spoke to Claire in agitated bursts.

"I'm sorry. Michael phoned. He's at the hospital…been in a car accident. I only stepped out of the room for a minute to take his call. She was asleep…at least I thought she was…I didn't want to wake her. I'd been about to lock the doors." Sally kept looking between Rosie and Claire. She was distraught and apologetic but didn't wait for any answer. Rosie was now her priority.

"I need to get her showered and into dry clothing." Sally stopped, looked at Claire, and repeated, "I'm really sorry."

Claire, who was rubbing the towel across her face, raised a dismissive hand as if to say it was okay. She was trying to feign calm, but Regan saw her agitation; how heavily she breathed. There was a connection between these three women that Regan had yet to understand.

As Sally disappeared with Rosie, she shouted, "Don't be here, Claire, when we come back. You know how you upset her."

Regan's confusion built. It was an odd thing to say, and it was said with compassion. Regan looked over to Claire who was still standing just inside the door. Her eyes were closed, and she hung her head as if she no longer had any energy left in her body. She looked like a defeated warrior who had fought her last fight and had nothing left to give.

A lump caught unexpectedly in the back of Regan's throat as her resentment gave way to guarded benevolence. Earlier, she had thought that Claire represented a real danger to Rosie, something that had been supported by Sally's previous comments. Yet now that picture looked skewed. There was a presence in this room, and Regan finally knew its name, tragedy. But what was the link? She had a feeling she was to find out before the night was over. The one thing she did know was that Claire was not a threat to Rosie.

Regan heard Sally talking away to Rosie next door and wondered if she should leave as well. Sally hadn't asked her to; her request had been solely directed at Claire. Regan decided she would stay. Sally had problems. Whoever Michael was, he was at the hospital, and worry was written all over her face. Regan would wait and see if there was anything she could do. She wasn't sure if Claire *could* do anything. Rosie did not want Claire anywhere near her.

She heard the hum of the shower stop and looked across at Claire again. She showed no signs of leaving. Regan's anger toward Claire took a backseat and assumed a temporary hold. These strange circumstances demanded that. She didn't want to be insensitive, but Sally would be back in the room in a minute—with Rosie.

"Sally's asked you to leave," she reminded Claire gently. She didn't want to add to whatever personal torture Claire was going through.

"I'm not deaf." Claire didn't look at her.

"I know you're not, but I think you ought to."

"I can't."

Claire was desolate and Regan understood nothing. She needed to know.

"What's going on here?" she asked.

Claire lifted her face to look at her; pain met confusion.

"Rosie's my partner."

Regan hated what she saw. Claire looked as if someone had reached inside her and ripped out all her insides. She was wretched.

"What?" Regan said.

Claire didn't reply; she didn't look able to.

"You said she was dead." Regan wished her statement hadn't come out as forcibly as it did. She wasn't trying to accuse.

Claire pulled herself straight and squared her shoulders. "She doesn't know me anymore."

"She's frightened to death of you."

"It's the disease," Claire said. "She's got Alzheimer's."

Alzheimer's? How could that be, Regan thought. Old people got this, not people like Rosie. She could only be in her forties.

"But she's too young," she said.

"I know."

Silence filled the room.

Sally reentered. "You still here?"

Regan and Claire answered "yes" in unison.

"Is she all right?" Claire asked.

"She's fine, but she won't be if you're still here when I bring her back in." Sally walked over and touched Claire's arm in kindness. "You know you have to leave. Go home, Claire."

Claire ran fingers through her wet hair as she released a quick breath of frustration. "You need to go see your son. Is he okay?"

At least Regan had the answer to one of her questions.

"Oh, I think so...I hope so," Sally answered. "I don't know. All I know is his car's wrecked." Sally looked desperate. "I can't leave Rosie."

Regan watched as the two of them mentally searched for an answer. It was obvious Claire wouldn't be able to help.

"I'll stay," Regan said. She searched Sally's face. "If you tell me what to do, I can stay."

Sally glanced across at Claire who nodded.

"If you're sure?" Sally's polite check didn't wait for an answer. "Bless you for this, Regan. I just need to see him and know he's okay." Sally spun to face Claire. "And I can't go anywhere while you're here. Please leave. There's nothing you can do. I'll put Rosie to bed, and she'll sleep like a lamb. She's worn out. We can talk tomorrow." She started pushing Claire toward the French doors.

"Give Michael my love...and if there's anything I can do—"

"—I know where to find you." Sally interrupted Claire in haste.

A smile based on some deep understanding passed between them, and Claire left.

Sally turned back to face Regan and took a deliberate sigh. "There are good days, and there are bad days. This is not a good day." Without waiting for any response from Regan, she clicked into command mode. She wanted to go see Michael.

"Right, love, I'll bring Rosie in now and get her settled. She's half asleep already so you won't have to do anything except be here. I'll leave you my number in case anything happens...which it won't."

When Sally led Rosie back in, she was unresponsive and unaware of Regan's presence. Sally led her to the bed like a tired child. Even before her head touched the pillow, she was asleep.

"She'll be like this all night." Sally checked Regan was happy with the arrangement one last time. "Are you sure you're okay with this?"

"Sure. You take as long as you need. Go sort your son out."

"If I do that, he may never leave hospital!"

Sally gave a nervous laugh as Regan watched her unpeel Rosie's clenched hands from her own. Sally caught her looking at Rosie's short nails.

"I have to keep them short or she digs them into her palms and really makes a mess." She finished tucking Rosie in and dimmed the lights. Regan followed Sally into the hallway.

"She really will sleep now so don't worry. Make yourself at home, and I'll be back as soon as I know Michael's okay."

Sally left, and Regan settled herself in for what was likely to be a long night.

It was almost dawn when Sally returned.

She looked drawn, and there were dark rings under her eyes, but she had a spring in her step. Michael's condition boded well.

Regan had slept in the chair by Rosie's bedside, and as Sally had said, she hadn't stirred.

"You didn't have to stay in here with her." Sally was apologetic.

"It doesn't matter; I've still managed to sleep. I thought it was safer this way. I could keep an eye on her. She had a bad experience."

"Maybe so, but all forgotten, I assure you."

Regan quietly arose and stretched, and then followed Sally out into the kitchen.

"How's Michael?"

"Very fortunate. He was going round a tight bend when that heavy rain hit. Another car was coming the other way and they collided. Both went off the road, and both cars are written off. Thankfully, neither of them are badly hurt, although Michael's going to look like a punching bag when all the bruising comes out. At least that's all it is, plus a dented ego. Men always like to think they're invulnerable and the stronger sex, especially behind the wheel of a car. It comes as a shock to their fragile psyches that they aren't. They've kept him in overnight—just to be on the safe side, and then Barry, my ex, will collect him. He was a lousy husband and a worthless piece of shit, but he occasionally does something unexpected, and rises to the challenge. He'll take Michael home and see he's okay." Sally let out a good-natured laugh, and it warmed Regan to see that the stress she'd worn before she left for the hospital was now gone.

"Let's have a cuppa." Sally was already filling the kettle.

Minutes later, Regan welcomed the drink as it kick-started her sleepy system.

She watched Sally wrap her cardigan around her large frame before sitting down. A chuckle escaped Sally's lips. "Well, that was a fun evening, wasn't it? Thank you for standing in, Regan."

"Glad I could help."

As Regan's body came back to life, so did the memories of last night. "Is it true that Rosie has Alzheimer's?"

It wasn't that she disbelieved what Claire told her last night; it was the shock that Rosie should have it at such a young age.

"I'm afraid so."

"Rosie told me she'd caught a virus in Egypt."

Sally gave an empty laugh. "Yes, I know. She thinks that sometimes. Apparently, she worked out there when she was younger. Sometimes she thinks she's back there. It's a bit of a common trait with Alzheimer sufferers; their minds do a sort of time skip. It's a bit like a jumping needle on a record. She used to talk about Egypt a lot. She talks less and less now as things progress."

"It's terrible."

It chilled Regan. Thank God, no one in her family had been cursed with this cruel disease, but its shadow stretched long. She knew friends and work colleagues who had someone touched by one form of dementia or another. Their stories were always the same. They spoke of how distressing it was to see someone loved disappear before their eyes. Gone, but not gone.

"Yes, it is, but we cope...most of the time." Sally looked uncomfortable as she recalled the unpleasant events of the previous evening.

Regan remembered something else, equally unpleasant.

"You know, you really shouldn't let Claire speak to you like that. She has no right."

"She has every right!"

Sally's quick, defensive response took Regan by surprise.

"She pays me to look after Rosie. The least she can expect is that I keep her safe. Claire was just scared last night and frightened. She loves Rosie. What happened was my fault. I thought I'd locked the doors. I can't believe I was so stupid."

An overload of information surged through Regan. She found it difficult to process. Rosie was Claire's partner. Claire loved Rosie. Yet Claire had kissed *her* back that day in the car. Her body had responded, her face flushed, and Regan knew passion was present. Rosie hated Claire, or at least was frightened to death of her. Regan witnessed that last night in the storm.

It would be too easy for Regan to believe the worst of Claire, Rosie's fear pointing to some heinous behavior from a de Vit. But Regan wasn't stupid. Every bone in her body told her that Claire could never do anything cruel toward Rosie. The look on Claire's distraught face last night said it all.

Sally interrupted her thoughts.

"I don't want to pry, but are you and Claire okay? I couldn't help noticing that you seemed on edge with each other."

"Understatement of the year." The sarcasm flowed, and Regan wished it hadn't.

"I thought the two of you were rubbing along nicely," Sally said.

"We were."

"But you're not now?"

"No. I've found out a few things about her that I don't like."

Sally raised her eyebrows, and her expressive eyes showed she was waiting for more.

"She's a de Vit!" Regan could almost hear the drum roll as she announced it, but all she got was a look of relief on Sally's face, as if her statement was unimportant.

"I know that."

"What you probably don't know," Regan continued, "is that Simon was knee-deep in debt and in with just about every de Vit investment house out there. They lent him shed loads of money, and when the recession came, they called it all in. From what I've discovered in Simon's paperwork, I believe it was the driving force behind him topping himself."

"Ah, well, I didn't know that. I'm sorry, love. But what's that got to do with Claire?"

"Right from the beginning, she's known how I feel about her family and she's listened to me rant on about them. Yet she's never told me who she is. I had no idea she was a de Vit. I discovered that from someone else. I have to ask myself why she wouldn't tell me."

"You've known me as long as you have Claire, but do you know my surname?" Sally said matter-of-factly.

"You're not a de Vit, too?" Unexpected humor crept into Regan's question providing a brief respite from the heavy topic. She was rewarded with a deep, chesty laugh from Sally as she shook her head.

"That's not the point, Sally. She should have told me. She could also have told me that she owned the apartment Simon rented, *which I now rent.* She didn't tell me that, either. Again, that information came from someone else. Did you know she owns this entire building?"

Sally was staring back at her sympathetically. "Yes."

Regan couldn't hide her frustration.

"She should have been more forthcoming, I admit," Sally said. "What was her excuse?"

"I haven't asked her. I don't want to know."

"Don't you think you ought to?"

"I don't want to know. I've heard what she's really like. I'm sorry if I sound paranoid, but all this dishonesty, it sours everything I thought I knew about her. I thought she was this wonderful, caring person who had time for my brother, and who tried to help him through the bad patches. I thought she cared for me in some way. I don't trust her anymore. She's a de Vit, for heaven's sake, and they're all a bad lot...Claire included."

Sally whistled. "I think you're being a bit hard. Claire doesn't march to the beat of anyone else's drum but her own. She liked Simon very much...we all did. Besides, she's got enough on her plate with Rosie. Things have been pretty rough lately."

"I think you only see one side to her."

"I don't," Sally said. "All she cares about is seeing that Rosie is looked after. It's why she's here. So she can do that. Claire's given up her career to do this."

"That's not what I've heard." Regan remembered what Cyn told her. "I heard she was thrown out of the navy."

Sally leaned back in her chair and frowned. "You heard wrong. She was very successful and destined for high places. Claire's chucked all that in for Rosie. I call that pretty admirable in my book."

Sally's words threw Regan off kilter. She didn't want to believe her. "I've heard other things."

"Oh, crikey." Sally cringed. "Not more. Like?"

"Like she was responsible for the death of a young girl when they were at school together. Claire bullied her, and the girl took her own life."

"Who told you that?"

"Cynthia Tennerson."

Sally nodded sagely. "She would."

"I called Claire on it, asked her if it was true. She didn't deny it."

"She wouldn't."

Regan was like a dog with a bone. "I'm told her family's influence and wealth got her out of a whole load of trouble, and that they packed her off to some finishing school in London."

Sally listened, murmuring the occasional response as she sipped her tea. Regan then watched as she deliberately placed her cup back in its saucer, put her hands in her lap, and eyeballed her.

"Regan, you're right, but you're wrong. Would you like to hear another version, more mine than Cynthia's?"

She didn't think it was going to alter anything, but it wouldn't hurt to hear Sally's take on things.

"Okay," Regan said.

"Yes, there was a young girl called Lizzy Brown, who was bullied at school—very badly—and she did end up taking her life." Sally sucked air through her teeth. "But you see, Cynthia has been a bit lean with the truth.

"It was never one person doing the bullying. There was a group of them in Lizzy's class. It's always the way of things, isn't it, that these sorts of people pick on the weaker element, and make their life a misery. Well, they targeted this girl and did all the usual nasty things. They called her names, harassed and tormented her. They broke into her locker and stole her books. They threw her gym kit into the pond. They were relentless as they teased, laughed, and sniggered at her. She was already a vulnerable kid full of anxieties and doubts, not helped by having parents who were going through a nasty and vitriolic divorce. One day, she just blew a gasket and hanged herself in the school library. She was only fourteen years old.

"The inquest didn't link her death to the bullying, although I always felt it should have. Their considered opinion was that she was an emotionally disturbed youngster whose balance of mind was disturbed by circumstances at home."

"You know a lot about this," Regan said.

Sally crossed her arms on the table and fixed her gaze on the table. She looked awkward. "I would. I was at the same school, although several years older. I was actually a prefect, and I regret to this day that I didn't see the depth of what was going on, and do something to stop it. There were also things going on in her home life. I should have seen that they were bad and getting to her."

"You couldn't have known."

"But I should have." Sally looked at Regan, a bittersweet smile on her face. "Lizzie was my kid sister."

Regan's breath caught.

"Oh, damn, Sally. I'm sorry." Regan's sense of guilt nearly suffocated her. Sally was such a lovely woman, and here she was, flinging doors wide open and revisiting painful times. It wasn't her intention to hurt her, and she kicked herself for putting sadness in her eyes.

"Don't be. You're right that Claire was a bully, but she wasn't alone. There were quite a few of them, and the ringleader of that veritable pack was an insidious little gremlin called Cyn Morgan, who you now know as Cynthia Tennerson. She was a vile, two-faced little shrew. Frankly, I don't think she's changed much."

Cyn hadn't told Regan any of this. Sally's dislike of the woman now made sense. But Claire? Claire employed Sally.

"How can you do this, work for Claire knowing what she did to your sister?"

"Let me tell you." Sally leaned like a conspirator across the kitchen table. "Claire was the only one of them who ever came to me and the family to apologize for her behavior. None of the others did.

"On the day of Lizzie's funeral, my parents just wanted family and close friends at the service. Some of the kids from school came, the nicer element. None of the bullies dared to show their faces, except one. Claire came. She sat at the back of the church and tried not to be seen. Mum saw her and caused quite a scene. She charged across to her like an express train and slapped her hard across her face. I won't forget that too soon. My brother and I had to pull Mum off."

"Claire should have stayed away," Regan said.

"Arguably, yes. But she was young. It was her way of accepting what she'd done and trying to put it right. A kid's perspective."

Regan pictured the scene. It wouldn't have been nice.

Sally continued.

"About a month after the funeral, the school held a memorial service for my sister, and it was as if she'd become posthumously popular. I watched a couple of the other girls linked to the bullying actually pretend to be mourning her loss. Cynthia had the nerve to go up to Mum and hug her, saying how sorry she was, and that Lizzie had been one of her friends, and how much she missed her. How's that for being two-faced? I wanted to throw her out."

"Why didn't you?"

"Mum was going through enough. We all were. Lovely though it would've been to kick Cynthia's arse out of the building, it would only have created a scene and hurt Mum more."

"Sally, I didn't know any of this." Regan felt awful.

"Of course you wouldn't." Sally reached across the table and grabbed Regan's hand. "Cynthia was never going to tell you. Somewhere in her mean little brain, she's erased all of her part in this."

"What a bitch."

Sally actually laughed.

"Not so long ago, Claire came back here with Rosie, looking for a full-time, live-in caregiver. Someone recommended me for the job. I'm a trained nurse and was looking for something more local. When I met Claire, we didn't even recognize each other. I only knew it was her because of her name. She didn't know me because I had my married name."

"Didn't it change things when you realized who she was?"

"All I could see was a desperate woman who was giving up everything to care for the person she loves. The more I've got to know Claire, the more I like and respect her. I sometimes wonder how she could possibly be that kid that taunted my sister, because I don't see anyone remotely familiar."

Regan was not giving Claire an inch. "Maybe you see the better side of her because of what you do for her…and she's grateful."

"No, no," Sally replied. "I've seen her rock bottom. You can't hide things there. Regan, I'm not trying to justify Claire to you. I just think you might want to step back and think again. You know the bit in the marriage vows, about to love and to cherish, in sickness and in health, till death us do part? She's into that. She really is. That's why she's the gardener. She can see Rosie every day and be close to her…as close as Rosie will allow. Claire was never kicked out of the military. That's all Cynthia talk."

Regan's head was beginning to ache. All her assumptions were being questioned, and she was finding it hard to hang on to them.

"Why does Rosie hate Claire so much?"

Sally shrugged. "I don't know. You'll have to ask Claire that. The easy answer is that it's the disease. I can only guess that somewhere in Rosie's disintegrating mind, her love has become distorted and paranoid. It happens a lot with dementia sufferers. Claire tried to look after her at home, but Rosie turned violent toward her. That can happen. So Claire put her into a care home, but that didn't work either. They didn't look after her well enough in Claire's eyes. That's why she came back here. She put Rosie in this place and employed me. There's another lady that sometimes covers when I need a break, but mostly it's me. Rosie is used to me…it works best."

Regan didn't know what to say. This was something else Claire hadn't told her. Yet she understood this particular omission. Was this what she'd wanted to tell her that afternoon on the way back from Torquay? Claire had wanted to tell her she was committed to someone else? Regan mentally slapped herself. This didn't matter anymore. There was no potential "us" between the two of them. Despite all that Sally said, Regan couldn't think any better of Claire; she *had* been deceitful.

However, Sally had shown her another side to Claire, and she knew she couldn't ignore it. It was now lodged in her like a splinter and would need attention of some kind. But not now.

Daylight was growing stronger, and she was flagging. Even though she had slept during Sally's absence, it was only cat napping. Regan was desperate for a shower and then to lie down and rest on a comfortable bed. Sally interrupted her.

"I can't see any bad in Claire. All I see is someone who loves someone deeply—someone who is now no longer here, not really. I call this love, real love. I'd like to think someone would love me enough to do that if the worst came to the worst." Sally paused. "I'm not sure that I wouldn't walk across hot coals for Claire."

CHAPTER SEVENTEEN

The following day, the worst of the weather was gone, but the rain stayed. It just drizzled its way down from above with monotonous continuity, and no one went anywhere, and nothing got done. That's how it felt to Claire.

The day after that was better. The sun sluggishly crept out from behind the clouds, and Claire managed to get a chainsaw to the tree bough that had fallen in the storm. She cut it into smaller manageable chunks that she could remove and later burn. Bonfire night was always a good time to get rid of the bigger stuff. She would just pile it up and cover it with a tarpaulin until November fifth arrived. Little did Guy Fawkes realize the favor he had done gardeners when he'd tried to blow up the Houses of Parliament all those centuries ago. It was the one time of the year when neighbors didn't complain about the smoke and flames. All you had to do was camouflage true intentions with a few pyrotechnics that imitated the Strategic Defense Initiative, and job done.

As she returned to the shed to get the wheelbarrow, she saw Regan at her kitchen window. Their eye contact lasted but seconds as Regan turned and walked away.

With a heavy heart, Claire pushed the barrow toward the cut wood that needed to be brought down to the side of the shed. She almost made it before an impulse hit her. She would see Regan now. She abandoned the barrow and walked up the lawn.

As she approached the front of the house, Regan was already there and coming toward her. This was unexpected. She'd imagined herself at Regan's front door, ringing the bell. She thought how their conversation would probably become heated again, and she wouldn't be able to say what she wanted. But the scenario in her head dispersed as Regan stopped in front of her.

Claire took a deep breath. "I was just coming to see you," she said. Her calm voice belied the butterflies that swarmed in her stomach. She soaked Regan's form in like a dry sponge on a wet surface. She looked lovely—fresh, young, and full of life.

Claire missed her and realized her own anger from the night of the party had faded, probably washed away in the storm and the other night's events. She had much to thank Regan for, stepping in to help Rosie when Sally needed to go to the hospital. She was also never one to hang on to animosity; it always seemed such a waste of emotional energy. Instead she thought of the good times; that always ate away at the bad.

Regan was dressed in a crisp sky blue blouse and tight black jeans. Claire caught the smell of soap and scent. She yearned for connection and wanted to reach out and hold her, to have Regan's arms around her and to feel her breath on her neck. She remembered everything about that kiss in the car and how Regan had made her feel. Alive. It had been so tantalizingly sweet. Now that was all gone. It was painful to have her so close, yet unattainable.

Claire wondered why she was here and figured something in her body language must have warned Regan that she was coming to see her. She guessed Regan didn't want her at the apartment. She would want to keep her at arm's length, and on neutral ground. Perhaps this was what it would become, acceptable distance? Even so, Claire was determined to say her piece and go.

"I saw you looking," Regan said.

The usual acid rancor Claire had come to expect of late wasn't present, and its absence gave her hope. She replied quickly, in case Regan blocked her words as she usually did now.

"I just wanted to say thank you for what you did the other night. I'm not sure what I'd have done if you hadn't stepped in."

Regan waved her hand with a vague gesture of acceptance. "That's okay. I'm glad I was able to help Sally and Rosie out."

Claire caught the deliberate omission of her own name. Its target hit bull's-eye. It stung.

"I hope you apologized to Sally."

Regan's comment wasn't unfriendly, and Claire actually smiled. "First thing I did the next morning."

She was surprised when Regan smiled back.

"I didn't mean to shout at her," Claire said. "She's incredible with Rosie. It was seeing Rosie out there in the storm. I was upset."

Regan nodded understanding. Claire saw her look back toward the apartment. She wondered if Regan was ready to leave, if she wanted this meeting over and done with, but when she looked back, she spoke.

"I didn't know Rosie's your partner. It must be hard."

How could Claire answer that? It was the worst of everything. How many times had friends and colleagues wanted her to "open up" and "share"? She lost count. The only person she wanted to tell was standing in front of her. She'd been ready to talk to Regan about it at their dinner, but it never happened. Now the opportunity was gone because Regan didn't care anymore. Regan was avoiding her like the Ebola virus ever since she pounced down to the shed and reminded Claire she was a de Vit.

Claire wouldn't waste her time.

"Shit happens." She gave her usual standard answer when others asked. They didn't really want to know what it was like. It was always a polite inquiry and then quickly on to another subject. Few had the stomach for the real answer, but from the beginning, Claire had sensed a connection with Regan, and a sense that she would really understand. It was too late now.

"Anyway, I just wanted to say thank you for helping." Claire turned to go, but in that split second realized she didn't want to. She didn't want to leave Regan. She wanted to stay with her, in her company, even if they no longer had anything to say to each other. Claire missed her so much. She was happy to stand here with Regan for hours, saying nothing and just breathing her scent in. Claire wished she knew what to say to bring her back to her. She turned back to face Regan and was amazed to see she hadn't left either, and didn't show any sign of leaving. Maybe she felt the same.

Claire stared at the woodpile still awaiting her attention, and she thought of the storm the other night, and of Rosie. The words fell from her lips without premeditative thought.

"No, actually, it *is* hard." She heard the tone in her own voice change, the usual emptiness fill her. "They say the human brain—the mind—is superior to that of a computer. Scientists want to create a machine with the capacity of human intellect and reasoning, give it independence, and yet they can't. It's because our creative intuitive logic is complicated, transcendent, and unable to be replicated." She looked hard at Regan. "Answer me this. Why then, can we take a malfunctioning computer, something inferior and dependent, run a system restore or set it back to default to make it function again? Yet we can't do that with the human brain? Where's the logic in that?"

Regan's eyes softened, and for a moment, Claire felt their connection again. But then a car drove up, a horn tooted, and Cynthia Tennerson shouted out to Regan that she had news for her.

The connection was short-lived. Cynthia's hail sounded far too friendly, and Claire reminded herself of the woman's dishonest part in distorting and wrecking any future she and Regan might have had. Cynthia was already out of the car, walking toward them. Claire wanted no part of this reunion.

She saw the awkward way Regan looked at her, as if she wasn't wanted. It was time for Claire to leave.

"Thanks again for the other night, Regan. Now you have to go. Your friend's here." Claire turned with as much dignity as she could and headed back swiftly to where she had left the wheelbarrow.

❖

Shit. Shit. Shit.

Regan was unhappy.

She was more than unhappy. She was upset and frantic. Something had just happened that she didn't like.

She stalked her apartment like a caged cheetah, moving up and down the same piece of carpet over and over again. It was destined to become threadbare.

Why did Cynthia Tennerson turn up at that precise moment? She interrupted something important. Regan was talking to Claire, and something was shifting between them—something making things better. Regan didn't understand what, but it pleased her. Then Cynthia arrived, and Claire walked off. Regan hadn't wanted her to. She hated their parting like that.

Regan continued to pace, resting joined hands at the back of her neck. Her heart raced like a panic attack. She was fretting.

Her mind kept switching from Claire to Cynthia, replaying what just happened. When she got up this morning, she'd no idea things were going to turn out like this. Things happened so quickly she wasn't prepared for. She *did* want to speak to Cynthia because she had things to tell her, but she'd wanted to do that in her own time, and when she was ready. This morning had preempted that.

Cynthia sodding Tennerson.

What a conversation they'd had outside in the car park.

Cynthia turned up to invite her to one of her dinner parties. "I'm terribly excited," she said. "I've managed to arrange some excellent guests. They're all in education and at the top of their profession. They're in a position to help you, Regan, with your career aspirations. If you sell yourself right and they like you, you'll find doors will open."

Cynthia appeared oblivious to the sequence of events she'd started earlier with her revelations about Claire. Regan felt sick that she'd been so childishly gullible. Cynthia probably hadn't even given their former conversation a second thought. She'd just chucked her grenades in and stepped back, not even interested in the damage she'd done.

Cynthia chatted away with her usual rapidity, and Regan felt she was being treated as a potential initiate member of some inner circle who, if she played her cards right, would be shown *open doors*. Cynthia clearly expected her to be honored by this, and Regan had no doubt the opportunity could prove lucrative, but the thought of the association made her stomach churn. It was too calculating and manipulated. Regan wanted to be chosen because of her abilities, not because she was part of some funny handshaking order. It was like selling her soul to the devil; favors given, favors returned in due course. She could never be part of anything like this.

Regan planned to confront Cynthia about her misrepresentations. She hated confrontation, but knew it had to be done. She was damned if she'd let her get away with all those untruths. She'd wanted to do this sooner rather than later and on her own terms, but it seemed her hand was forced, and the time was now. She could only imagine how unpleasant this would be and how Cynthia would take it all. Cynthia was unlikely to handle rejection well.

"I'm going to have to decline your offer of dinner," Regan said.

Cynthia was taken aback at the announcement, but assumed it was a conflict of dates. "Given the importance of this dinner to your future, I think you ought to rearrange your diary, Regan."

Regan heard the edge of control and patronization in the tone. She steeled herself.

"No, Cynthia, you misunderstand. I won't be coming to any dinner party you arrange. Call it a conflict of interest."

"A conflict of interest?"

Regan told her what Sally had said, of things that had happened decades ago when Cynthia had been at school.

Cynthia spluttered with indignation.

"Good heavens, that was years ago. Why would you want to dredge something like that up?"

"Because you did, remember?" Regan said.

"You don't expect me to remember some minor school event from way back? It's long past and forgotten."

Sally had warned Regan of Cynthia's selective memory. She didn't like the term "minor" either.

"But you do remember Claire's part," Regan said.

"Well, she's a de Vit, and it's always such a pleasure to see people like that get their comeuppance. Those moments always stand out."

"So you really don't remember your part in it?" Regan asked.

"My part?" Cynthia hissed like a snake. "I had nothing to do with it. Why would I have any involvement with some feeble-minded child who wanted to end it all?"

"That's not what Sally said."

"Really?"

"Really. She said you were part of the group that teased and harassed her sister, and actually added that you were the ringleader."

Cynthia bristled and huffed. "Ridiculous. Sally is a bitter woman with a broken marriage who looks for excuses around every corner. If her family had been less fractured and more resilient, that silly girl might be alive today. Just because she couldn't handle the pressures of life, don't hang the blame on me."

Her dismissive, insulting tone toward Sally and her family stuck in Regan's craw. She was determined not to lose her temper. It'd already got her into trouble.

"I'm sorry, Cynthia, but I don't believe you."

"I do hope you're not calling me a liar."

That was precisely what Regan was doing.

"I'm afraid I am, Cynthia. You also lied about Claire being court-martialed out of the service."

"I never said that," Cynthia snarled.

"You implied she'd been thrown out."

Cynthia retreated behind excuses. "I'm sure someone told me that. I can't be responsible for what I hear. I was only repeating it."

Cynthia was like Teflon, nothing stuck to her and certainly no acceptance of blame. She was beginning to show her true colors. The more she spoke, the more Regan saw the person Sally described.

"I think you're being very silly, Regan. You're listening to all the wrong people. I find that immature and naïve of you."

Regan sucked her lip before answering. "And I find you a rather mean, sour individual who holds grudges."

"You don't know what you're talking about." Cynthia was dismissive.

"Oh, I think I do. The worst part of this is that I let you play with my…immaturity, and my vulnerability, and my worst fears. What sort of person does that make me? I was too quick to accept everything you told me."

Cynthia stared at her. "I told you the truth."

"Only as you want to see it."

"If you side with that little lesbian, then you're an even bigger fool than I thought." There, it was out. Cynthia's shining glory. She was homophobic. Regan's intuition *had* been right.

"I'm not siding with anyone, but if you play with fire, Councilor, beware you don't get burned. You could have kept the past quiet and no one would ever have known what happened all those years ago. But you can't help yourself, can you? Your petty vindictive nature, you have to blacken Claire's reputation—"

"—reputation? She doesn't have a reputation, certainly not a good one anyway."

"—blacken her reputation," Regan repeated with emphasis, "while hiding your own involvement. Not content with that, you lied about her military service. I don't like your tactics, or the way you undermine people. You're a councilor and you're supposed to be above these sorts of things, or maybe I am naïve. I believe that office belongs to people who are above reproach and who try to be pillars of society. I'm afraid I find you severely lacking."

"How dare you speak to me like this? I've tried to help you. I've invited you into my home, and frankly, gone to a lot of effort to gather people around who might be able to help you. I've treated you as a friend."

"And you lie to your friends? I'd be a fool to trust you."

To say Cynthia was displeased was like calling Mount Etna a hill. Her nostrils flared, and she was panting like a racehorse after the Grand National.

"You little idiot. You don't know what you're doing. I've been in this game a long time, and I have power. I can make things happen... or not." Regan heard an edge of warning. "You do not want to cross me."

"Nor you, me," Regan countered. Altercation and argument were not her thing, but dear Lord, she was actually enjoying this. Looking at how galled Cynthia was, she wondered how many people ever stood up to this woman. And Regan hadn't even lost her temper. She was proud of herself, and she was far from over.

"One final thing, Cynthia. I don't know if Claire is a lesbian or not," Regan wasn't going to confirm that nugget of information, "but I am. Perhaps it's only right that you should know, for heaven forbid you'd have me to one of your dinner parties. How the neighbors would talk."

Cynthia bristled with disgust, and her eyes narrowed. "I think we're done here." She glared at Regan. "You've made your bed, now go lie on it. I can see I've wasted my time on you." She didn't say another word as she got into her car and drove off.

Regan had returned to her apartment shaking. Her initial instincts had been right. Cynthia was not a nice person, *and* she was dangerous. Regan sighed. If Cynthia was as influential as she liked to think she was, then Regan had just shot herself in the foot by announcing her sexual preference. Every educator this side of Stonehenge would now know. Would that wreck her job opportunities? Were people still that narrow-minded? Time would tell, but at least she'd been honest. Something Cynthia hadn't. Regan felt good.

What didn't feel good was how she felt when she thought of Claire. Her heart sank and she turned miserable. She was beginning to realize she'd made a mess of things. Worse, she'd been hostage to her own stupid temperament and volatile anger.

And what of her anger?

It was fading. It started to fade the day she bumped into Claire at Simon's grave. She *knew* Claire was there because she was Simon's friend, not because of any silly guilt complex. One thing Cynthia *was* right about, Regan was an idiot. She'd made some terrible mistakes that she now might have to pay for. Regan assessed the damage.

She could see that there were things Claire had done, or hadn't, that she didn't like. She didn't understand why Claire had acted like that, but it was only right that she should have given her the opportunity to explain. Regan now realized that she wanted to hear Claire's side of things.

Bit bloody late.

Regan was emotionally thawing, and especially after that damn key was pushed under her door. It shocked Regan into a state of enlightened awareness. The key kick-started her common sense and gave her a not too irrational fear that she might just have buggered up. She was losing, or had already lost, Claire.

It seemed she was being bombarded with more information about Claire, and most of it indicated that she was a thoroughly decent human being. The one blot was something she'd done as a teenager, but even Sally forgave her for that. If Sally could forgive her, then what business was it of Regan's? None. And then there was Sally's comment that she'd walk over hot coals for Claire. That was not an insignificant statement.

Regan wanted to talk, and listen, to Claire. Perhaps she'd known the minute she saw Claire this morning from her kitchen window. It was why she'd gone down to see her. As they'd talked, Regan sensed a lessening of hostilities between them. It gave her hope that there might still be a chance of…something.

But then Cynthia turned up and she saw the way Claire looked at her. She was misreading everything, and she hated the way Claire referred to Cynthia as "your friend." Regan caught the look of utter disappointment on her face, and before she could put anything right, Claire left.

It mattered to Regan what Claire thought. Probably the same way it had mattered to Claire what Regan *wrongly* thought of her.

The worm turns.

Regan sat on her couch and placed her head in her hands. When she finally looked up, she spotted the key that Claire had returned. It was on the top of a small, laminated table by the door. Regan put it there when she picked it up. It was still there. She didn't have the heart to do anything with it. It was Claire's key. Simon gave it to her because he trusted her. Regan wished she'd kept her mouth shut, and that the key hadn't been returned.

Oh, I've been a fool.

Regan knew she'd made a huge mistake and one she hoped she might be able to sort. She couldn't stop thinking of how much Claire was suffering, coping with Rosie, and what she'd given up. Claire didn't need Regan's dreadful behavior. She needed support, kindness, and understanding…like she'd given Simon. Of course, Claire had bailed Simon out of some of his debts. She was his friend. Why had it taken Regan so long to realize all this?

Neither had Claire reacted adversely, and thrown her out of the apartment. Regan had expected that. Claire never lashed out either. Every time they'd bumped into each other, Claire remained civilized and polite.

And what of me? I'm irrational, bad tempered, and have anger issues.

Regan felt ashamed. *I've hurt Claire. I've been cruel.* Maybe Claire was better off without her anyway.

She looked at the key again on the table.

She prayed. "Give me a chance to put things right," she spoke out loud. "Please don't let it be too late."

❖

Claire hated food shopping, but if she wanted to live, it was one of those things that had to be done.

Claire looked at her list and mentally checked off the items as she moved through the supermarket adding what she needed to her cart. At least she didn't feel she was wasting time. The last few days it had done nothing but rain so she couldn't do anything in the gardens, parts of which now looked more like the Somme than a manicured, genteel place to commune with nature. No doubt the good weather would return, but right now, it was like her mood, bleak.

A perverse side of her was glad it was raining. It meant she had a rational excuse for not being at work. She wasn't trying to avoid it. There were still some boughs to be cut up that lay like large chunks of charcoal on the lawn, and on further examination, another part of the tree that needed to be lopped. The lightning strike had hit the tree hard and she hoped it would survive. Once the rain stopped and she could get out there again, she'd see what could be done.

It was her heart that was grateful for the opportunity to abstain from work for it meant she didn't have to bump into Regan. Seeing her the other day with Cynthia left a sour taste in her mouth. Regan was choosing her new friends.

Claire willed her mind off the depressing subject and looked at her list again. Almost done. There were a few other things to find, and then she could go home.

As she turned into the household aisle, she spotted her.

Regan was standing at the other end. Claire froze, and in those nanoseconds of paralysis, she saw Regan look at her. Claire then did something she'd never done in her life. She diverted her gaze and pretended she hadn't seen her, casually glancing over at the mops and plastic buckets before turning her cart out of the aisle and then dashing madly for any other area that would provide cover.

Moving like a demented shopper rushing to get first hands on sales items, she zigzagged her way through the store until she felt safe.

She ended up in the pet food aisle facing a box of salmon crunch biscuits with a black and white feline licking its lips. Grabbing her breath, she reasoned Regan wouldn't come here. She furtively glanced around wondering if store security were now eyeballing her on CCTV, the strange woman breaking land record speeds in a confined zone.

"Al, we've got a weird one in cat food."

Claire could almost hear the message being relayed to some man in uniform "on the ground" who would conveniently appear near her and then watch her like a sparrow hawk waiting for the kill. But no one turned up.

Slowly, she relaxed and gazed up at another shelf in front of her. There were bright colored boxes neatly lined up, declaring the words, "We care for your pussy." If the whole incident weren't so surreal and ridiculous, she might have laughed. That would confuse security. They'd assume she wasn't a shoplifter, but a vulnerable adult from some local care home.

Gritting her teeth, she moved cautiously toward the checkout counters. For the first time in her entire supermarket experience, there was one free and the middle-aged assistant was idly examining her nail extensions. The woman scanned her items before announcing, "If you spend another fifty-nine pence you get a ten-pound voucher off your next gasoline purchase over thirty pounds."

"What?"

"I said if you spend another fifty-nine pence, you get ten-pound voucher off your next gasoline purchase over thirty pounds."

Claire spotted Regan heading toward the check out area. She bent down low, and the checkout assistant gave her an odd stare.

"Bad back. Torn a ligament. Can't stand too straight," Claire lied.

"Oh, I know. I did that in the garden last year," the assistant said. "I was trimming my hedges. It took months until I could stand straight. I found hot baths helped."

This was ridiculous. All Claire wanted to do was get out of the store, unseen, and with her shopping.

"So, do you want to?" The woman was studying her nails again.

"What?"

"Do you want to spend another fifty-nine pence to get the ten-pound voucher off your next gasoline purchase over thirty pounds?"

Exasperated, Claire looked around and threw a packet of chewing gum in with her shopping. Her response was like activating a chain reaction. The checkout assistant rang the last item, announced the amount, and handed over a voucher.

"Do you want assistance with packing?" she asked.

Claire had already pushed everything into three plastic bags. "No, thanks, I'm done." She handed over cash and waited for her change.

"You be careful," the checkout assistant said.

"Eh?"

"Lifting bags too heavy…it'll only aggravate your back." It was kind meaning advice.

"Oh, right. Yes. Thank you. I'll take care.

Claire walked out of the store moving low to avoid being seen. If security *was* watching her, she must have looked like Quasimodo. She swiftly made her way back to her vehicle. It was only when she got home and began unpacking that she allowed herself time to think.

Why had she behaved like that in the store? It really wasn't adult behavior. She'd deliberately avoided Regan who would know she'd done it *deliberately*. What would she now think? *Oh, damn.*

Claire reasoned she'd done it because the relationship—what relationship—was going nowhere fast. After all this time of being dead inside, she'd opened herself up to someone, and was now hurting. She was sick to death of hurting. This wasn't how it was supposed to be. Regan had turned against her and was all chummy with Cynthia Tennerson.

She felt thoroughly sorry for herself. During the day, it was fairly okay. Her head ruled all thought. It told her to be realistic and rational. She had enough going on in her life at the moment, so why add to it? She managed to convince herself that she didn't need a relationship, or the worry of one, and that in time, she and Regan would probably manage to coexist around each other. Slowly, things would go back to how they'd been before Regan appeared.

The nights were different. This was when her heart took ascendancy. She would try to sleep, and fail, and her heart would *chatter* away, reminding her that she didn't want to go back to how things had been—lonely. It told her that she deserved a chance to move on and that Rosie wanted this. It told her to stop feeling guilty whenever she thought she might begin a new life *without Rosie*. Her heart would tell her to not give up and that she should trust her instincts, and give Regan a chance. It was precisely because she didn't know what was going on between her and Cynthia that she ought to at least find out.

This mental state of civil war left her feeling tired and irritable. She forgot appointments and people's names, and made silly mistakes. She'd gone to get vehicle fuel and only realized she didn't have her purse when she'd topped up and went to pay. Fortunately, she was a regular, and the manager was cautiously understanding. She'd rushed home, grabbed the cash, and returned and paid. But it was all embarrassing. Claire knew she couldn't go on like this. She needed to sort herself out.

The next few days dragged. Regan tried to phone Claire, but her calls went unanswered. She was being ignored. It didn't surprise her. Claire was returning some of her own medicine. She knew Claire saw her the other day at the supermarket. She'd even waved to Claire in the car park as she saw her leave, but she'd got no response.

I guess I've asked for this.

Regan wasn't the depressive sort, but she was right now. She wanted to speak to Claire badly, but the way things were going, that wasn't about to happen too soon. Her miserable state was at least broken by some good news.

She was being offered a chance to visit the mathematics faculty at a nearby university. They were inviting her to have a look around and discuss research opportunities. She'd only written in a couple of weeks ago, and the fast response was unexpected. It seemed her usual ploy of job seeking—she who writes in first—was paying off.

Maybe they liked her educational background and her areas of research interest. A thought entered her mind. If Cynthia was going to stir shit, maybe she hadn't got to this institute yet. She grinned. Maybe she had, and the faculty was full of *out and proud* mathematical geniuses. Whatever, they were asking to meet her. There was hope.

It was partially because of this positive news that she went into town to see the apartment letting agent. Given the difficult situation she found herself in with Claire—increasingly looking like all her own fault—she was taking the bull by the horns. She wanted to stay in the place, and at the moment, she was only on a six-month lease. Her question was simple. If she wanted to stay longer, was that possible? Regan figured she might as well find out now whether Claire would be looking to finish the arrangement. The answer that came back surprised her. Not only was *the owner* willing to allow further extensions, subject to adherence to the lease, but if she wished to purchase the place at a later stage, this would be considered. Claire was being very obliging, and Regan was grateful. It was a small sign that if they could never be friends again, at least they might coexist with more grace. Anything was better than what they had at present.

Another positive—although Regan considered it arguable—was that a date was set for the inquest into Simon's death. It marked the end of a bad period in her life. Closure might now be possible. She welcomed it as it meant she could fully concentrate on moving forward, and sorting her life out. If she didn't think too much on the mess between her and Claire, things looked positively chipper.

She banished her depression and strode downstairs to Sally and Rosie's, feeling a need to get out and talk.

"Cuppa?" Sally's cheery face and robust stature met her at the door.

"Love one," Regan said.

Sally always welcomed her as if they were old friends. She never felt as if she was intruding.

"I just thought I'd find out how Michael's doing," Regan lied. She *did* want to know, but that wasn't why she was really here. Sally gave her one of those looks that implied she knew that, but she went along with the deception.

"Oh, he's a resilient chap, and doing fine. He's off work for a while, but he should be back to normal pretty soon."

"Glad to hear it, and Rosie? No after effects?"

Sally breathed out like a pantomime horse. "She's fine too, thank God. If she'd caught a chill or anything because of me, it would be awful. She's ill enough as it is."

Regan saw the concern splattered across Sally's face. "You didn't do it on purpose, Sally. Your mind was elsewhere."

The mitigating evidence barely lightened her heavy looks. "I know that, but when you're dealing with someone increasingly frail, you don't need things like that happening. This disease does not need a helping hand."

"Where is she?"

"Next door, asleep. Mornings are usually her more responsive periods, when she's more lucid, but that's been slipping lately. She sleeps more, and even when she's awake, she's not really with us. Lately, she's looked at me and I wonder if she isn't forgetting who I am." Sally sighed. "I wish I'd known her when she was well."

Regan saw, and liked, how attached Sally was to her patient. It warmed her. It was good to know someone really cared for Rosie. That was never a guarantee when people became vulnerable and needed help.

"I know so little about Alzheimer's, other than what it is...the obvious. Do you think it's hereditary?" Regan only surface read articles that occasionally popped up in the media, and she always avoided the television documentaries. They depressed and frightened her.

"Depends what you read," Sally answered. "Not in Rosie's case. No one in her family has had it, but it can be in the genes. They call that familial Alzheimer's. I've known plenty of patients with no family links at all."

"How much time has she left?"

Again, Regan was struck with how much Sally cared for Rosie. The question produced an unguarded stab of pain, only to be replaced by a look of quiet acceptance. It was plain she considered her patient more than an income.

"How long's a piece of string?" Sally answered. "Rosie is young. She has a young body, full of young organs. The trouble is, as the disease advances, it does its job. It makes the brain forget to do what it has to. A lot of patients simply die of malnutrition. Their body forgets *how* to eat, *how* to swallow. They get weaker.

"As things progress, so do the chances of infection. Their immune system breaks down. Even when one infection is cured, it often comes back and eventually may not respond to treatment. Often the person can't even tell you they don't feel well because they've forgotten how to communicate, or understand. We have to hope we see the signs before things become too serious."

Regan understood. "I couldn't do this sort of work. I've only known Rosie a short while, but I already feel attached to her. How do you cope, day in, day out, watching someone like this fade away? It must affect you."

Sally gave a wan smile. "I don't think about it too much. I just try to do my job."

"Claire must be relieved she has you."

Sally idly pulled at an earlobe. "I'm not sure she felt that way the other night."

"Stop beating yourself up. You said yourself, Rosie's okay."

"Yes, I know."

"But it does make you want to live for the day."

"No kidding." Sally laughed. "I live in fear of forgetting where I've put my car keys, praying it's not an early sign. But as Claire is very fond of saying, no one knows what the compost heap of life holds for us."

Thinking of Claire made Regan flinch.

"How is Claire? I haven't seen her around much." Regan tried to sound upbeat.

"She's fine. She touches base several times a day to check on Rosie."

Regan hadn't seen her.

"You two still not talking?" Sally asked.

Regan held her arms up in mock defeat.

"Sally, I've made a real mess of things, and now Claire thinks I'm best buddies with Cynthia. I'm not."

"Why don't you tell her that?"

"Because she isn't around; she's avoiding me and won't answer any of my phone messages."

Sally looked lost for words.

"But you should be proud of me, Sally."

"I should?"

"Oh, yes." Regan actually grinned.

"What have you done?"

"I told Cynthia Tennerson what I thought of her."

The smile that radiated on Sally's face deserved to be photographed and hung in a portrait gallery. "Oh, and I missed it! How did she take it?"

"I think I can safely say she hated every minute, and will never darken my doorstep again."

"Wouldn't I have liked to have been a fly on the wall."

"She's homophobic too." Regan thought of the unpleasant remarks Cynthia made toward Claire's sexuality. They still stung.

"Doesn't surprise me."

"I don't think there's a redeeming feature anywhere inside Cynthia. Why the hell I didn't suss that when I first met her, I don't know. I didn't think I was that bad at reading people. You should have said something."

"Not my place," Sally said. "People have to make their own minds up."

Regan paused. "I haven't done a good job at reading Claire either, have I?"

It wasn't said as a question, and she didn't expect Sally to answer.

Sally shrugged and her brow puckered. "Can I ask you something?"

This was going to be one of those deep, meaningful questions, but Regan consented with a nod.

"Why the hurt, Regan? Why this *huge* level of hurt? Has Claire really done something that justifies it? It just seems out of proportion. Don't get me wrong, I do understand. Claire *should* have told you a few things, but your reaction seems top heavy. I'm wondering why, especially as I can see you still care for her. Am I missing something?"

Regan raised steepled fingers to her face and exhaled slowly into them.

"I've been asking myself that, too. I'm not proud of any of this," she admitted. "I suppose it's got a lot to do with trust. All my life, I feel I've put a lot into relationships with people, but never got the same level back. Even Simon let me down. Then Claire comes along, and for the first time in my life, I thought, here is someone I trust, and more, someone I can really care for, and love. We didn't have a great start, but the more I got to know her, the more I found myself giving her a level of trust I've never given to anyone else. It's all happened so quickly." Regan shook her head in bewilderment. "When I found out she'd kept all this information from me... information I think is important and that I think she should have told me, it's been a huge blow." She looked at Sally. "I thought she cared for me, too. I feel rejected. You don't keep things from someone you care about. It hurts.

"I'm not perfect, Sally. I'm just human with all the usual bag of frailties. No one likes to feel they're being lied to, especially when they're in love with someone."

"Ah, that four lettered word," Sally said softly. "Now I begin to understand."

Regan didn't respond.

"And you feel it's over?" Sally asked.

"I do. Not that anything ever really started."

"You don't really," Sally said.

"What do you mean?"

"You don't really think it's over. You've slipped up, Regan. You said when you're in love with someone. Present tense."

"Does it matter? Claire's not talking to me. She's walked away. It takes two to make things happen."

"You're going to give up then?" Sally said.

"I'm not sure what else I can do, except wait and hope Claire talks to me...if she ever does."

"Hmm," was the only reaction Regan received.

"You must find this all unacceptable, Sally. Here I am talking to you about a relationship with a woman who is already in a relationship. Don't you find it wrong?"

"No." There was no hesitation in Sally's response. "Claire needs a life, and she hasn't got one anymore with Rosie. If you're genuine and can offer her that, you've got my full backing. Just don't play games with her. She's had enough."

"I can't offer her anything anymore."

"I think the two of you need to talk."

"I am trying." Regan's retort only earned a raised eyebrow. "Any bright ideas?"

"Me?"

"You're full of wisdom, and sensible."

Sally's mouth dropped open. "You're seeking relationship advice from me? Ye saints, you've picked the wrong one here! I can assure you I'm no font of wisdom in these matters. My marital relationship is littered with disaster after disaster. Even though we're divorced, I still occasionally want to kill my ex and peel all the skin off his body. I'm not really sure, Regan, that you should be looking to me for this sort of advice. All I can say is that I'm quite sure an opportunity will arise giving you both a chance to talk, and when it comes, just don't mess up."

Regan wasn't convinced.

"Do not mess up," Sally repeated.

"I'll try my best."

Sally nodded. "That's all you can ask for. Think of that compost heap in life."

Regan tried to, but all she could think of was the look on Claire's face as Cynthia arrived in the car park. Regan was going to have to try *really hard*.

❖

Claire stood in front of the tree and stared at the woodpile for the umpteenth time realizing she hadn't got a clue what she was doing. She wasn't thinking, and the chore in front of her was going nowhere.

She'd given up the other day moving all the wood to the shed because of bad weather. Now it was better, she was determined to finish the job. But her mind wasn't on the task. She couldn't stop thinking about the self-satisfied look on Cynthia Tennyson's face as she'd approached Regan in the car park, or her own immature behavior in the supermarket.

She wondered if her mind had been on this task the other day too because there was still wood that needed chainsawing if she had any hope of moving it. She'd already lopped a smaller bough down to make the tree safe.

With a heavy heart, she started the chainsaw and pushed the metal teeth into the bough. Suddenly, a piece of wood flew up and hit her in the face.

"Damn it!" She cut the motor. Blood already streamed down her face as she removed her heavy gloves. *You idiot.* She should have been wearing a protective helmet and goggles. They were still in the shed. She'd been so distracted by her thoughts she'd forgotten them. Now she was gushing blood.

Before she had time to work out where the blood was coming from, she heard Sally shouting as she ran down the lawn toward her.

"What have you done?"

Sally grabbed her face in her hands and started inspecting the damage.

"Piece of wood ricocheted up and hit me in the face."

"I can see that. You've made a right mess. I think your eyes are okay, but you'd better come in and let me see to this."

Claire wanted to say she'd be okay and would sort it, but she knew better. She'd no idea what she'd done, only that her face hurt and there was blood…lots of blood. Sally was a trained nurse. Putting herself in Sally's hands was a no-brainer.

Minutes later, she was seated in the kitchen eyeball to eyeball with the nurse as she inspected, prodded, and poked her face.

"Does that hurt?" Sally asked.

"Yes."

"And that?"

"Yes."

"There?"

"Ouch! Bloody 'ell, Sally. Yes, it all hurts."

"That's good, no nerve damage." The positive assessment held no pity. Sally leaned back. "You're very lucky. Apart from a few nasty cuts, you've got away with it." Sally tweaked her nose. "And this isn't broken."

Claire yelped in pain, but Sally appeared oblivious as she reached for the antiseptic. It produced a smell Claire loathed as it always reminded her of hospitals.

"Ouch...that stings," she hissed as her wounds were cleansed with the astringent.

"Don't be such a baby," Sally said.

"You're supposed to be a carer."

Sally's eyes narrowed. She ignored the insult. "Why weren't you wearing your safety kit?"

"I forgot."

"Since when have you ever forgotten anything important like that? Never. Your mind was elsewhere."

Claire didn't answer. She wasn't going to give Sally the satisfaction of knowing she was right. "Rosie okay?" she changed the subject.

"Yes. She's asleep."

Claire was grateful for small mercies. If she hadn't been, she wouldn't be in the kitchen now, and Rosie would be screaming like a banshee.

Sally wiped salve into a small gash on the bridge of her nose. Its sting was unexpected, and Claire recoiled back into the seat.

"Keep still. I can't fix this if you keep flinching."

"Did you actually qualify as a nurse?" Claire whinged.

"Yes, I did. Now stop bellyaching," Sally said. "You're worse than my son." Her eyes narrowed again as she inspected her work. "You're not going to be pretty when all the bruising comes out."

"Damn it. I should've been paying attention."

Sally leaned back again and looked at her with disgust. "Yes, you should. Claire, you're going to have to sort this before you kill yourself."

"What are you talking about?" Claire knew exactly what the topic was, and Sally knew she knew. She remained looking at her like a lab rat, saying nothing.

"Well?" Sally demanded.

"Well, what?"

"What are you going to do about Regan? You can't keep avoiding her. You're two adults who obviously *like* each other."

"Has she said something?"

Sally was disappointed with her response.

"If she has...and I'm not saying that...I'm not going to break confidences." Sally paused before adding, "But she obviously cares for you."

"You think?" Claire retorted with just too much enthusiasm. Her face already felt tight, and her sarcasm and facial expressions cost her dearly. The shaping of the words hurt, sending a sharp pain up her nose into her forehead, where their sound resonated like a TV with the volume up too high. She was going to have the mother of a headache. If it felt this bad now, what was she going to feel like later on?

"Yes, I do. You're both lovely people who seem hell-bent on misreading each other. Stop letting your delicate constitutions interfere with your future."

"You should tell her that," Claire muttered stubbornly as she thought again of Cynthia.

"Am I going to have to kidnap the two of you and lock you in a room together?" Sally's exasperation showed.

"I don't think you understand—"

"Oh, shut up. I get it, and so should you." When had Sally become so sadistic?

"There's too much anger and emotion between you both for this to be ignored. You're both tromping around like lovesick cows, determined not to show how you each feel, and letting small inconsequential things get between you. Now bloody well do something and sort this out."

"I've tried that," Claire said sullenly.

"Well, try again."

"It won't work."

Sally pushed a cotton bud up her nose to soak the blood.

Claire groaned and thought how heartless the ministering angel was. "Do you have to do that?" she mumbled.

It was clear Sally did, for she gave no quarter and the activity continued in silence.

"She's been trying to find you," Sally finally said.

Their eyes met, and Claire must have looked guilty because she saw Sally frown and purse her lips. "What have you done?"

Claire grabbed Sally's hand, the one that was sticking the bud up her nose, and she pulled it away. Sally waited patiently for an answer, and Claire wondered if this was how it felt being at a confessional. Would she feel absolved of all failings and weaknesses if she confessed? *Father, I have sinned.*

"I've been a bit of a prat, Sally. I saw Regan in town and ran away. She saw."

"Oh."

"It wasn't very adult, was it?"

Sally's rigid body language relaxed, and for the first time since Claire had entered the kitchen, she caught a glimpse of kindness.

"When my ex was having one of his many *secret* affairs, I washed all his underwear in a detergent I knew he was allergic to."

Claire tried to smile, but the swelling wouldn't let her. "What happened?"

Sally looked like a cat that had discovered how to open a birdcage full of canaries. "He came out in the most awful rash all over his body. He itched and scratched where you don't really want to see a man itching and scratching. But it worked. The current hussy of the moment left him rather fast, any amour dampened. I suspect she thought he had crabs."

Claire raised an approving thumb.

"The moral of this little tale, Claire, is that we don't always get to behave like grown-ups."

They shared a smile, or at least Sally did. Claire's face was swelling up like a puff adder. She dreaded what she looked like.

"Well, I wish I had," Claire said.

Sally reached out and squeezed her hand. "It's up to you, but why not have another go at the talk stuff? I bet she'll listen. She's in love with you, you know."

Claire studied Sally's face. She clearly believed what she'd just said. Why couldn't Claire? She kept seeing Cynthia's sneering smile.

Sally continued cleaning Claire's face and didn't mention the matter again.

When Claire left, Sally called a taxi and instructed her to go straight home and rest, and to take a few headache tablets. "You're going to need them."

Claire didn't doubt it. Her headache was growing.

"And look on the bright side." Sally grinned as she waved her off. "You still have your teeth."

❖

"Oh, my God!" Regan cried out as she stared at the discarded chainsaw resting at the side of a pile of logs strewn across the lawn. She saw a blood-soaked glove beside it, and more splashes of red on a piece of freshly cut wood. Her mind put two and two together. With alarming mathematical dysfunction, she produced a double-digit number. This wasn't good. A chainsaw, a blood-stained glove, more blood over wood, and no Claire.

She ran across the lawn to the French doors and knocked on the glass. She was relieved when Sally's cheery face appeared seconds later.

"I think there's been an accident," she breathed heavily as the door opened. "There's blood over by the—"

"Calm down," Sally said. "Claire's had an accident, but she's okay. I've sent her home in a taxi. You'd better come in."

Sally stepped back and Regan entered. Rosie was in bed, apparently watching TV. She didn't acknowledge Regan's presence. Neither did she really seem to be taking any notice of the program. Though her eyes were on the screen, she looked spaced out. Rosie was staring into nothingness.

"She's had a bad night," Sally said in a low voice. "Nightmares."

Regan watched as Sally made a show of locking the doors. "Wouldn't want Rosie to wander out, would we?" The guilt on Sally's face was real, the memories still raw. "Come on through to the sitting room," she whispered.

Although Sally offered her a seat, Regan remained standing. Her heart was still pumping with shock. She waited for Sally's explanation.

"The silly fool wasn't wearing her safety equipment, and a piece of wood flew up and hit her in the face. There was lots of blood, but nothing broken, nothing serious. She'll survive."

Regan exhaled heavily. She was relieved. Her mind had conjured up all manner of scenarios, none of them good. She'd gone into panic mode the minute she'd seen the blood. Thank God, Claire was okay.

She felt her legs shaking, and she fought an intense desire to burst into tears. It was only Sally's quiet composure that held her back. If anything happened to Claire, she'd go nuts. She didn't want to admit it, but the reason she was in the garden in the first place was not simply to take in the air. Her real modus operandi was to *accidentally come across* Claire. She wanted to try again and talk to her.

Content that Claire wasn't lying prostrate in some herbaceous border and bleeding to death, Regan left Sally's. Suddenly consumed with a desire to do something concrete and useful, she headed back toward the chainsaw to secure it. The fact that Claire hadn't done that told Regan her injuries were bad enough despite the reassurances Sally had given. She stepped over some of the wood and picked up the heavy piece of equipment, then walked back down the lawn toward the potting shed.

When she entered, she saw all Claire's little terracotta pots lined up on the bench like military soldiers on display, each with a tiny sapling barely bigger than her thumb, and destined to grow into whatever.

A wave of sadness came over her, and her heart ached. The scene before her looked wrong. It was empty. This was where Claire hung out most of the time, and she was supposed to be here. It was her place, ministering to her beloved plants...and watching over Rosie. Regan understood that now.

Claire's absence only echoed in the space like a foghorn out at sea. Regan yearned to have her here now. She wanted to see her and to know she was all right. She wanted to reach out and take her in her arms and tell her she was sorry she'd been an idiot.

The saw weighed heavy in her hand, and she placed it on the floor. She gazed again at the army of seedlings. She picked up a little pot and with great care, studied the tiny plant that was nothing but a couple of infant leaves. Claire's imaginary voice whispered in her ear, telling her to "Step away from the plants." Regan couldn't help smiling, and her eyes began to sting. "Let's hope I can sort this out with your mum," she said to the plant before placing it back down carefully with the others.

She scanned the shed and spotted a heavy metal lock-up cabinet in a far corner. It looked like the place where Claire would keep valuable tools. There was only one problem. It was locked.

Regan groaned. She couldn't leave the tool here unsecure and unattended. Though the area wasn't brimming with errant criminals ready to conduct some chainsaw massacre, it was a piece of equipment to be respected. It needed locking away. As she glanced down at her feet where the saw rested, an irrational impulse came over her. This was the closest thing she had to Claire. She would take it back to her place and look after it until Claire came back.

The humor of the moment didn't escape Regan. She would face Claire on return and announce, *"I've been caring for your chainsaw."* It would be seen as the ultimate act of love, and they would live happily ever after.

Regan wished it was so simple.

Over the next few days, she rang Claire many times and left messages. Still her calls went unanswered.

CHAPTER EIGHTEEN

The car engine purred as Regan approached the apartment building.

She spotted Claire almost immediately. She was leaning against the boundary stone wall that led down to the coastal path. It was the one they had walked together not so long ago, and when things between them had been better.

She took a deep breath, steeling herself. This presented a perfect opportunity to talk to her, but as she exited the car, Claire stood and came over to her. Their thoughts seemed attuned, though Regan wondered what the topic of conversation would be, surely not pleasant. She hadn't seen Claire since the dreaded "Cynthia" moment when she'd eyed her like a traitor and walked away.

As Claire drew nearer, Regan gasped.

"Good God, look at your face!"

"I'd rather not."

"It's horrible." She was looking at a nostril filled with congealed blood, a black eye, and bruised face.

"Thank you." Claire's response was lackluster.

Regan winced. "That could have come out better, but you know what I mean."

Claire's light nod assured her she'd not already botched any chance of reunion.

"It's okay." Claire's facial movements were restrained and minimal. Regan could see why. Everything looked tight and swollen, bruised and painful. Sally was right. Claire was lucky.

"Is it?" Regan asked, aware her words held subtext.

Claire sensed this too, for it took her a while to answer.

"I've still got a massive headache, but it's getting better. And as long as I avoid mirrors, I'm fine."

"I'm glad. Sally told me what you did."

"Not to be repeated."

Not that Regan was in any way grateful for what happened to Claire, but it was providing a topic of conversation that was far lighter than the one that lay waiting. It was the gentle ground before things of greater importance took priority. Regan sensed their imminent arrival.

"I've tried to phone you several times," she said.

"I know. I wasn't sure I wanted to answer." At least Claire was being honest.

Regan nodded. Why would Claire want to speak to her after everything that had happened?

"Can I say something?" Regan asked.

Claire's eyes narrowed, as much as they could. "Still?"

Regan ignored the flip of sarcasm.

"I just want to say that I apologize for what I said to you in the shed, the manner in which I said it, and for my consequent behavior, especially when I know you've been trying to offer an olive branch. I behaved badly."

"Yes, you did." Claire was pulling no punches. Regan accepted that. Claire's admonishment continued. "You never gave me a chance to say my piece."

"No, and I'm sorry, Claire. I've always had a short fuse, but lately…" Lately, Regan knew she'd been acting well outside her box, and she wasn't proud. Hot temper or not, this behavior *wasn't* her. It was extreme and she hated it. More, she hated the damage it had done. She probably did have some mitigating factors in there somewhere, but they didn't justify the hurt she knew she'd inflicted on Claire.

Claire was giving her apology solemn reflection, and Regan found it difficult to read her. Facial expressions were important at times like these, but Claire's weren't there, thanks to a lump of wood.

"I think we need to talk," Claire said. "Do you think that's possible? Two-way communication, this time?"

"Yes." Regan ignored the reprimanding tone, and her answer was somber and serious. She was grateful for this offer. This time, she intended to show Claire how different she could be. She would act like a rational individual.

"This isn't an easy place to keep avoiding each other," Claire said. "And it sounds as if you're keen to stay on."

It was clear she was referring to the conversation Regan had just had with the letting agent.

"Yes, I am, and thanks for letting me stay."

Regan smiled to show her gratitude and hoped Claire understood how much her magnanimous offer meant. The apartment was all she had left of *family*. It was silly the way people attached themselves to places and possessions. They became little pieces of memory to be seen or held when loved ones were no longer around. It was just things bereaved people did, it was part of being human.

"I expect you still have questions you'd like answered." Claire wasted no time.

"I do." Regan was honest. "But they don't seem so important now." She realized her statement could be misread. It hadn't come out right, and she saw the quick cut of pain in Claire's eyes. She tried to correct things, but her words came out jumbled. "No, what I meant is they're still important, and I would like to hear your side of things. I just meant they aren't so dominant and out of proportion...huge. I didn't mean I don't care anymore because I don't care for you—"

Claire raised a hand. "Okay. Stop. I've got it."

After a few seconds, Claire asked, "Who cleared, and stacked the wood?"

They were back to safe, holding conversation.

"I did," Regan answered. She'd spent most of a day finishing off the job Claire had been unable to. She'd ended up enjoying it. "No, actually, that's not entirely true. I started the job but then, one by one, many of the residents came out and helped. I can't tell you how popular you are. Everyone wanted to chip in. Even Grace came out and raked."

Claire's eye's softened, and Regan saw how touched she was.

"Do you know what happened to my chainsaw?"

"Yes. I've got it up in my place."

Claire looked surprised.

"Well, I couldn't lock it away in the shed, so I thought it was safer up there." Regan thought of it, sitting on her kitchen floor in the corner on a large sheet of plastic.

A crease formed with difficulty on Claire's forehead. "It stinks of fuel."

Regan grinned. "No kidding. I'm grateful I don't smoke. I'd have ignited by now if I did." She paused before adding, "That might have solved our problem." She was rewarded by a flicker of humor in Claire's eyes.

"And someone's been watering my plants."

Regan assumed she meant the army of seedlings in their military rows on the bench inside the shed.

"Me," Regan replied with casual nonchalance. "I've been developing my nurturing skills. I don't think I've killed any."

Claire tipped her chin forward in acceptance. "Thank you for that. I've been worried about them, but I couldn't do anything. This headache's been a beast."

"Maybe you should go see a doctor."

"I did. I'm all right. I've just got to be patient. It is getting better…slowly."

"It doesn't look it."

"Yes, you said," Claire said wryly.

Pleasant chat evaporated and left a silence. Regan sensed the elephant between them grow larger. She took the lead, forcing a nervous smile. "Why don't you come up and let me reunite you with your chainsaw? We can have a drink if you like and talk there."

But Regan's idea didn't register as acceptable to Claire. It was clear she didn't like the idea.

"I won't if you don't mind. If you could drop the saw off in the shed sometime. No rush. I'll probably be there again from tomorrow."

A cavern of emptiness filled Regan and her smile disappeared. Her offer was rejected and likely with it, the chance of doing any real damage limitation. Was everything good over between her and Claire?

"Sure." She tried to sound upbeat.

"I don't think what we have to say will take too long," Claire added. "We might as well stroll around the gardens."

Regan's disappointment grew. Claire *was* keeping her distance. But if this was the way Claire wanted it, then she wouldn't argue. At least they were talking. It was a start. Regan hoped she'd be able to claw her way back into Claire's affections at a later date when time might gentle all the unpleasantness. For now, she would honor Claire's terms.

They walked down to the garden and through the laburnum tunnel that had been spectacular back in May, along with the azaleas. It was one of Regan's favorite places to walk in an evening. She hoped the two of them weren't about to create memories that would forever spoil the place for her.

"I'm going to answer your charges," Claire said. "When I've finished, if there's anything you still want to know, you can ask."

Claire's hardnosed approach continued.

"You asked why I didn't tell you that I'm a de Vit. I wasn't hiding that. It's just at the beginning, the need to tell you never crossed my mind. By the time it *did*, I was getting more than a little worried that I had to be careful *how* I told you."

Their eyes met. Claire's were full of cold resolve.

"Whether you believe me or not, Regan, I was planning to tell you this at dinner, but that got cancelled, and then, well…the rest, as they say, is history.

"You're probably thinking that I should have told you earlier given everything you'd started to tell me about Simon's financial investments and the link to the de Vit name. There were certainly opportunities."

This was exactly what Regan was thinking.

Claire stopped walking to deadhead a flower. "I *should* have told you earlier, but I didn't. Why? Because I felt I was up against this huge wall of hatred you were building. It was targeted at my family, and by association, at me. I didn't want to blow it."

Claire looked at her and the tension in her body relaxed. "I was growing very fond of you, Regan, and I didn't want to ruin things. I didn't want to risk spoiling everything. I wanted you to get to know *me* first, that you would then trust me enough to know I'd never have done anything to hurt Simon." She cast the dead flower to the ground and resumed walking.

"Simon was my friend, and I was his. Our talks were always two-sided. I valued his support and understanding as much as he did mine. We saw each other at some of our lowest times. Simon knew I was a de Vit, and it never bothered him."

"I was shocked when I found out you belong to that family," Regan said.

Claire stopped abruptly and faced Regan.

"I'm a de Vit. It's just a name," she said sharply. "But since we're on this subject, let's define the boundaries of the term family. Do you feel responsible for the wider elements of yours? I mean aunts, uncles, cousins, and so forth." The question was rhetorical. "Do you feel that what they do reflects on you?"

"No, of course not."

"So, we're talking close family here? Mother, father, siblings?"

Regan could see where this was going. She didn't answer, and Claire continued.

"Now we've defined those boundaries, let me tell you how proud I am of *my* family, and why. My parents live in London and are happily married. Dad is semi-retired now, but he was a financier, a capital investor who ran his own business. You'll have to take my word on this if you can, but he wouldn't shake a leaf from a tree. He's an honest, decent man who I love to bits. He's always been my moral compass. He gives back far more than he takes, much to my mother's chagrin. She wants him to do less and enjoy life more, but he's stubbornly resistant. He sits on several charitable boards. He won't give these up because he knows he makes a difference.

"My mother is also from independent wealth." Claire eyeballed Regan. "That isn't an apology. It's the side of the family where much of my money comes from. A much loved grandmother passed away and left me a considerable sum, including this place. I don't know why she chose me. Maybe she liked sailors. Maybe she was a closet lesbian." Claire shrugged. "Anyway, I'm rich. What can I say?" She didn't wait for an answer.

"I have one brother who drives my father crazy because he doesn't understand money in the slightest. All he's interested in is his lovely zany wife. They are breeding more children than is decent. When he isn't increasing the world population, he designs and builds computers for a company in Essex." Claire paused. "Is this boring you?"

"No." It wasn't. Regan was finally learning more about Claire, but at such cost.

"Now, if you want to talk about the wider boundaries of the de Vit family and the money hunters? Yes, they're out there somewhere in packs. Do I feel akin to them? Not at all. I chose a career in the military, and until Rosie became ill, that and Rosie were all I cared about. If I'm honest, there are a couple of relatives I wouldn't turn a garden hose on if they were on fire, and I do have a cousin who is currently doing time for grievous bodily harm. I'm surprised Cynthia didn't tell you that, too."

Before Regan had any opportunity to clear the air about Cynthia Tennerson, Claire was off again.

"Simon did owe me money. He was in arrears with his rent. The utility companies were also hounding him for payment and threatening to turn off everything possible if he didn't pay up. Yes, I wiped his debts, including the utility bills. I took over the payment of those. Why did I do this? Because Simon was my friend, and I am a stinking rich de Vit. I wish he was still living there now, totally free of charge. I told Simon I never wanted to see a penny of what he owed. I just wanted him to find his feet and sort himself out. There was never going to be a huge bill I'd eventually call in…and Simon understood that. The question is, do you?"

"Yes, I do." Regan's reply was quiet. She was ashamed.

Claire studied her, and Regan wondered if she sensed that too. She hoped so. When Claire spoke again, this time she seemed gentler.

"There are things in life more important, Regan, than soaking someone for money when they're down and haven't got it." She paused. "Don't you think I wouldn't give everything I own if it would bring Rosie back? Money or love? It's a no-brainer." Claire put a hand to her forehead and frowned. Regan suspected her headache was worse.

"As for what I did to Sally's sister? Yes, I'm guilty, and I have no excuse." Her eyes narrowed in pain. "Maybe one day, you'll let me tell you about that, but…" She flinched. "Right now, I'd rather leave it."

Regan reached out and gently touched her shoulder.

"Thanks for telling me this, Claire. You're right. I should have trusted you. I got everything wrong, and I'm sorry. But right now, you need to go home and rest. You shouldn't be here."

"Have I answered all your questions? Are we done talking?"

Claire's eyes were closed. It was clear she was in pain and uncomfortable. Regan couldn't help herself as she touched the side of her face. A voice inside her told her she was doing the wrong thing, that it was the wrong time, and that she had no right. But still she did it. She half expected a hand to swipe her touch away, but it never came. Instead Claire opened her eyes and stared blankly at her.

Regan sighed.

"I've no more questions, Claire. At least none of the awful ones from the potting shed." She gave a feeble smile. "As for being done talking, I hope not. I couldn't stand it if we didn't talk again. I want to make amends if you'll let me."

Claire didn't answer. She stepped back.

"You're right. I need to go home. I'm sorry about this." She waved a hand around her face. "I'm not firing on all cylinders." As she began to walk away across the lawns toward her vehicle, she turned back. "Just pop the saw down when you can and leave it in the shed. I'll lock it up when I'm next in. Thanks."

Regan watched Claire drive off and prayed it wasn't the end of everything. Claire had left no clues as to how things might continue between them.

She hung around the gardens for a while thinking on the rather cool, formal conversation that had taken place. Words replayed in her mind. *I was growing very fond of you. I didn't want to ruin things… risk spoiling everything.*

Sadness cut into Regan, for those words registered an ending, something now past. And yet, there had been something in Claire's eyes that suggested otherwise. Regan hoped she was right. Time would tell.

She plodded slowly back to her apartment aware that she didn't know what to do next. For the want of something to take her mind off things, she grabbed the chainsaw and returned it to the potting shed.

More than a week passed, and aside from seeing each other occasionally, and waving cordially, they didn't talk. Not because either of them wanted to avoid the other, but the comfort of an opportunity, an excuse, didn't present itself. Regan suspected they were both lost at how to reconnect.

So on a cold morning, when the summer sun didn't want to put in an appearance, Regan felt a bounce in her step when she was presented with a reason to seek Claire out. She waited until she saw Claire moving around at the shed and headed down there.

"I saw you from the kitchen window. Hope you don't mind company?" Regan hid her nervousness in a light, upbeat tone as she put her head around the shed door. She was rewarded with a faint smile. On the way down, Regan had worried she wouldn't be welcome, but she didn't sense that here. Maybe her suspicions were right, that they both wanted to "join the dots" again, but weren't too sure how.

She continued to build on her casual, easy manner as she sauntered over to the bench where all the little pots were. The seedlings were growing.

"How are you all?" she said, leaning into them and talking in a nurturing voice as if to children. "I've missed you, but hey, you're growing strong." She glanced up. Claire now stood at the other end of the bench.

"It looks like they've survived my care."

Claire's smile grew. Regan's nervousness receded.

"Not a single one has died. In fact, I think they've thrived in my absence. They've clearly taken to your ministering." Claire sounded friendlier than the last time they'd spoken.

"Did you get the saw?" Regan asked, even though she could see it in the corner by the metal lockup.

"I did. Thank you."

"You look better."

"I am. Thanks."

"Weather's turned chilly," Regan added.

"Yes, but it's only a blip. They say warmer weather will be back by the end of the week."

"Hope so. I hate the cold, and it's too early for autumnal days." Regan's nervousness seeped back. She was running out of things to say, and where once they'd never struggled for conversation, that comfortable flow of words wasn't present.

"Headache better?" Regan said.

"All gone," Claire answered.

Regan's conversation bank was exhausted, and in its absence she looked at Claire, smiled like an idiot, and shrugged. She was beginning to question why she was here. She wanted to ask a favor but wasn't sure its request would be well received.

"How's the job search going?" Claire asked.

"I've got an interview the beginning of next week, up in Exeter. And another university has asked me for more detail."

Claire seemed genuinely pleased. "Good. Looks like it's all coming together."

"Yeah, looks like it's all coming together," Regan repeated like a parrot. She grimaced, making a face. This wasn't easy.

"You haven't—"

"I wanted to—"

They simultaneously spoke.

"You first," Regan said politely.

"No, you."

Regan waved her hands in front of her in a vague gesture of defeat. "It's been a week, and I wanted to come down and see how you are." She released a large sigh. "And I wanted to ask a huge favor."

"A favor?"

"The date for the inquest is through. It's this Friday. I'm told I don't have to go, but I think I want to. It'll help me find closure. The only trouble is…" She stared at Claire and sighed again.

"You don't want to go alone," Claire said.

"No. I don't." Regan leaned against the bench, wanting its support. Her legs felt heavy, her earlier bounce gone. "I wondered if—"

"—I'd go with you?"

Thank God, Claire understood.

"Yeah. I've no right to ask, but I'm not sure I can do this by myself, and I thought, given your close friendship with Simon, you might want to—"

"Yes."

"What?"

"Yes, I'll come with you," Claire said.

Relief flooded Regan. "Oh, you've no idea how grateful I am. I'd do it by myself, but I don't want to, and the only person I want there with me is you. *Thank* you, Claire." Her gratitude oozed. "And I think Simon would want you there as well. We're the only two people who knew and cared for him. It seems right."

"Of course, I'll come. Just let me have the details."

"Sure. I'll drive," Regan added.

Claire shook her head, and for a minute, Regan expected her to say that she'd meet her at the inquest. She was wrong.

"I'll drive us there, Regan. You don't know what state you'll be in when it's over. I know it's only a formal procedure to record the verdict, but these things can be upsetting."

Regan wanted to decline the offer, but common sense told her Claire was right. She agreed.

Time stretched and conversation died. Regan recognized that she'd achieved her aims. She'd broken the proverbial ice and introduced a slow thaw, and she'd managed to get Claire to go with her to the inquest. It was time to leave while she was ahead.

"Well, I can see you're busy catching up. I'd better leave you to it."

"Gardens don't stop even when you do," Claire answered.

"I'll ring and let you have the details for the inquest."

As Regan turned to leave, she said, "You will answer this time, eh?" She smiled at Claire and was pleased to see a smile returned.

"I will."

"And I'll see you little guys later," Regan spoke to the plants as she left.

❖

Claire stared around the room as she listened to the coroner conducting his inquiries. If anyone had asked her later what exactly was said, she couldn't have answered. Her mind was elsewhere. She was conflicted. Regan was seated next to her. She was quiet and subdued, and every now and then, she would take a tissue and wipe her eyes, before returning it to a sleeve where it was tucked away.

Not so long ago, Claire would have had no hesitation in wrapping an arm around her to offer support. But something inside her remained tight, and she couldn't. Twice, Regan had turned on her like an uncontrollable dog, and Claire was loath to give her any opportunity to do that again. In fairness, Regan had apologized and Claire did not doubt her sincerity. Nevertheless, she didn't want to put herself in the way of harm again. She'd suffered much this second time around and wasn't keen to go through it again.

Claire's dogged resistance didn't hide the fact that she remained attracted to her. Several times, as Regan moved, Claire caught a whiff of her familiar perfume. It intoxicated her. No matter which road she took, Claire was torn.

Distracted from the room's proceedings, Claire's thoughts continued to ramble. What sort of relationship was she prepared to have with Regan? They were going to be in close proximity as Regan was making her intentions clear. She wanted to remain in the apartment and might also consider buying the property later on. How would Claire cope with that arrangement? Could she handle distancing herself and cutting off her own emotional reemergence?

Claire let out an involuntary sigh that drew Regan's attention. Regan smiled at her with such warmth, clearly thinking she was upset over Simon. Claire was happy to let her think that; it was easier. She certainly wasn't going to admit that she was summing up her options of friendship like a numerical equation.

She crossed her arms, angry with herself for being indecisive. If only she wasn't so tired, but she wasn't sleeping. Part of that had to do with the accident. Only now as the swelling reduced could she get comfortable. Another reason for her insomnia was her doing. She could not stop thinking. Her brain fired up into hyperactivity at night, and she couldn't switch it off. All she could think about was Regan.

She spent hours and hours weighing up the pros and cons of what type of relationship they should have. She had choices. It could be a business one, that of a renter to a tenant. It could be friendship. It could be something more. Claire wasn't stupid. For all her distancing, she was still drawn to Regan. If ever that option was to take seed, then how did Regan feel about Rosie's presence? It wasn't a usual scenario for romancing. Eventually, as the analytical area of her brain tired, carnal desire inevitably crept in. That kept her awake, too. Claire *wanted* to trust Regan again, but was afraid.

She felt a nudge, and it brought her back to reality.

Regan was leaning in close, her voice low. "Thank God, that's over."

Claire felt gentle breath on her skin, but before she could analyze its effect on her, Regan was standing and straightening her jacket.

The inquest was over and Claire had daydreamed her way through it to the point of total ignorance. She didn't even know what the verdict was. She was just thinking how to cover up this heinous omission when Regan provided the missing information.

"I suppose a verdict of suicide is inevitable given the findings."

"Are you happy with that?" Claire asked.

"It's the truth. I'm just glad this is all over. It feels like a weight's been lifted from my shoulders."

Claire thought she did look *lighter*. Regan was standing erect, stretching and pushing her shoulders back with military guard precision. In Claire's eyes, she was radiant, with her black hair shining and her face relaxed as she smiled.

Regan turned and stared at her with intensity.

"Thanks for coming with me, Claire. I expect you didn't really want to come."

Claire was about to feign that she'd never thought otherwise, but there was an expression on Regan's face. It told Claire that she understood, that her decision to join her was costly, and possibly against her better judgment. Regan was no idiot—not all the time, anyway. She knew they were both struggling to find their footing with each other.

An interruption occurred as several people came over to Regan. They were all speaking sympathetic words and shaking her hand. Claire waited patiently. When they left, Regan turned to her.

"Let's get out of here."

They walked out of the inquest and into welcome fresh air. Both ran across the busy road to where the Jeep was parked.

Regan noticed the spring in her step as she hopped onto the sidewalk the other side of the road. That energy hadn't been there this morning. She'd felt heavy as she'd risen and prepared for the day. But now she was invigorated. It had been a long time since she'd felt like this, long before Simon had taken his life.

"Funny ol' thing," she said, as they closed the vehicle doors in unison.

"What?" Claire delayed starting the engine.

"This seems to be turning into a day of new starts...new beginnings. Before we left this morning, I got a phone call from the realtor who's selling my house. There's a couple who keep going back to look at it. It seems they want to buy it and have put in an offer."

"That's great," Claire said. "A good one?"

"Not bad. I've accepted in principle and instructed the solicitor to start the ball rolling."

"I'm really happy for you."

Claire's generous response lifted Regan's already happy disposition. "Even better," she continued, "it seems they want to complete as soon as possible. It could be sold within a few months."

Claire swiveled toward her, her face warmhearted and open. Regan could have almost thought that nothing bad had ever passed between them.

"All I've got to do now is get a job, Claire. I hope I don't blow the interview."

"You won't disappoint them."

There was affection and warmth in Claire's soft words, and Regan fought to not misread their kindness. At any other time, she might have turned the moment to intimate advantage, and she battled a desire to slide across and get closer. She didn't move. She knew Claire was holding back, and Regan respected that. The day was going well, and she wasn't going to ruin it by doing something stupid. She forced her thoughts to other things.

"Thanks again, Claire, for letting me stay in the apartment. It means a lot."

"I know it does, and I meant what I said. If at some later stage you want to purchase the place, you can, but I don't think you should rush it. Get used to living there and see how you settle in. See if it really is what you want. It's not going anywhere...and I don't plan to evict you." They laughed.

Claire jangled the car keys and started the engine.

Regan wasn't looking forward to Claire dropping her off at the apartment. She would disappear, and Regan would then have to wait until the next golden opportunity presented itself to be with her. She didn't want to lose Claire today. Not yet.

"I don't know about you," Regan said, "but I could do with a drink and something to eat. Will you let me buy you lunch?"

She half expected Claire to turn her down, or at least come up with some excuse, but the idea seemed to please.

"That sounds good to me. Let's go find somewhere."

Regan couldn't hide her elation. She wondered if Claire saw.

❖

They ended up at a pub along the coast road that looked out over high cliffs down onto the ocean. It was rumored the place had once been the rendezvous point for smugglers centuries earlier, although no one had ever come up with real evidence to support that. Nowadays, it was much used by tourists during the summer and ramblers all year round.

It was a shabby building that needed a good lick of paint, but the food was above average. If you didn't mind the smell of dirty boots or clumps of mud on the old, original flagstones, then it was a decent place to stop for refreshments.

Claire was grateful the place wasn't as crowded as it usually was as they ordered lunch. Normally, there was at least one coach load of people here.

She watched as Regan bought a couple of cool lagers, joking about something with the barman. He was all smiles and male virility charm, clearly locking on to the fact that she was a woman not wearing a ring and game for the chase. Claire suffered a ping of jealousy, resenting that anyone might dare chat Regan up. That reaction surprised her. It was something she'd have to think about when she got home.

They sat outside at a wooden picnic table and waited for lunch to arrive. The sunshine was warm, and they both relaxed. Claire's earlier thoughts at the inquest resurfaced, and with them, something she wanted to know. It was suddenly important to her decision-making processes. Regan's answer would help her decide what type of relationship she wanted with her.

"Mind if I ask you a question?" Claire said.

"Sure." Regan smiled.

"Cynthia."

Regan's smile disappeared, and she reached for her drink. When she placed it down, she moved the glass around in tiny circles before looking at Claire. Claire sensed her discomfort.

"That day you saw the two of us together outside the apartments, you should have stuck around, Claire. I challenged Cynthia on what she'd told me about you. I told her I'd discovered it was all lies. She didn't like it."

"She wouldn't," Claire said.

"She told me I was a fool to cross her. I'm guessing I might find out why later on."

Claire listened to Regan's half laugh. Cynthia was treacherous, but she wouldn't cross Regan. Regan now knew too much about her. Cynthia was still a bully, but she was more a coward. She wouldn't want to jeopardize anything. Claire didn't think Regan had anything to worry about.

"I take it you aren't chummy anymore," Claire said.

Regan's eyes widened in shock. "We were *never* chummy. She was simply a conduit that I stupidly believed was giving me information I sought regarding the de Vits. I ended up being fed more than I needed...and complete lies. Thank God someone opened my eyes to what a nasty piece of work Cynthia Tennerson is. I only wish I'd been more astute and less the idiot, and that I'd discovered it before I ruined things between you and me. I should have known she was lying without having to be told. I should have trusted *you*."

Claire saw regret on Regan's face.

"Can I ask who your source was?" Claire asked.

"Sally."

Claire burst into laughter. She could just picture Sally being given the opportunity to vent about the great Councilor Tennerson. She'd be puffing and snorting, stabbing at the air. Sally was no fan.

"What am I missing?" Regan asked.

"Sally loathes her."

Regan's confusion gave way to understanding. "Ah, then I haven't missed anything. I've got that. I imagine you're not too keen on her either."

Claire shrugged and said nothing.

The subdued response puzzled Regan. "Doesn't Cynthia's behavior rattle you?"

"I'd be a liar if I said it didn't," Claire said. "She's an immoveable force, a bit like bad weather. She reminds me of a tornado. You can never predict where she's going to strike, only that wherever she does, she'll do damage."

"She must have upset a lot of people. It surprises me she hasn't been thrown off the council. Couldn't you do that? You must have influence?"

Disgust filled Claire, and she looked sharply at Regan. "I don't have that sort of influence, and would I lower myself to her level? Never." She shook her head. "No, I'm patient. She has upset a lot of people. Somewhere along the line, she'll tie her own noose. Though I admit I'd be happy to supply the rope."

"How can you be so calm? She's dangerous and manipulative. You should be livid...incensed, riled up." Regan was shaking her hands in the air. "After everything she's said about you."

Claire smiled. There was something rather nice about having Regan on her side. It was a change. Maybe they were bonding again. She was glad she'd decided to do lunch. She almost hadn't. "Well, maybe tomorrow, after I've had a good night's sleep, I'll be incensed and riled up. But right now, I'm hungry."

The look on Regan's face was a picture. She didn't understand Claire's philosophical, laid-back view. A small voice whispered inside Claire that the option of a purely business relationship with Regan was looking distant.

"You're not natural." Regan's banter was friendly.

"I never said I was," Claire teased back.

Their lunch arrived.

When nothing but crumbs remained on their plates, Claire suggested they take a walk up to the lighthouse on the hill. It was on the other side of the road and about half a mile up a gentle gradient.

"I expect you'd also like to know why Karen turned up?" Regan said as they crossed the road. She hadn't had an opportunity to tell Claire.

"Only if you want to."

Claire's casual response didn't fool Regan. She heard the disguised interest. She wondered what Claire thought of Karen's almost intense need to see her, a need strong enough to make her drive all the way south.

"She came to tell me she was willing to leave the school so I could go back if I wanted. She surprised me, Claire. It's a generous offer. But I told her I no longer want to teach at secondary level and that I'm looking at a career change. I also told her I'm staying here."

"How did she take that?" Claire was guarded. Regan found it difficult to read her.

"She understands. I've told her to stay on at the school and not mess with her chances of being the next head." Regan paused. "I expect you wondered if she was here to ask me to go back to her."

Claire stopped walking and looked at her. "I wasn't sure. I *was* sure that you weren't interested in that. You told me that, and I trust you."

Claire's response had a dual effect on Regan. It implied she trusted her. But Regan hadn't trusted Claire. Her guilt rose again. But there was also something in what Claire said, *I trust you.* Present tense. It was a strange thing for someone to say who no longer had any interest in someone, unless…

Regan didn't push it. Small steps.

"Karen also wanted to tell me how sorry she was about Simon."

"She's gone then?"

"Gone, Claire. I'm glad but I'm also pleased we've parted on better terms. It closes everything."

Claire nodded.

They neared a building that was once the lighthouse. It no longer was. It was now a bijou residence with several expensive cars outside. The place smelled of money.

Regan studied it. The deluxe property didn't appeal to her, and she was saddened that the original charm of the building was lost. Sticking a rectangular, single-story building onto the side of the tall conical shape hadn't helped. Neither had the several gaudy modern statues in what attempted to be a garden. The building was reduced to a garish, loud blob on the crest of a hill.

"Why do people do this?" Regan said. "They have to spoil things, don't they?" It wasn't really a question, but she saw that Claire agreed.

"I guess the building is no longer fit for purpose, and it's been an easy way the local authorities can rid themselves of its responsibility," Claire said.

"If only the planners had been more sympathetic," Regan said. "Can you imagine how rough it must be *living* here in the winter?"

"Not for me."

"Nor me," Regan said.

They walked beyond the lighthouse to a point where there was a good view of the bay. For a while, they stood in amiable silence and enjoyed the scene.

"I'm glad we did this," Claire said.

"Me, too."

They looked at each other, and Regan felt something good pass between them, like an acknowledgement that they might be able to move forward. It filled her with hope. Maybe she could be forgiven. She'd learned much of late, most of it about herself, and her shameful behavior. But why learn lessons if you can't use them later? She wanted another chance with Claire. If it came, this time she wouldn't ruin it.

They started to walk back.

"Mind if I ask you a question?" Regan asked. She wanted to test if a level of trust was back.

"Go ahead."

"The other day, when we were talking, you mentioned what happened to Sally's sister. You said you'd maybe tell me about that one day. If it's none of my business, Claire, just say. I won't be offended. But Sally told me what happened. She told me about Cynthia's part in it too, something Cynthia didn't tell me."

"She wouldn't."

"Sally's very fond of you, you know?"

Claire came to a slow halt, her manner pensive. "Thank God for Sally. I won the lottery the day I found her. Rosie took to her straightaway." She paused. "You'd like to know what happened."

"You don't strike me as the bullying type, and I can't imagine you were ever a friend of Cynthia's."

"I was young and foolish. The stupid things we do at that age. You never think of consequences, but my actions helped push Lizzie over the edge.

"I've no excuse, Regan. Nobody made me do what I did. I was born with a brain and knew right from wrong. I was a clever student who did well in scholarly things, but socially, at school, I never felt I belonged. It was probably because of the silver spoon stuck in my mouth." Claire gave a halfhearted laugh.

"It's one of the reasons Dad sent me to the local school. He wanted me to be around folk who didn't have unlimited financial resources and who worked hard to make their living. He said it would be good for me. Since the school had a good reputation and was top in the exam league, it suited.

"Like any youngster at a new school, I wanted to fit in. I let a small group of girls lure me into their circle. Suddenly, I was socially accepted and felt part of the *in crowd*. For a while, I let go of my own common sense and moral compass. I should have known better. I learned how wrong I was at cost."

"Sally said Cynthia was the ringleader," Regan said.

"She was, but no one can make you follow if you don't want to. I did something heinous and very wrong. Along with that crowd, I harassed Lizzie. We called her names, laughed at her, and made her the butt of cruel jokes. She couldn't take it. The day she died, I wanted the earth to swallow me up. I caused her so much misery. If only I'd been nice to her. She was actually a sweet kid, just horribly shy and uncoordinated. I've regretted it ever since."

"Your dad took you away from the school?" Regan recalled what Cynthia had said.

"He did not!" Claire looked aghast. "He made me stay there for another term and suffer the consequences. I was treated like a leper, and quite right. Dad made me do penance."

Regan found Claire's youthful behavior incongruous. She'd never been a bully, or been their target. She guessed she was lucky. It wasn't Regan's place to apportion blame. If Sally forgave her, that was good enough.

They resumed walking, this time their bodies closer, their arms occasionally touching. Regan longed to link arms, but it was still too soon.

"How long has Rosie been ill?" Regan's question met with no resistance. It seemed a level of trust was back.

"It's difficult to say when it first started. So many early symptoms went undetected. Both Rosie and I thought things were manifestations of stress. Rosie even thought it was iron deficiency." Claire gave a hollow laugh. "We tried eating healing foods, trying to counter some mysterious unbalance. Of course, neither of us wanted to face the inevitable. We were always looking for rational excuses." Claire looked across at Regan. "She's fifty-two, you know."

Regan balked. Even now, ravaged by illness, Rosie didn't look her age.

Claire continued. "She was always very fit and full of energy. I used to tell her she had Peter Pan genes in her somewhere." Claire fixed her gaze on a container vessel far out at sea.

"At the beginning, we really did think that work stress was the cause of the problems. Rosie was a lecturer in contemporary and future defense security at King's College London. Later, King's and the military ended up in an academic partnership. Quite a few of the King's lecturers started teaching at the Joint Services Military College in Wiltshire."

"Is that where the two of you met?"

"Yes. I was an officer in the navy and on a lengthy staff course there. Rosie was my tutor, and we clashed like hell at the start. She was older and thought I was a snotty young know-it-all." Claire smiled. "Well, I was pretty bright. We knocked heads a few times, but eventually my abundant wit and charm ground her down. Romance grew. When I finished the course, we were an item.

"By the time we knew it was Alzheimer's, Rosie could no longer teach. I got a compassionate posting so I could be at home with her. That worked for a while, but then things got worse. She'd drive off without paying for car fuel, or walk out of a store with unpaid goods. Sometimes, she'd just disappear. I can't tell you how many times I've had to call the police to report her missing. She became paranoid, no longer really knowing who I was, only that I was stealing from her and was out to hurt her. Sometimes she was quite violent. I couldn't cope.

"I found her a good care home, but she hated it…and I hated it. She deserves better than that. I left the navy and brought her down here where I can look after her."

Claire stopped talking, and it seemed as if the memories threatened to overcome her. Regan reached out and touched her arm gently.

"Are you all right?" She watched as Claire struggled. "We don't have to talk about this. I don't mean to hurt you."

Claire lifted her head as if she'd sorted whatever demon was present. "It's okay. I'd like to tell you, if you don't mind listening."

Regan nodded, and they resumed their stroll.

"Why does she hate you so much? Is it the disease?" Regan couldn't understand how two people so in love could have such hatred come between them.

"Yes, in part," Claire answered. "When Rosie knew what was happening to her, she begged me to leave her. She said she didn't want me to see her disintegrate. She started to push me away. Of course, I ignored it. But I suppose somewhere, her desire to see me live my life and her continual pushing me away…it's morphed into some dark obsession. As the disease has grown, it's warped her mind. That hatred, born out of love and of best intentions, has taken over."

"You must miss her terribly."

Claire looked at her. Her face hid nothing. Every miserable emotion she'd gone through in the last few years was written there.

"At first, losing her was awful. Every advancing stage was torture. But she's been gone for so long now, time dulls."

Claire reached out to hold Regan's arm. She swung it in a friendly shake.

"Do you know, Regan, I used to feel so guilty because I stopped feeling the pain. I still feel guilty. It's receding, but every now and then I catch myself thinking that when I'm happy, I shouldn't be. Silly, isn't it? There's nothing I can do.

"I think I've stood on the edge of madness, but I've walked back from it. I've learned to accept that the woman I loved simply doesn't exist anymore. That helps. It's what Rosie was trying to tell me. She didn't want me to be a prisoner to a ghost. It's taken time, but I understand now. Although understanding and acting on it isn't always easy."

"What will you do now Rosie doesn't know you anymore?"

Claire spoke with fervor. "But I know her, and while there's breath in my body, I will continue to look after her. I'll see her needs are met, and with dignity. I know she'd have done the same for me."

Regan understood. She more than understood. She was proud of Claire. Everything about her made sense now, as did Sally's comment of walking over hot coals for her. Regan had been a fool.

They walked again, back over the road and past the pub, toward the car park.

"Thanks for sharing this," Regan said. "I feel I know you better. I've wanted to."

"Really?" Claire feigned mock surprise. "We haven't done very well so far, have we?"

"No, but that's my fault. Just try to dig deep and forgive me. That's all I ask."

Claire said nothing.

When they returned to the apartments, Alice Gordon, a young woman in her early thirties, and an architect, spotted them. She waved her hands animatedly around her head to get their attention before bouncing over to the car and talking to Claire even before she had time to get out. The look of relief on her face was evident.

"Oh, thanks the stars. I thought I'd not see you before I went." Her Scottish lilt filled the air.

"Claire, I've a problem. BMW are coming to collect my car tomorrow for a service. I was going to work from home and hand them the keys. But now the office has called and I've to go to London tonight. I don't want to cancel the service. There're a few problems with the car that need sorting. Would you be able to give them the keys tomorrow morning, and then get them back on return?"

Regan hung around the back of the Jeep trying hard not to listen in, but it was difficult not to. She grinned. This was one of the reasons Claire had cited when asked why no one knew she was a de Vit and owner of the property. She could see what Claire meant, and more, how much it meant to people here to be able to turn to *the gardener*.

"I can do that, Alice. No problem."

"Brilliant. You're magic. I'll pop back in and go get the keys."

"Do you want a lift to the train station?" Claire asked.

"No, I've ordered a taxi, but thanks. You're the best."

Alice ran into the building.

Regan nodded to Claire. "I get it. The gardener can do things a de Vit can't."

Claire didn't look vindicated. "A mild deception, yes, but one with many benefits, and for everyone."

Regan awkwardly figured their day together was at an end. She thanked Claire again for her support and was heading for the front door when Claire called out to her.

"I don't suppose you'd like to go to the theater? I've got tickets to a play."

Regan turned back excited. Claire was asking *her* out. "I'd love to. Which one?"

"Can it be a surprise?"

It could have been a trip to see a biologist dissecting a rat's innards. Regan would have said yes. She couldn't believe that Claire was inviting her anywhere. She wasn't going to have to wait or plan another "golden" opportunity.

"Yeah, okay."

"Great. We'll talk later then."

"Later then." Regan sounded like an awkward teenager invited out on a first date. She was just struggling with what to do or say next when Alice came to her rescue. She was running back out of the building, waving a key fob at Claire.

"I'll leave you to it," Regan said, making her exit with as much dignity as she could. When she entered the building and glanced back over her shoulder, Claire was watching her, smiling.

Regan couldn't help but whistle a tune as she ran up the stairs two at a time.

CHAPTER NINETEEN

Regan found it difficult not seeing Claire as much as she'd like, but she didn't want to push things. She thought it best to let Claire migrate to her and in her own time. Besides, she had the theater trip to look forward to.

It wasn't as if she was standing idle. She still had a small secondary job writing mathematics questions for an examination board. It kept her brain occupied, and she was grateful right now for the money it brought in. She also spent some time with Sally, and occasionally sitting and trying to engage Rosie in conversation. It was getting less and less productive, and Rosie seemed to be increasingly uncommunicative and in a world of her own.

When Regan's proverbial hands drew idle, she thought only of Claire and of how much she missed her.

Several times, she saw her in the grounds, and always very early. One morning, Regan rushed out with the intention of inviting her up for a coffee. She'd assumed she was on her way to the potting shed. Instead she saw Claire drive off. Regan thought it odd. Why drive off when you've only just arrived to start the working day?

Her opportunity to get together with Claire came later.

It was while she was studying a road atlas and working out the best route to get to one of her interviews that her attention was drawn to a place called Fidget Bottom Arboretum.

The bizarre name grabbed her attention.

She researched it on the Internet. The more she learned, the more a plan built in her head. She'd pick a good day and then, if her own personal allure didn't draw Claire like a magnet, maybe the delights of the place would. It boasted several miles of paths leading through over 3000 species of trees and shrubs. There were also over 300 types of wild flowers. That would do the trick. No self-respecting gardener could turn that down. Sometimes Regan admired her guile and sheer cunning.

So one early morning, again when she saw Claire out on the lawn, Regan ran outside. This time she caught up with her. Regan suggested the outing for the next day but was thrilled when Claire proposed they go today.

"The weather's great. Why wait?" Claire said.

Regan wasn't sure if her magnetism had pulled, or if it was the mention of the trees and shrubs. Either way, she was going to spend time with Claire. Her plan had worked.

The arboretum proved worthy of the entry cost. It covered a lot of ground, and they spent their time strolling and chatting their way around the many footpaths. They didn't rush and followed the recommended route that was on the small map they'd been handed.

They discovered the delights of three small lakes. They were remarkably called Top Pool, Middle Pool, and Bottom Pool. They found a big square farmyard full of every different type of poultry possible. It was called The Hen Square. Later, the map took them through a delightful spot full of different varieties of fern, called The Fernery.

"Whoever's named these places, their imagination knows no bounds," Regan stated dryly.

Claire was laughing, and yet she wasn't.

It was beginning to worry Regan. All day, Claire wasn't her usual self. She was subdued. Throughout their conversations, and there were many, Regan sensed a subtle detachment between them. At first, she thought Claire's reserved demeanor was a safety thing, and that she was still keeping her distance. But as the day moved on, Regan felt it was something more.

Just before they'd left the apartments that morning, Regan had been speaking to Sally, and she'd said something strange.

"Be nice to Claire today."

At the time, she thought it was another of Sally's therapeutic chunks of advice, counseling her to not bugger the delicate road to recovery that she and Claire traversed. But now she wasn't sure.

Claire was tired. There were dark rims under her eyes that weren't there a few days ago, and her usual energetic self wasn't present either.

They came to an area called Poplar Dingle. It was a gentle place full of majestic trees that surrounded an area where people could picnic. Despite the beautiful weather, they were there alone. Regan chanced an opportunity.

"Let's sit for a while and listen to the breeze in the trees," she said. She wandered over to a set of wooden seats and sat down. Claire followed.

Regan wasted no time.

"What's wrong?" she asked.

"Wrong?"

"You're not here. It's as if your mind is someplace else."

She watched as Claire started to bluff her way out of the question but then changed her mind mid thought. Her shoulders dropped, and when she looked again at Regan, she appeared exhausted.

"I'm sorry. I know I'm quiet. I don't mean to be. It isn't you." Claire didn't even have the energy for much voice. And though Regan was glad of the qualification, it didn't remove her concerns. She thought again of Sally's words that morning.

"Something's happened. Rosie?"

Claire eye's widened. She nodded.

"Sally says you've been spending time with Rosie…chatting to her," Claire said. "It's good that you've done that. Anything that keeps her engaged mentally. You've been very kind, but you won't have to do it any longer."

"What's happened?" she asked again.

"I didn't think this would hurt so much," Claire answered flatly. "I've known this was coming…Sally's always warning me it would. But you're never ready."

Claire sounded calm and controlled, but Regan wasn't fooled. She watched as Claire kept rolling the fingers of her left hand into her palm. She was upset.

"Rosie hasn't been too well the last few days. We've had the doctor out a couple of times. She's had a temperature, won't eat, and has been having terrible nightmares. I've been helping Sally and sitting with Rosie."

The statement soaked into Regan's mind. The last time she'd sat with Rosie was about five days ago. Rosie had been quiet, but apparently fine. What brought a frown to Regan's face was imagining Claire *sitting* with Rosie. That scenario was warped. Rosie didn't normally allow Claire anywhere near her. A chill ran through her. Was Rosie *that* ill? Was Rosie dying?

"Is she very ill?" Regan was afraid to hear the answer.

Claire pinched the bridge of her nose.

"She's had a urinary infection. The doctor's got her on antibiotics and she's getting better now. I've been staying at her side all night. Just before I saw you this morning, Sally managed to get her to eat. It's a good sign."

Regan realized why she kept seeing Claire so early in the mornings and then leaving. She had sat with Rosie several nights. It explained why Claire was drained.

"You must be shattered," Regan said.

"I'm fine. Don't worry." Claire smiled at her.

"You've been able to sit with her then?" Regan said. Not everything had yet been said, and Claire seemed to recognize that Regan knew that.

"Sally warned me this would happen."

"What?"

"She doesn't know who I am anymore."

"Didn't she stop knowing who you are a long time ago?" Regan thought of the fear Rosie had of Claire.

Claire gave a half smile. "Yes, but at least she knew enough to hate me. I'm not even that anymore. There's no recognition. Nothing. It feels like the final cut." There was a moment's hesitation before Claire said, "It's why I can finally sit with her. You won't have to now."

"Oh, Claire." Regan placed a hand on hers. "I'm sorry." She hated this disease. To say it was cruel was an understatement. "Perhaps the infection...this will be a temporary lapse." She looked into Claire's eyes. "She might hate you again in a few days." Her attempt at humor found its mark and earned a light laugh from Claire.

"You say all the right things." Claire smiled at her, her eyes full of thanks. "Maybe you're right, Regan, but...it's the beginning. It's the beginning of the end. Poor Rosie."

Claire turned her face away for a second, and when she glanced back, Regan saw tears rolling down her cheeks.

Regan couldn't help herself. She wrapped Claire in her arms and held her tight. It was the most natural thing to do. And Claire let her do it. Regan bent and kissed the top of Claire's head, smelling the scent of her shampoo. She wanted to protect her. She wanted to give her back life and all of its joys. How absurd it was that not so long ago, she'd tried to despise her. But life was full of ebbs and flows. Regan was thankful she'd sorted the right from wrong.

She wanted Claire in her life. She didn't know if Claire wanted her, or if she might not be *able* to want her, not while Rosie was still alive. She sensed Claire's guilt. Regan only knew she didn't want to lose her. She was willing to accept her presence in whatever capacity was offered. If that was only friendship, so be it.

Claire stood as if she were embarrassed. She wiped her eyes roughly with the back of a sleeve. Regan sensed she didn't want to talk about Rosie anymore, so she said nothing. Claire was coming to terms with what had happened.

As they walked back toward the visitor center car park, Claire allowed Regan to place an arm around her shoulder. Its support and warmth felt good, and she leaned into Regan's body and found comfort there.

For a while, Claire didn't even think. They walked in silence, and she allowed the rhythm of their pace to comfort her. When she did think, she thought of Regan's kindness, both to Rosie *and her.* It couldn't be much fun being with someone like her today. She hoped she hadn't ruined Regan's adventure, but suspected she had, although Regan wasn't giving anything away.

Before they turned the final corner that led to the center, Claire apologized.

"I'm sorry. I've spoilt your day."

Regan stopped, dropped her arm from Claire's shoulder, and stared at her with incredulity.

"You haven't," Regan said with vigor before wrapping her arm back around her. "You're here...with me."

Nothing else was said as they finished their walk, but Claire thought much. She was discovering something. She doubted her relationship would Regan would be one based purely on friendship. Something inside her was shifting, and an answer was growing plain.

Chapter Twenty

It was late, but Claire didn't want to go home.

The way the diffused lamplight fell on Rosie's face, she seemed almost well again. The usual pale pallor that rested on her features wasn't visible.

Claire watched the rise and fall of her breath as she sat by her bedside.

She knew she ought to go home and catch up on sleep, but it had been so long since she'd been able to spend time with Rosie. She didn't want to leave her.

Sally said nothing but understood everything. She would bring Claire a cup of tea every now and then.

Rosie slept. She had been sleeping ever since Claire arrived, over three hours ago. Like a sentinel, Claire used the time to watch over Rosie and to think back on their times together. The memories were many, and they were good.

She reached and took Rosie's hand. She held it to her lips and kissed each finger before laying it back on the bed and holding it in both of hers. She closed her eyes. She felt the softness of Rosie's skin on hers and imagined they were holding hands again, like they used to do. Sleep crept over her, and she dreamed. Her dreams were sweet and Rosie was in them, walking and laughing again.

She moved in her slumbers and jolted awake. She still held Rosie's hand. She glanced up and was surprised to see Rosie looking at her. For a second, she feared Rosie might return to her old state and scream, but she just gazed at her with big blue eyes.

"Hello, Rosie," Claire said gently.

Rosie didn't answer.

"I'm Claire. I'm just sitting with you if that's okay."

Still Rosie said nothing.

"You won't remember me, but you and I go back a long way. We've always been there for each other. I've loved you, and you've loved me. That's just the way of it."

Rosie studied her, but it was like someone looking at something they didn't know or understand. It saddened Claire. All that intellect and sentience, all that love was gone. She felt Rosie's hand move in hers.

"I miss them," Rosie said.

Claire looked up at her and smiled. "What do you miss, Rosie?" She loved hearing her voice again. It had been so long.

"They don't grow here. It's too hot."

Claire waited. Her patience was rewarded.

"I miss them." Rosie frowned, and she looked hard at Claire. "They're my favorites."

"You miss the flowers?" Claire said.

"Do I know you?"

"I'm Claire, Rosie. You know me."

"They're my favorites."

"Which ones, Rosie?" Claire knew the answer. She would always know the answer.

"I miss them. Do I know you?"

"I'm Claire, Rosie. I'm your Claire."

Rosie stopped talking. Claire found herself wiping tears from her face. Five minutes later, Rosie's soft voice broke the stillness in the room.

"Forget-me-nots. Are they my favorites?"

Claire nodded. "Yes, they are, Rosie. They have always been your favorites."

"I miss them."

Rosie drew quiet, and though she occasionally looked at Claire, Claire knew she didn't see her. But she remained with her by her bedside. She continued to study the face she had once loved and kissed.

Some time later, she took Rosie's hand, brought it to her lips, and kissed it. She thought of Regan.

"I'm going to try to let the guilt go now, my darling. But you know I'll always be here for you...right up to the end."

Claire rose and leaning over, she kissed Rosie on the forehead. "Good night, sweetheart."

Claire left the room and went home.

CHAPTER TWENTY-ONE

"Y ou see? I'm a good driver, too," Regan said in mock defense as she rounded a country lane en route to Torquay and the theater.

"I never said you weren't," Claire answered. Regan loved her husky timbre.

"No, but I can see you're still peeved because I've talked you out of driving us there in your Jeep."

"I'm not peeved at all," Claire said defensively.

"Yes, you are. You're such a *sensitive* gardener," Regan said. "But I'm damned if I'm going to sit in a theater smelling like a compost heap."

Claire yielded, but her eyes danced with humor. Regan laughed.

There was another, unspoken, reason why she didn't want Claire to drive. When Regan returned, Claire told her how she was spending time with Rosie. She no longer stayed the night, and at Sally's insistence, was catching up on her sleep. Though Claire had loosened up and was more relaxed than the time at the arboretum, Regan knew she was still weary. It was emotionally draining coming to terms with the changes in Rosie.

Regan reached a hand across and rested it on Claire's thigh. "I'm only joking." Her tactile move was rewarded, as she noticed the slightest flush of cheeks from Claire. That was the beauty of pale skin; it gave away everything.

"Well, just be careful. I'm *sensitive*," Claire said.

For a while, they fell silent but for the occasional road directions from Claire.

Regan gave life to their next topic of conversation.

"I can't believe how close I came to losing all this."

Her statement confused Claire.

"You bought these tickets as a surprise. Because of my stupidity, we almost didn't make this."

She heard Claire sigh. "You're not going to apologize again, are you? Because I don't think I can stand it."

Claire wore the same practiced patience that Grace sometimes did around George. It tickled Regan.

"As long as you know how sorry I am for my bad behavior. It's important to me that you really understand that."

"Okay, I hear you. Now shut up, and change the disc."

But Regan didn't.

"I'm grateful that we're at least able to do this because it tells me we're fixing things. It's just..." She faltered.

"It's just what?" Claire said.

"It's just that I want to know we can at least be friends, *real* friends. I don't want us to be occasional companions."

Claire didn't answer, and her silence worried Regan.

"I am right, aren't I? We're friends now? You wouldn't be taking me to some mystery theater production in Torquay if we weren't?" It didn't ease Regan's concerns that Claire now looked uncomfortable. And was still quiet.

"This is where you say something, Claire."

"You want to know if we can be friends?" She hesitated a while before answering. "I don't think that's possible."

Regan's heart stopped beating as her hands gripped the steering wheel.

"No?" She felt her eyes sting. She blinked hard.

"No."

Every snatched glance at Claire troubled Regan. Nothing looked positive. She feared her expectations of a wonderful evening were about to be dashed. Maybe she should have kept her mouth shut. She did now as she waited, sensing that Claire had more to say.

"I don't think *friends* is what either of us wants to be, do you?" Claire said.

Regan didn't understand, and she decided on straight talk.

"I only know I don't want to lose you, Claire."

Claire's face remained unreadable, and time dragged painfully. When Claire spoke again, Regan felt her heart flutter in hope.

"I don't think I want to lose you, either." Claire's voice was soft.

Regan fought to keep her attention on the road. "So?" she asked.

"So, why don't we try again? Start things slowly and see how they work out?"

"Define slowly."

"Well, we could start by seeing how this evening goes. Then maybe we could go for dinner one evening—"

"Like on a date?" Regan interrupted.

"Like on a date," Claire confirmed.

Regan's heart regained routine rhythm. Her hands relaxed on the wheel.

"Would you like that?" Claire asked.

"Of course, I would." Regan thought her crazy to even ask.

"Okay then."

"Okay then," Regan repeated.

Claire glanced across at her and smiled. Regan smiled back.

"Phew, that was tense." Regan sighed.

"No, it wasn't. We were just *defining boundaries*."

Regan recalled a previous conversation. She changed the subject.

"So, where exactly are we going?" she asked. "This mystery stuff is killing me. I need to know what direction to go in."

"All in good time, you'll see." Claire said.

❖

Claire laughed.

It had nothing to do with the humorous antics of Madame Arcati, the delightful eccentric medium who threw herself into a psychic trance on stage, eliciting bellowed roars of audience laughter in the packed, cozy theater.

Regan was laughing too, enjoying every moment of Noël Coward's play, *Blithe Spirit*, and oblivious that she was being covertly watched by Claire.

Claire loved looking at her. She was nothing like Rosie. Rosie's face had been full of soft curves and gentleness. With her large, expressive eyes and pale coloring, she'd been a damned attractive woman. Many had called her stunning. How often had Claire sensed the confusion of male colleagues who couldn't believe such beauty existed only for her, and in a lesbian relationship?

Regan's appeal was more androgynous. It was less flattering. Her strong jawline and sharper features lent her a pleasant face that was more handsome than blessed with feminine attractiveness. Yet it was full of its own charm, and it drew Claire to the point of intoxication.

Something hilarious happened on stage, and Claire shifted her attention back. She felt as light as a feather and happier than she had been in a long time. She thought it curious that, of late, every time she set eyes on Regan, her heart would lift, and she wanted to smile. It was Regan who made her happy. She was learning to love everything about her. She loved her swagger, the way she flicked her hair when she was making a point, and the way her northern dialect curled around the words.

I'm in love.

She wished they were alone in the theater. If her wish was granted, she would turn and kiss Regan. But there was no puff of smoke and no fairy granting such desires. Regan was still laughing at her side, unaware of what was going through Claire's mind. Claire mused that she might have to return to see this play again. She was distracted and paying it no attention.

Simon popped into her thoughts. She wondered if he was watching the two of them from up above. He'd always wanted her to meet Regan. Maybe he had secretly hoped they might get on. Was he aware of what was developing between them now? She hoped so.

The play finished. After lengthy and deserved standing ovations, they exited the building, swept up in the throng of theatergoers all avidly talking of the wonderful performance. Regan was one of them.

"I can't believe that was an amateur production."

"They're very good, aren't they?" Claire said.

"Outstanding. We'll do this again."

Claire nudged her to the edge of the sidewalk to allow the mass to pass.

"Let's go somewhere for a drink," Regan suggested.

They linked arms as they searched. The streets were full of people. It was the height of the tourist season and everywhere was packed. The crowds jostled and fought for space. Claire pulled Regan closer in case they became separated in the bustle of movement.

They found a pub. It was crowded and loud, and neither could hear the other talk. They left as soon as they finished their drinks. Outside, it was now dark, and the town was a mass of night lights and street revelers.

As they strolled back to the car, still arm in arm, Claire didn't want the evening to finish. They would have the journey back, but it wasn't the same. She couldn't look into Regan's eyes. She couldn't hook her arm through hers. She deliberately slowed their pace and kept pulling Regan toward shop windows pretending to be interested in what they had to offer.

Regan grew amused. If they moved any slower, they would stop. She wondered if Claire's lack of motivation to get home had anything to do with not wanting their time together to end. If it was, the feeling was mutual.

"This has been such a great evening," Regan said.

"Thank you for coming tonight," Claire answered.

"Thank *you* for asking me."

Claire turned her attention from a shop window and stared into Regan's eyes. Regan realized they were both speaking in whispers. The moment was suddenly intimate.

Claire surprised Regan as she took one of her hands and kissed its palm several times. The touch of her lips sent electric shocks through Regan.

"This has been a wonderful evening," Claire spoke quietly. "I don't want it to end."

The words were wrapped in yearning, and Regan thought she heard their desire, their need for something more. When she looked into Claire's face, she knew she was right. Her eyes burned with intensity and glistened in the streetlight.

Claire pulled her forward along the sidewalk in silence. Regan's heart raced.

They passed a narrow alleyway dimly lit to their side, and without thinking, Regan sidestepped into it and its welcoming shadows.

She pulled Claire toward her, wrapping arms around her small waist. She edged in closer and kissed her. She met with no resistance.

"I can't help myself. I've never felt like this before," Regan said.

"You haven't?"

Regan felt the warmth of her breath, smelled the scent of her body. It was calling her. She wanted more.

"I think I might be in love with you," Regan said.

"You've loved before."

"Not like this, I haven't."

Claire leaned back to look at her, her face full of curiosity. Regan wanted to memorize every subtlety of feature and lock it away in her head forever.

"It's always been passionate and hot, lust driven," Regan said. "That's probably why my relationships never last. You're different. You're in here." Regan took one of Claire's hands and placed it over her heart. "I want to be with you. I think of you all the time. You can set me on your mantelpiece, and I'll be happy. Take me home with you, and let me care for you."

Claire pulled her back in close. The embrace was tight, and it sucked the air from Regan's lungs.

"God, I love you," Claire whispered. "I've been afraid to say anything, in case you didn't feel the same way."

Regan laughed gently into her neck. "Couldn't you tell?"

Claire laughed back. "Ever since that walk at the arboretum, that's when I knew. It was when you said I hadn't spoilt your day because I was there with you."

Claire kissed Regan's throat. It sent tremors through her, and she hugged Claire tight, wanting to crush her so close they might merge into one.

"That was a beautiful thing to say, darling," Claire whispered.

Darling.

Claire called her *darling,* and for a moment, Regan thought her feet left the ground.

They both jumped as a young couple ran into the alleyway, almost colliding with them. There was a look of love in their eyes, and it didn't take much guessing that the young boy and girl considered this a favored spot for a passionate kiss, too. Their surprise was only surpassed by the look of acceptance that someone else was sharing their special place. The lovers looked at one another, laughed, and then ran off.

Regan couldn't hide her own surprise as Claire turned back to her and lifted her arms and placed her hands around her head. She pulled Regan down to her and gave her a series of lingering kisses on her lips.

"That bit you said." Claire spoke between kisses.

"What bit?" Regan was having difficulty breathing. She was aroused.

"Where you said I made you feel different."

"Yeah."

"The bit about past relationships always being passionate and hot, lust driven," Claire said.

"Yeah."

"Does that still apply?" Claire asked.

Regan stepped back, stuttering. "I thought we were taking things slowly."

Claire's eyes were dilated. She was aroused, too.

"This is slowly," she replied. "This is my slowly. I can't answer for yours."

Regan's breathing sounded erratic. Claire's eyes narrowed amorously, and a willful smile formed on her lips.

"Oh, bugger," Regan said.

"Something wrong?"

"Yes, something is wrong."

Claire stared at her, her eyes wide open. Her face was all innocence.

"Don't look at me like fat wouldn't grease a pan," Regan said. "You *know* something is wrong. How the hell am I supposed to drive us home tonight feeling like this?"

"Feeling like what?"

"Feeling like I'm not going to be able to concentrate on my driving because my mind is on other things."

"Really," Claire purred. "And what is your mind on?"

"Making love to you as soon as possible."

"Maybe we should get a room, then."

"Maybe we should."

"We'd better go find one, then."

"We'd better go find one quick," Regan said.

They rushed up to the hotel room with teenage enthusiasm, laughing as Regan struggled to enter the card the correct way into the door device. Once inside, they fell against a wall, still laughing in between the kisses.

Regan went to put the light on, but Claire stopped her. She slowly raised a hand to Regan's face and drew it gently down until her thumb rested on her lips. She parted her lips and kissed her lightly.

There was something about the act that chased their frivolity away. Alone in the room, the solemnity of what they were about to enter into, took over. Regan went quiet. She held Claire's waist in her hands.

They didn't part. They stood there connected, yet not moving.

"You're thinking," Claire said.

Though Regan's eyes were still unaccustomed to the darkness, she sensed the smile on Claire's lips.

"No, I'm not," she answered.

"Yes, you are. I can hear you. You're worried that I can't move on. You're thinking of Rosie."

"I haven't said that."

"No." There was understanding in Claire's voice, no demands.

Regan was lost for words.

Claire continued. "You're wondering if your *investment* in me will be worth it."

Regan *was* thinking of Rosie, and what that might mean—to Claire. "You make me sound like a calculator, someone without heart. I'm not into investment strategies," she whispered back.

"But you're thinking it."

Regan tightened her hold on Claire. "If we're talking strategy, the question might be if this is a short, medium, or long term investment."

"And you favor?" Claire asked.

"It's said that if you lock up assets for the long term, the rewards are likely to be higher, less dangerous."

"You should have gone into finance," Claire whispered ardently. "Just so you know, the answer is yes."

"The question?"

"Yes, I can move on," Claire clarified.

"Rosie's shoes are pretty big to fill."

"They are, but I think you have big feet."

Claire drew closer to Regan, running her fingers through her hair. The sensation set Regan's groin on fire. Claire brought her face up to Regan's so their lips almost touched.

"When the navy took me away from Rosie, I could be in a room full of people, but I was always lonely because she wasn't there. No one filled my heart like her. We had that connection, you see. We were soul mates."

Regan's eyes were adjusting to the dark, and she could now see Claire's face. Love stared back at her as Claire continued.

"It's that bond with another human being, the one that tells you that no matter where you are, how far away you might be, there's another living soul on this planet who feels for you the way you do for them. It lets you know you aren't alone. I feel that way when I'm with you, Regan Canning. I never thought I'd experience that again, but I do…and I have no intention of losing it."

Regan pushed closer into Claire, and their lips met as they wrapped their arms closer around each other. Their kisses became more passionate.

No words were spoken but for the occasional gasp or groan as their needs became more urgent.

"I'll draw the curtains," Regan panted.

"No, leave them." Claire said.

"Someone might see."

"We don't want the lights on. I want to make love to you in the streetlight. I want to imagine I'm still in that alleyway with you."

"Jeez," Regan grunted. "Have I got myself a wild, uncontrollable gardener?" Her heart pounded so hard in her chest, she wondered if Claire could hear it.

If she could, Claire said nothing. She only moved her hands seductively over Regan's body. Regan felt her trembling. Claire's own control was slipping fast.

"Make love to me, darling," Claire gasped.

With breathless energy, Regan snaked her head low and around Claire's neck before planting small kisses on her lips. Claire thrust her body forward and into Regan's.

Regan moaned.

Claire responded by slipping a leg in between Regan's, her thigh touching the juncture of her sex.

"Thank God for second chances," Regan whimpered.

"Third," Claire said.

"Third time lucky. Whatever."

"Life is full of chances, Regan, except we don't often see them. They can pass us by in the blink of an eye, and then they are gone. Sometimes you just have to grab the chance and hang on for dear life, see where it takes you."

Regan knew Claire was in danger of losing herself, and Regan wasn't far off, either. She caught her staring at the double bed before them.

"Come to bed with me?" Regan asked. She pushed her hips close into Claire's and slipped her hands onto firm buttocks, pressing hard.

"Yes," Claire said.

Passing car lights streamed across the ceiling of the room. Occasional voices echoed up from the street below as Claire lay on her back with Regan above her.

The bed creaked and sheets stuck to her hot, sweating body as she tried to control the building desire between her legs.

But Regan would not go there. Not yet. She was taking her time and devouring her with kisses that went from light, chaste ones to those of a longer, more passionate nature. Claire adored them all as she opened her mouth wide to accommodate the commanding, dominating tongue.

Her breasts rose as she arched her back. Her breathing turned labored as she fought to hold herself from coming. Regan wasn't helping. She was rubbing up and down her as she licked a meandering pathway to her neck, across her collarbone, and down onto her breasts. Regan circled a nipple with a wet tongue before teasing and tugging it with her mouth.

Claire moved her hands up into Regan's hair. It felt like silken threads running between her fingers.

"Please, go lower," she begged. "I'm ready."

"Patience," Regan whispered as she continued attending to Claire's breasts.

Claire squirmed as Regan pressed her mound powerfully against hers and grinded them together rhythmically before pushing upward. She felt her vagina stretch. It was ready, and open, and wet. She was desperate and could wait no longer. She begged.

"Now, Regan, please. I've waited so long."

This time Regan obliged. Regan heard the urgency in her voice and knew her time had come.

Artful fingers entered her. Claire lost herself as they moved in and out to the cadence Regan set.

She closed her eyes as her breathing quickened. Lust consumed her, and she felt free, riding high, and higher on wonderful debauchery. This was what it might be like to be libertine, to be a fast and loose woman who cared for nothing but carnal desire. Except Claire did care more. Her body involuntarily thrust itself down on Regan's probing.

She wallowed in the pleasure giving as they rocked together, feeling what it was like to be overfed and drunk with passion. She cried out as she climaxed. Regan did not stop. She started slowly pumping again, gently probing deeper with each movement.

Once more, Claire's excitement grew. She felt the swelling and upsurge rise in her again. The crescendo built faster this time, and when it reached its high point, she moaned. As her trance-like state slowly ebbed, her awareness returned.

Regan stretched her body up so her face was next to hers. She was kissing her neck, her cheek, her lips, with feather kisses, before lying peacefully at her side.

Claire slipped an arm around Regan's waist and placed a leg across her.

With little breath left in her, she whispered, "Thank you, my love."

Regan tilted her head and seizing a chaste moment, she kissed her again. It was gentle.

"Okay?" Regan's voice was dreamy and distant.

"Very okay." Claire pulled her close, wrapping her tighter in her arms.

"I love you," Regan whispered as more car lights stretched across the ceiling.

Claire adored the way her voice sounded during their lovemaking. It was deep and raw, full of sex. She hoped it was a voice reserved only for her now. Always.

"I love you," she answered.

Regan moaned as she nestled her face into the crease of her breasts and rested there. Claire smelled the scent of sex between them. As she did, something faint stirred again between her legs. It was a calling, but she wanted to let Regan rest.

"Do you think," Claire said, "that if I was a little attracted to another woman and wanted to start something wonderful with her...do you think she could accept that my love comes with responsibilities—"

"—as in caring for Rosie?" Regan interrupted.

"Yes."

"I think that if that person was the right one, she would, without hesitation, say yes."

Claire leaned up on an elbow and stared hard into Regan's eyes. Regan did not shy from their intensity. She raised a hand and pushed stray hair from Claire's face.

"It would show her the compassion that person has for her ill partner, to care for her in sickness and health. I think that *other* person would feel damn lucky to find someone like that. To love and be loved in return."

Regan's answer warmed Claire.

"Do you think *you* might ever think about becoming that person?"

Regan choked. "Hell of a time to ask!"

Claire feigned apology and rested back on the pillows.

Regan now rose on an elbow. "I think after the passion just shared in this bed, that person would be bloody disappointed if she wasn't at least considered."

"Bloody disappointed?"

"Yeah. Something like that. I'm no poet laureate. I've a scientist's logic. I dig numbers. What do you want, a poet?"

Claire nestled closer, moving on top of her. "No, darling. I think you'll do just fine."

Claire slipped a hand down between them.

"What are you doing?" Regan's eyes were wide.

"I'm going to make love to you again."

"Jeez, woman. You're going to kill me."

They linked arms as they left the hotel, stepping out onto the sidewalk.

Claire started to turn left toward where the car was parked, but Regan tugged at her and pulled her in the opposite direction.

"What are you doing?" Claire asked.

"You need to go back to that little shop on the high street," Regan said.

Claire looked confused.

"You need to go back to the shop that you were looking in yesterday evening on the way to the theater. The one that was full of second-hand stuff and you said was clutter."

Still the penny wasn't dropping. Regan smiled.

"It was in the window," Regan continued. "You couldn't take your eyes off it, and you were so disappointed that the shop was shut. You know you want to go back and buy it."

Regan kept dragging Claire along the street and in the direction of the shop. "I saw you looking at it, that tiny pot with the plastic forget-me-nots in it."

Claire stopped, shocked. "But I never said anything."

Regan grinned. "You didn't have to. I could see it in your eyes. You want that pot for Rosie because of how much she loves those flowers."

"Am I so easy to read?"

"Only to me, because I'm in love with you." Regan hooked her arm in the crook of Claire's and moved her along. "Let's go back so you can buy it"

"I thought I could put it near her bedside. She'll see it then when she's awake."

"I think it's a lovely idea."

"How do you know Rosie loves forget-me-nots?" Claire asked.

"She told me."

"She did?"

"Not in so many words, but she kept pointing them out and asking Sally about them, all the time. They obviously still hold some significant meaning." Regan paused. "And why else would *you* plant them all around on her patio?"

"They were her favorites. She always loved spring flowers best. She made me plant them all over the garden."

"Look, we're here and the shop's open." Regan pointed at the window. "It's still there. Go get it."

Claire disappeared inside the shop and a few minutes later, returned with the pot. "It's only a silly cheap thing," she said.

"They're the things that mean the most," Regan answered.

They linked arms again and began walking back toward the car.

"Thank you, Regan," Claire whispered.

Regan pulled her closer.

Chapter Twenty-two

Claire received the phone call from Regan while she was turning soil in an old vegetable patch.

"What are you doing later?" Regan asked.

"Later?"

"Like about four o'clock this afternoon?"

"What I'm doing now, turning soil."

"Can you meet me in town, say at Mario's?"

Mario's was the coffee shop on the harbor and where they had walked the coast path to that first time. Why would Regan want to meet Claire there? She sounded furtive.

"Yes, of course." Claire wondered what the mystery was. "Any particular reason, other than to see me again?"

"Just be there."

"What are you up to?" Claire asked.

"Stop asking questions. Just be there."

Regan was about to ring off, but Claire stopped her. "Hang on a minute. If I turn up, then I've a demand."

"What?"

"It's your turn to pay. You left me with the bill last time."

"Fair enough. I pay." Regan sounded happy. "See you later."

The call ended.

Claire had no idea what Regan was up to. She only knew she was up to something.

When Claire arrived at the coffee shop, Regan was already there and waiting.

"You're late," she sighed.

"I'm not," Claire said. "You're early."

She grabbed a seat and pulled herself up close to Regan. "Now, what's this all about?"

"Wait for the coffee. It's ordered. Then I'll tell you."

They waited several minutes. The coffee arrived.

Claire took a sip and then blatantly gazed at Regan in expectation. She actually saw Regan grow bashful and shy as she reached into a pocket to reveal a small blue box.

"It's not what you think." Regan was self-conscious. "But it's important."

Claire didn't know what she thought. Her mind hadn't even time to contemplate a ring...which Regan was warning her it wasn't. The box was placed in front of her.

"You can open it," Regan said.

Claire touched it first before slowly removing the lid. Inside she found a solid silver chain. As she drew it from the box, an attachment revealed itself. It was a silver key that hung from the chain's center. The significance of the gift was not lost on her. When she looked back at Regan, her eyes misted over.

"Do you like it?" Regan asked.

"Of course I do. I love it." Claire's voice crackled.

"It's the key to my heart," Regan gushed, her face red. "You better not lose it."

Claire reached out and ran her fingers down the side of Regan's face. "Never."

"Oh, and this, too." Regan pulled something out of another pocket. It was a house key. Claire recognized it straightaway. It was the key Simon had given her. It was the one she'd pushed back under Regan's door.

Claire was in danger of bursting into tears.

"This one will be much more useful," Regan said. "But it comes with one condition."

"That is?"

"It has to be used regularly."

Claire smiled as she took Regan's hands in hers.

"I'll keep your condition. It's safe." Her smile grew wider. "And I shall start using it immediately. Would this evening be too soon?"

Regan cupped her hand in both of hers as she said, "This evening will be perfect."

About the Author

I. Beacham grew up in the heart of England, a green and pleasant land, mainly because it rains so much. This is probably why she ran away to sea, to search for dry places. Over the years, and during long periods away from home constantly travelling to faraway places, she has balanced the rigidity of her professional life with her need and love to write.

Blessed with a wicked sense of humor (not all agree), she is a lover of all things water, a dreadful jogger and cook, a hopeless romantic who roams antique stores, an addict of old black and white movies, and an adorer of science fiction. In her opinion, a perfect life.

I. Beacham can be contacted at: brit.beacham@yahoo.com

Books Available from Bold Strokes Books

A Reunion to Remember by TJ Thomas. Reunited after a decade, Jo Adams and Rhonda Black must navigate a significant age difference, family dynamics, and their own desires and fears to explore an opportunity for love. (978-1-62639-534-3)

Built to Last by Aurora Rey. When Professor Olivia Bennett hires contractor Joss Bauer to restore her dilapidated farmhouse, she learns her heart, as much as her house, is in need of a renovation. (978-1-62639-552-7)

Capsized by Julie Cannon. What happens when a woman turns your life completely upside down? (978-1-62639-479-7)

Girls With Guns by Ali Vali, Carsen Taite, and Michelle Grubb. Three stories by three talented crime writers—Carsen Taite, Ali Vali, and Michelle Grubb—each packing her own special brand of heat. (978-1-62639-585-5)

Heartscapes by MJ Williamz. Will Odette ever recover her memory or is Jesse condemned to remember their love alone? (978-1-62639-532-9)

Murder on the Rocks by Clara Nipper. Detective Jill Rogers lives with two things on her mind: sex and murder. While an ice storm cripples Tulsa, two things stand in Jill's way: her lover and the DA. (978-1-62639-600-5)

Necromantia by Sheri Lewis Wohl. When seeing dead people is more than a movie tagline. (978-1-62639-611-1)

Salvation by I. Beacham. Claire's long-term partner now hates her, for all the wrong reasons, and she sees no future until she meets Regan, who challenges her to face the truth and find love. (978-1-62639-548-0)

Trigger by Jessica Webb. Dr. Kate Morrison races to discover how to defuse human bombs while learning to trust her increasingly strong feelings for the lead investigator, Sergeant Andy Wyles. (978-1-62639-669-2)

24/7 by Yolanda Wallace. When the trip of a lifetime becomes a pitched battle between life and death, will anyone survive? (978-1-62639-6-197)

A Return to Arms by Sheree Greer. When a police shooting makes national headlines, activists Folami and Toya struggle to balance their relationship and political allegiances, a struggle intensified after a fiery young artist enters their lives. (978-1-62639-6-814)

After the Fire by Emily Smith. Paramedic Connor Haus is convinced her time for love has come and gone, but when firefighter Logan Curtis comes into town, she learns it may not be too late after all. (978-1-62639-6-524)

Dian's Ghost by Justine Saracen. The road to genocide is paved with good intentions. (978-1-62639-5-947)

Fortunate Sum by M. Ullrich. Financial advisor Catherine Carter lives a calculated life, but after a collision with spunky Imogene Harris (her latest client) and unsolicited predictions, Catherine finds herself facing an unexpected variable: Love. (978-1-62639-5-305)

Soul to Keep by Rebekah Weatherspoon. What *won't* a vampire do for love... (978-1-62639-6-166)

When I Knew You by KE Payne. Eight letters, three friends, two lovers, one secret. Can the past ever be forgiven? (978-1-62639-5-626)

Wild Shores by Radclyffe. Can two women on opposite sides of an oil spill find a way to save both a wildlife sanctuary and their hearts? (978-1-62639-6-456)

Love on Tap by Karis Walsh. Beer and romance are brewing for Tace Lomond when archaeologist Berit Katsaros comes into her life. (987-1-162639-564-0)

Love on the Red Rocks by Lisa Moreau. An unexpected romance at a lesbian resort forces Malley to face her greatest fears where she must choose between playing it safe or taking a chance at true happiness. (987-1-162639-660-9)

Tracker and the Spy by D. Jackson Leigh. There are lessons for all when Captain Tanisha is assigned untried pyro Kyle and a lovesick dragon horse for a mission to track the leader of a dangerous cult. (987-1-162639-448-3)

Whirlwind Romance by Kris Bryant. Will chasing the girl break Tristan's heart or give her something she's never had before? (987-1-162639-581-7)

Whiskey Sunrise by Missouri Vaun. Culture and religion collide when Lovey Porter, daughter of a local Baptist minister, falls for the handsome thrill-seeking moonshine runner, Royal Duval. (987-1-162639-519-0)

Dyre: By Moon's Light by Rachel E. Bailey. A young werewolf, Des, guards the aging leader of all the Packs: the Dyre. Stable employment—nice work, if you can get it…at least until silver bullets start to fly. (978-1-62639-6-623)

Fragile Wings by Rebecca S. Buck. In Roaring Twenties London, can Evelyn Hopkins find love with Jos Singleton or will the scars of the Great War crush her dreams? (978-1-62639-5-466)

Live and Love Again by Jan Gayle. Jessica Whitney could be Sarah Jarret's second chance at love, but their differences and Sarah's grief continue to come between their budding relationship. (978-1-62639-5-176)

Starstruck by Lesley Davis. Actress Cassidy Hayes and writer Aiden Darrow find out the hard way not all life-threatening drama is confined to the TV screen or the pages of a manuscript. (978-1-62639-5-237)

Stealing Sunshine by Tina Michele. Under the Central Florida sun, two women struggle between fear and love as a dangerous plot of deception and revenge threatens to steal priceless art and lives. (978-1-62639-4-452)

The Fifth Gospel by Michelle Grubb. Hiding a Vatican secret is dangerous—sharing the secret suicidal—can Felicity survive a perilous book tour, and will her PR specialist, Anna, be there when it's all over? (978-1-62639-4-476)

Cold to the Touch by Cari Hunter. A drug addict's murder is the start of a dangerous investigation for Detective Sanne Jensen and Dr. Meg Fielding, as they try to stop a killer with no conscience. (978-1-62639-526-8)

Forsaken by Laydin Michaels. The hunt for a killer teaches one woman that she must overcome her fear in order to love, and another that success is meaningless without happiness. (978-1-62639-481-0)

Infiltration by Jackie D. When a CIA breach is imminent, a Marine instructor must stop the attack while protecting her heart from being disarmed by a recruit. (978-1-62639-521-3)

Midnight at the Orpheus by Alyssa Linn Palmer. Two women desperate to make their way in the world, a man hell-bent on revenge, and a cop risking his career: all in a day's work in Capone's Chicago. (978-1-62639-607-4)

Spirit of the Dance by Mardi Alexander. Major Sorla Reardon's return to her family farm to heal threatens Riley Johnson's safe life when small-town secrets are revealed, and love may not conquer all. (978-1-62639-583-1)

Sweet Hearts by Melissa Brayden, Rachel Spangler, and Karis Walsh. Do you ever wonder *Whatever happened to...*? Find out when you reconnect with your favorite characters from Melissa Brayden's *Heart Block*, Rachel Spangler's *LoveLife*, and Karis Walsh's *Worth the Risk*. (978-1-62639-475-9)

Totally Worth It by Maggie Cummings. Who knew there's an all-lesbian condo community in the NYC suburbs? Join twentysomething BFFs Meg and Lexi at Bay West as they navigate friendships, love, and everything in between. (978-1-62639-512-1)

Illicit Artifacts by Stevie Mikayne. Her foster mother's death cracked open a secret world Jil never wanted to see…and now she has to pick up the stolen pieces. (978-1-62639-472-8)

Pathfinder by Gun Brooke. Heading for their new homeworld, Exodus's chief engineer Adina Vantressa and nurse Briar Lindemay carry game-changing secrets that may well cause them to lose everything when disaster strikes. (978-1-62639-444-5)

Prescription for Love by Radclyffe. Dr. Flannery Rivers finds herself attracted to the new ER chief, city girl Abigail Remy, and the incendiary mix of city and country, fire and ice, tradition and change is combustible. (978-1-62639-570-1)

Ready or Not by Melissa Brayden. Uptight Mallory Spencer finds relinquishing control to bartender Hope Sanders too tall an order in fast-paced New York City. (978-1-62639-443-8)

Summer Passion by MJ Williamz. Women loving women is forbidden in 1946 Hollywood, yet Jean and Maggie strive to keep their love alive and away from prying eyes. (978-1-62639-540-4)

The Princess and the Prix by Nell Stark. "Ugly duckling" Princess Alix of Monaco was resigned to loneliness until she met racecar driver Thalia d'Angelis. (978-1-62639-474-2)

Winter's Harbor by Aurora Rey. Lia Brooks isn't looking for love in Provincetown, but when she discovers chocolate croissants and pastry chef Alex McKinnon, her winter retreat quickly starts heating up. (978-1-62639-498-8)

The Time Before Now by Missouri Vaun. Vivian flees a disastrous affair, embarking on an epic, transformative journey to escape her past, until destiny introduces her to Ida, who helps her rediscover trust, love, and hope. (978-1-62639-446-9)